An Exhilaration of Wings

The Literature of Birdwatching

Edited and with

an Introduction by

Jen Hill

D1488037

PENGUIN BOOKS

PENGUIN BOOKS
Published by the Penguin Group
Penguin Putnam Inc., 375 Hudson Street, New York, New York 10014, U.S.A.
Penguin Books Ltd, 27 Wrights Lane, London W8 5TZ, England
Penguin Books Australia Ltd, Ringwood, Victoria, Australia
Penguin Books Canada Ltd, 10 Alcorn Avenue, Toronto, Ontario, Canada M4V 3B2
Penguin Books (N.Z.) Ltd, 182-190 Wairau Road, Auckland 10, New Zealand

Penguin Books Ltd, Registered Offices: Harmondsworth, Middlesex, England

First published in the United States of America by Viking Penguin 1999
Published in Penguin Books 2001

10 9 8 7 6 5 4 3 2 1

Copyright © Jennifer Hill, 1999
All rights reserved

Audobon in the West, compiled, edited and with an introduction by John Francis
McDermott, University of Oklahoma Press. Copyright © 1965 by University of
Oklahoma Press. *The Natural History Prose Writings of John Clare*, edited by Margaret
Grainger. Reprinted with permission of Curtis Brown, Ltd, London, on behalf of Eric
Robinson. Copyright Eric Robinson, 1984. *On the Wings of a Bird* by Herbert Ravenel
Sass. By permission of Doubleday, a division of Random House, Inc. *A Naturalist in
Indian Territory: The Journals of S. W. Woodhouse, 1849–1850*, edited and annotated
by John S. Tomer and Michael J. Brodhead, University of Oklahoma Press, 1992.

Illustrations reproduced with the assistance of Cornell University Library,
Cornell University.

Manuscripts of Gilbert White housed in the British Museum.

THE LIBRARY OF CONGRESS HAS CATALOGED THE HARDCOVER EDITION AS FOLLOWS:
An exhilaration of wings : the literature of birdwatching / edited
and with an introduction by Jen Hill.
p.   cm.
ISBN 0-670-88724-2 (hc.)
ISBN 0 14 10.01801 (pbk.)
1. Bird watching Quotations, maxims, etc.   I. Hill, Jen.
QL677.5.E95   1999
598'.07'234—dc21   99–21043

Printed in the United States of America
Set in Fournier   •   Designed by Francesca Belanger

Except in the United States of America, this book is sold subject to the condition
that it shall not, by way of trade or otherwise, be lent, re-sold, hired out, or otherwise
circulated without the publisher's prior consent in any form of binding or cover other
than that in which it is published and without a similar condition including this
condition being imposed on the subsequent purchaser.

PENGUIN BOOKS

AN EXHILARATION OF WINGS

Jen Hill is a graduate of Stanford University and received a Ph.D. in literature from Cornell. She lives in Reno, Nevada, where she teaches at the University of Nevada at Reno.

Praise for *An Exhilaration of Wings:*
The Literature of Birdwatching

"A good many of the usual suspects are here—Thoreau, John Muir, and the like—but Hill also includes a generous selection from the unjustly neglected John Burroughs, and a good deal from Florence Merriam, whom I didn't know before this, but find delightful." —*The Philadelphia Inquirer*

"This lovingly organized anthology of notes on birds contains entries by the English diarist Gilbert White that read like haiku, and solutions to the mysteries of what nesting flamingos do with their legs and how fish hawks, or ospreys, seem actually to attract their prey." —*The New Yorker*

"An illuminating introduction to the history of birdwatching as conveyed through a storehouse of revealing and beautifully written excerpts spanning a period from America's colonial past to the early twentieth century ... Hill's interesting collection enables the reader to see the remarkable position of birding as an activity that is, on the one hand, experiential on a personal level, and on the other hand, completely interconnected with politics, social history, art, literature, and science." —*The Urban Audubon*

"This lovely collection will evoke for birdwatchers a sense of the birds they have missed, the birds they have sought, and the centuries-long company they keep out there alone in the field. And for those unhappy few who don't know the pleasures of birding, they will find them here and perhaps learn something of the thrill of sightings in the wilderness, in woods, at the shore and in cities and backyards." —George Levine

"Through her selections and juxtapositions, Jen Hill has put together an anthology fascinating not only to those interested in birds, but to those interested in people who watch them. We reveal ourselves in what we admire or dislike—or simply are blind to—and nowhere is this more apparent than in our response to the songs, plumage, and habits of birds." —James McConkey

for my grandmother
   A. Mildred McDonald
with love
   J. Mildred Hill

I have heard of "love me, love my dog," but I never heard of "love me, love my bird."

Maria Edgeworth, *Belinda*, 1801

Acknowledgments

This book owes much to many people and many resources.

For their hard work and patience I am indebted to my agent, Clyde Taylor, and my editor, Paul Slovak.

Joseph Kastner's *A World of Watchers* is not only a well-written history of birdwatching, but helped me conceive and contextualize my introduction. Bethany Schneider and the many Cousins of Book and Bowl provided good-humored and useful feedback on that section.

For early encouragement I thank Russell Bourne, Frances Hill, Dorothy Mermin, and Stephanie Vaughn. Thanks go to Kirsten Manges for handling details and to Lisa Baskin, who suggested Charlotte Smith as a source and generously allowed me to use her copy of Smith's *A Natural History of Birds*. Thanks also to Dennis Daneke and Karen Harrison for introducing me to birdwatching, Montana-style.

I could not have completed this book without the patient staff and resources of Cornell University Library, especially those of the Division of Rare and Manuscript Collections at Kroch Library. I am particularly indebted to Katherine Reagan, Mark Dimunation, Elaine Engst, and Laura Link for their input, hard work, and good cheer.

Finally, warmest thanks to Larry Cantera, for encouraging and indulging my love of birds, books, and research, for his good conversation on long road trips, and for suggestions that made this book more interesting and more readable.

In any work that seeks to represent a variety of voices, there will be some that are overlooked. I decided early on to privilege unknown and difficult-to-find birdwatching voices, and this has been, necessarily, at the expense of better-known, best-loved sources. Since unique spelling and punctuation contribute to the texture and accuracy of the collection, I silently corrected only those archaic spellings and names that seemed unduly jarring.

Contents

Introduction

We are so in the habit of focusing our spy-glasses on our human neighbors that it seems an easy matter to label them and their affairs, but when it comes to the birds—alas!, not only are there legions of kinds, but, to our bewildered fancy, they look and act exactly alike. Yet though our task seems hopeless at the outset, before we recognize the conjurer a new world of interest and beauty has opened before us.

—Florence Merriam, 1889

Any history of birdwatching must begin rather arbitrarily. No doubt people have watched birds as long as there have been people to watch birds.

For many, the spirit of birding dates to Sir Thomas Browne, an Englishman who in 1662 assembled a rough list of birds for what would later become his *Notes and Letters on the Natural History of Norfolk*. "There is also a lesser sort of Agle called an ospray wch hovers about the fennes & broads & will dippe his claws and take up fish oftimes for wch his fote is made of an extraordinarie roughnesse for the better fastening & holding of it & the like they will do unto cootes," he wrote, as if to resume a conversation with a nature-loving friend. "Stares or starlings in great numbers," he continues later. "Most remarkable in their numerous flocks wch I have observed about the Autumne when they roost at night in the marshes in safe places upon reeds & alders. wch to observe I went to the marshes about sunne set. where standing by their usuall place of resort I observed very many flocks flying from all quarters. wch in lesses than an howers space came all in & settled in innumerable numbers in a small compasse. Great varieties of finches and other small birds wherof one very small calld a whinne bird marked with fine yellow spotts & lesser than a wren. there is also a small bird called a chipper somewhat resembling the former wch comes in the spring & feeds upon the first buddings of birches & other early trees." It is the second passage that identifies Browne as a birdwatcher: he seeks the marshes at sunset, he knows the starlings' habits, the diet of a chipper in the spring.

By 1737, *A Natural History of English Song-Birds* had appeared, having as its frontispiece perhaps the earliest picture of birdwatchers. A man and a woman sit at the edge of a field. The man holds a nest with three openmouthed chicks, and his well-dressed female companion points at the birds as if to reach for them, her brow wrinkled in what could be thought—or is it concern? Perhaps wonder? Behind them in the bushes lurk two men, one of whom holds a branch up out of his sight line as they peer into the field beyond. These are eighteenth-century birdwatchers, complete with gaudy caps, breeches, full skirt, and daring décolletage, but recognizable to their modern-day counterparts by the intensity of their interest: the woman's gaze, the tension in the body of one of the men in the bushes as he cranes past his companion's shoulder. Birdwatching, it appears, had arrived.

Despite these ancestors, it is impossible to say when, exactly, birdwatching emerged as a practice distinct from the larger category of natural history. Mention 1789 to most people and they recognize the date of the French Revolution. For the history of birdwatching, the date was just as revolutionary: it marked in England the publication of Gilbert White's *The Natural History of Selbourne*. White's compact, casually chatty text with its local focus ushered in a new way of documenting the natural world. Earlier volumes about birds—Browne's included—were encyclopedic and sought only to classify, name, and describe species. Often the result of elaborate information- and specimen-gathering voyages, they employed a new scientific nomenclature that categorized the natural world in a comprehensive and comprehensible knowledge system. But while the project enabled an organized and thorough knowledge of the world, the lists of birds it generated were as dry as the dead carcasses shipped back to scientific societies in England from the edges of a rapidly expanding empire. White, a rector of the Church of England and an avid naturalist, took a different approach. Concerned less with naming and discovery than with careful and methodical observation, and with a curiosity contentedly bounded by his immediate surroundings, White wrote an engaging series of deceptively simple letters in which he made connections between species and habitats and, in the case of birds, posed a series of questions about the behaviors he witnessed in his neighborhood. Not only did White's book serve as a primer to a new kind of field method, but in his joyful anecdotes we recognize an obsession. *The Natural History of Selbourne* was an immediate popular success, and has never been out of print since.

While the rural rector was observing young cuckoos deposited in titlark nests in the English countryside, William Bartram traveled through the American South, recording the flora and fauna of the colonies. In 1791 the record of his journey appeared in England and America as *Travels Through North and South Carolina, Georgia, East and West Florida*. True enough, Bartram's journey was directly linked to the earlier, classificatory scientific project—he undertook it as a paid specimen gatherer for an English client—but by focusing on live birds, their surroundings and actions, the young Quaker from outside of Philadelphia revolutionized the understanding of birds. A poet and an artist, Bartram sought connections between the human and the natural in his observations of nature. His method combined detailed factual lists of birds with close observation of their habitats and behavior, through which runs Bartram's deeply held personal identification with the beauty and diversity of the outdoors. His *Catalogue of Birds of North America*, published separately, was true in style to the categorization efforts of earlier in the century and identified 215 species. But the *Travels* are full of revolutionary observations of migration and bird behavior that resulted from Bartram's holistic approach to the natural world. His reputation was such that President Thomas Jefferson asked him to accompany Lewis and Clark's expedition in 1804, only to have the naturalist decline, citing age and ill health. Still, all explorers and scientists who followed took a bit of Bartram with them, for the confessional nature of his work detailed the link between person and place, between scientist and subject, that had previously been ignored.

Bartram's readers in England included the poets Coleridge, Wordsworth, and Shelley, and if his birdwatching influenced the nascent Romantic movement, it's almost certain that the values of the Romantics promoted birdwatching. Wilderness areas that had been perceived as "hideous and desolate," as William Bradford observed on arriving in New England in 1662, were now valued for their evocation of the sublime. The heavily cultivated and shaped gardens of the Enlightenment were passé; wilderness was all the rage. By the 1830s places that had previously been seen as bleak and forsaken—the Lake District in England and the Adirondacks and Berkshires in the United States—were established tourist destinations. At first, "the wild" was valued primarily for its larger, more dramatic aesthetic, and travelers recorded only their experiences of the larger landscape. Eventually, though, artists like those of the Hudson River Valley school of painters revealed the natural world in all its detail, making visible the flora and fauna of wilderness. And, in 1838, John James Audubon's *The Birds of America* turned the focus of the new generation of nature lovers to birds.

In America, the shift from taming the wilderness to appreciating it followed increasing urbanization and industrialization in the cities. Britain also saw increased industrialization, and in both places changing work patterns and readily available manufactured goods introduced a new way to spend time: leisure.[1] *Mary Barton*, Elizabeth

---

[1]Ironically, the encroachment of the railroad and of urban factories and smokestacks along waterways were a very real threat to native bird populations. But many birds adapted to their new urban surroundings—as many a New York City dweller today will attest—which led to an entirely new kind of bird-watching: the pursuit of the urban bird.

Gaskell's novel of the working poor in Manchester, describes entire families using their free hours on weekends and evenings to stroll and picnic in meadows and downs on the outskirts of town. Job Legh, a working-class naturalist, "takes a day here, and a day there, for botanizing or going after insects" and spends not only all his free time, but all his spare money, on his hobby. Leisure time provided the opportunity for the amateur pursuit of natural history by all classes, and the literature of natural history available to the amateur grew exponentially. The young science of ornithology was especially open to contributions made by nonprofessionals. Indeed, with the help of an opera glass and careful, detail-oriented observation, the committed amateur could rapidly become a specialist in the science of birds. Rich and poor, birdwatchers shared what they knew with each other and gradually formalized networks to exchange information in the form of clubs and journals in the nineteenth century, both in the United States and in England. Books about birds—accounts of scientific explorations of exotic locations, backyard birding tips, habitat and identification treatises—abounded and found a huge popular audience.

Women made up a significant proportion of the new birdwatchers. If in the Romantic period women had been equated with nature, the Victorian period of the midcentury had them dressing like birds. Elaborate feathered hats were the rage and even simpler millinery styles relied heavily on feathers for decoration. The hidden cost of such a high trade in feathers was the decimation of rare bird populations. Often, the birds were still alive when feather hunters cut off their wings and threw the still-struggling bodies into the ocean to drown. Women by the hundreds of thousands joined in opposition to such appalling butchery of "feathered innocents and the consequent death of the[ir] nestlings,"[2] and swelled the ranks of both the Royal Society for the Protection of Birds and the Audubon Society. Members of the RSPB paid two shillings and signed a

[2]From a resolution by the General Federation of Women's Clubs (United States, 1907).

pledge vowing not to wear the feathers of any bird other than the ostrich.[3] In addition to their public roles of political advocacy, women like Olive Thorne Miller and Florence Merriam made new friends for birds with popular, reader-friendly accounts of bird behavior that reached out to a new generation of young readers whom they hoped to convert to birdwatchers and conservationists.

While the mobilization of friends of birds and birdwatchers helped formalize the conservation movements of the late 1800s, their own methods demanded scrutiny and change. Many early bird-watchers observed birds in their habitats just long enough to shoot them—Robert Penn Warren described John James Audubon as "our most famous killer of birds"—and the methods of specimen collec-tors were difficult to break, despite the Audubon Society motto, "Two birds in the bush is worth one in the hand." Bird's-nesting and egg collecting were accepted popular hobbies in the nineteenth cen-tury, especially for young boys. *Tom Brown's Schooldays*, that quin-tessential novel of Victorian boyhood, devotes an entire chapter to a bird's-nesting expedition. The boys work together successfully to hoist the youngest, most agile member of the expedition up to a magpie's nest. "All right—four eggs!" he cries. "Take 'em all!" shouts one of his companions. When they get bored of robbing nests, the boys collect pebbles to throw at the birds, hoping to bring them down in midflight. These practices continued well into the twentieth century. Indeed, nonsensical as it may seem, it was not uncommon for "scientific" people to slaughter birds in efforts to determine species' agility and flying behavior. But all along, people such as the English poet and naturalist John Clare decided that they would not kill or otherwise interfere with birds in their habitats. America's most famous writer about nature, Thoreau, chose to pur-chase a telescope to facilitate birdwatching early in his career, writing, "In some respects methinks it would be better than a gun. The latter brings them nearer dead. The former alive."

[3]Fittingly, the first president of the RSPB and, until her death in 1954, the only president the organization had for its first sixty-five years was a woman, Winifred, Duchess of Portland.

Since bird populations are highly susceptible to human predation and to changes in environment, birders were among the first to call for environmental regulation and protective legislation both in the United States and in Britain. As early as 1791, a statute was introduced into the assembly of the state of New York calling for protection of pinnated grouse, locally known as Heath-Hens, in Queens and Suffolk counties. The chairman of the assembly read the title incorrectly as "an Act for the Preservation of Heathens and Other Game," which seemed to astonish the northern members, "who could not see the propriety of preserving *Indians*, or any other heathen." The casual way in which the politicians discussed Indian removal places this very early indeed in American history, but lest one think that early citizens valued avifauna over native peoples for sentimental reasons, it is important to note that legislation such as this was enacted with the object of maintaining bird populations as an exploitable resource. It would be more than a century before conservationists and birdwatchers made great changes in environmental policy.

Among the most vocal and visible birders in the United States in the early part of this century was Theodore Roosevelt. He recounted after his presidency, "People looking into the White House grounds and seeing me stare into a tree no doubt thought me insane." To which his wife added, "And as I was always with him, they no doubt thought I was the nurse in charge." His years in office were high-profile ones for the outdoors and its inhabitants. After establishing the national parks, he took a birding expedition to Yellowstone in 1903 with John Burroughs. (Few people read Burroughs anymore, but the famous naturalist and friend of Walt Whitman influenced a wide readership with his essays on bird life.) Roosevelt would later create the first national bird sanctuary at Pelican Island, Florida, to be followed by many more. Fittingly, after his years in the Oval Office, the next presidential position he took was in a chapter of an ornithology club on Long Island.

Theodore Roosevelt wasn't known for his keen eyesight—he is, after all, the only president on Mount Rushmore wearing glasses— but many of his acquaintances remarked on his almost uncanny ability to hear birds and identify them through their calls alone. Such thorough knowledge is the mark of the complete birder, because despite its name, bird*watching* is an experience of the ears and intellect as much as it is of the eye. Experienced birders acknowledge that identifying elusive birds requires a kind of certainty that eludes all but the most conscious of viewers. To sight and identify a prothonotary warbler demands a level of concentration that alters the entire act of seeing. And a little luck, besides. True birders require sharp eyes, but they also require *vision*. In the words of Gilbert White, they must "be able to distinguish birds by their air as well as by their colors and shapes."

And because, when observing birds, today's birdwatchers echo White's actions of more than two hundred years ago, birding connects us to our history—not only a history of the natural world, but the history of human experience. Bartram had it right as early as 1791: we are not separate from the natural world. In the nineteenth century, some went so far as to claim birds as a sort of missing link to the biblical past, and engaged in detailed debates outlining the species that were sure to have inhabited the Garden of Eden. But biblical history aside, the writers collected here remind us both of our past and of the timeless pleasure of birdwatching. Their prose instructs and reveals, and manages to carve out a little quiet space in which a connection is made between reader, writer, and bird, across time and space.

Whether the triumphs of a rare sighting or a big day are shared with birding companions or jotted in a private journal, birdwatching is about seeking connection. Arguably, behind the urge to look at birds is a desire to see ourselves—if not in their behavior, courtship rituals, and territory squabbles, then in the realization that birds are *not us*. We have killed birds, tamed them, put them in cages, and have even succeeded in making some species extinct, but ultimately, they elude us. By doing so, birds offer us an opportunity to be surprised and affirmed, to know that there exist some things that exceed us—free, wheeling spirits that call to us, only to soar beyond our grasp.

Far-away birds have fine feathers.

Though the egg be small, still a bird will come out of it.

Sweet is a bird's voice where he was born.

The bird is known by its feathers.

Birds do not light on only one branch.

> —Traditional Gaelic proverbs
> From Alexander Robert Forbes's *Gaelic Names of Beasts
> (Mammalia), Birds, Fishes, Insects, Reptiles, Etc.*, 1905

Getting Started

There is news in every bush.
—John Burroughs, *Wake Robin*, 1893

Use your eyes. Use them and have faith in them.

Use your eyes and trust them. And go out and listen to the birds. Oh, if we would listen more often to the singing of the birds!

—H. R. Sass, *On the Wings of a Bird*, 1928

The best way is the simplest. Begin with the commonest birds, and train your ears and eyes by pigeon-holing every bird you see and every song you hear. Classify roughly at first,—the finer distinctions will easily be made later. Suppose, for instance, you are in the fields on a spring morning. Standing still a moment, you hear what sounds like a confusion of songs. You think you can never tell one from another, but by listening carefully you at once notice a difference. Some are true songs, with a definite melody,—and tune, if one may use that word,—like the song of several of the sparrows, with three high notes and a run down the scale. Others are only monotonous trills, always the same two notes, varying only to length and intensity, such as that of the chipping bird who makes one's ears fairly ache as he sits in the sun and trills to himself, like a complacent prima donna. Then there is always plenty of gossiping going on, chippering and chattering that does not rise to the dignity of song, though it add to the general jumble of sounds; but this should be ignored at first, and only the loud songs listened for. When the trill and the elaborate song are once contrasted, other distinctions are easily made. The ear then catches the quality of songs. On the right the plaintive note of the meadowlark is heard, while out of the grass at the left comes the rollicking song of the bobolink. . . .

Having begun sorting sound, you naturally group sights, and so find yourself parceling out the birds by size and color. As the robin is a well-known bird, he serves as a convenient unit of measure—an ornithological foot. If you call anything from a humming-bird to a robin small, and from a robin to a crow large, you have a practical division line, of use in getting your bearings. And the moment you give heed to colors, the birds will no longer look alike. To simplify matters, the bluebird, the oriole with his orange and black coat, the scarlet tanager with his flaming plumage, and all the other bright birds can be classed together; while the sparrows, flycatchers, thrushes, and vireos may be though of as the dull birds. . . .

With these hints in mind, go to look for your friends. Carry a pocket notebook, and above all, take an opera or field glass with you. Its rapid adjustment may be troublesome at first, but it should be the "inseparable article" of a careful observer. If you begin work in spring, don't start out before seven o'clock, because the confusion of the matins is discouraging—there is too much to see and hear. But go as soon as possible after breakfast, for the birds grow quiet and fly to the woods for their nooning earlier and earlier as the weather gets warmer.

—Florence Merriam, *Birds Through an Opera Glass*, 1889

There is room for difference of opinion as to whether certain birds are "as big as an English sparrow" or not. Moreover individuals differ.

—Hubert Lyman Clark, *The Birds of Amherst and Vicinity*, 1906

Strangely enough, not only country boys and girls, but their fathers and mothers, not only confuse swallows and martins with one another, but these with the swift! Yet they are readily distinguishable. All, it is true, have long, pointed wings, and forked tails: but their coloration is very different.

—W. P. Pycraft, *Birds in Flight*, 1922

For examining adult birds in the field, good vision and a notebook and pencil are the chief requisites, though an opera- or field-glass may often be used to advantage. Warblers, vireos, and other active birds that live by foraging may be quietly followed as they flit from tree to tree. In this way it is not difficult to discover the character of their food and about how much is consumed during a given interval of time. Now and then there will be favorable moments when it is possible to see for a certainty just what is taken. Cuckoos, kingfishers, flycatchers, and other birds that are more or less sedentary must be watched, an hour or two perhaps, from one position,—an occupation not nearly so irksome as it looks on paper.

—Clarence M. Weed and Ned Dearborn, *Birds in Their Relations to Man*, 1903

America offers a fine field to the ornithologist, and even a traveller who is usually careless of the study of natural history, cannot fail to be delighted with the variety of beautiful birds which he will see in merely passing through the American forests, more particularly in those of the States. Red birds, blue birds, and yellow or Baltimore birds (a species of starling), will frequently fly across his path; turtle doves are constantly alighting in the road before him; a large, magnificent species of woodpecker, with a red crest, usually termed the woodcock, will sometimes make his appearance; a great variety of the same genus, particularly a small species with a marked plumage of black, white, and crimson, are almost always in sight; he will be startled and deceived by the mew of a catbird,—and his eye and ear will be attracted by the brilliant plumage of a blue jay, the singing of the mocking-bird, the melodious flute-like whistle of the wood-thrush, or the instantaneous buzz of the passing humming-

bird. Considering the wildness of the country, I was very much surprised at the scarcity of the larger birds of prey; a small brown vulture, commonly misnamed the turkey-buzzard, is however an
exception.

—Godfrey T. Vigne, *Six Months in America*, 1832

Avoid the highways when you take a walk. Even if well shaded,
they are abandoned now to the pestiferous English sparrows; and if
you are really intent on a good tramp of a few miles, do not turn
aside for a stretch of swamp. If you have any fear of wet feet, be
properly shod before starting. It too often happens that the sights
best worth seeing come to you when in a bit of wet meadow. The
swamp-sparrows, that are such sweet songsters; the marsh-wrens
and the king-rails and soras will not come to the dry ground at the
edge of the meadow and sing and show themselves for your benefit.
If you want to enjoy them, you must go to their haunts; and once
there, if you are really fond of birds, you will never regret it. There
are neglected, tangled, briery nooks in every neighborhood that will
repay frequent visits. There some of the best bird-music is to be
heard. In an old field I know of, too barren to be worth cultivating,
and unpleasantly strong with the odors of Jamestown wood, there is
every summer a whole colony of Carolina wrens, and their songs are
not excelled by any of our birds, except certain thrushes and the
rose-breasted grosbeak. In this field, too, I am sure of finding scores
of garter-snakes, and the pretty creatures add a charm to the place.
Finally, nowhere else are there so many gorgeously-colored dragon-
flies as about this same neglected weed-grown field. By very many,
walks are thought to be enjoyable only in what is commonly called
pleasant weather.

What constitutes a pleasant day, as distinguished from an
unpleasant one, is not very clear. If I have seen something new,
that day is pleasant, however the thermometer registers or the winds
blow. Surely, too, after a month of sunny days, a steady, pouring
rain is delicious, not to look at merely, but to be about in it. It is
charm enough to tempt one out to see how the birds and mice and

squirrels, and the snakes, frogs, and insects pass their time when it rains. The cunning you will see displayed by them will compensate for the soaking you may get.

—Charles C. Abbott, *A Naturalist's Rambles About Home*, 1885

One cannot, unfortunately, watch all birds, and of those that one can it is difficult not to say at once too little and too much: too little, because one may have only had the luck to see well a single point in the round of activities of any species—one feather in its plumage, so to speak—and too much, because even to speak of this adequately is to fill many pages and deny space to some other bird. All I can do is to speak of some few birds as I have watched them in some few things.

—Edmund Selous, *Bird Watching*, 1901

The first law of field work is exact observation, but not only are you more likely to observe accurately if what you see is put in black and white, but you will find it much easier to identify the birds from your notes than from memory.

—Florence Merriam, *Birds Through an Opera Glass*, 1889

It matters not how one may limit it, the word "Observations" has a terrific sound. Let a man say merely that he watched a robin (for instance) doing something, and no one will shrink from him; but if he talks about his "Observations on the Robin-Redbreast" then, let these have been ever so restricted, and even though he may forswear to call the bird by its Latin name, he must expect to pay the penalty. . . . I have *watched* birds only, I have not *observed* them.

—Edmund Selous, *Bird Watching*, 1901

Coming up lately from Bridgewater by the Great Western, I kept a good look-out for birds. Starlings were in flocks. The jackdaws were making a great noise, and very busy getting their nests ready, about the towers of Exeter Cathedral. All the way along the line from Taunton to Paddington the rooks were sitting on tops of the trees, and in many cases the hens were sitting on their eggs. The last rookery I saw was in the Marylebone Road, where there were sixteen nests.

There is round the base of the rook's bill a white skin. It is said by some that the feathers have been worn off on this part by digging in the ground. My opinion is that it is naturally devoid of feathers, though it is curious to observe that the young rooks have feathers at the base of the bill, which afterwards disappear. The ravens and jackdaws retain the feathers at the base of the bill all their lives.

—Frank Buckland, in George C. Bompas's *Life of Frank Buckland*, 1885

When the mind is distracted by sorrows it cannot shake off, it boots little that the chirp of the chestnut-sided and cerulean warblers is sharp and penetrating; that the call of the black-throated green, black-throated blue and myrtle warblers is somewhat harsh; that the Maryland yellow-throat expresses his alarm or disapproval in a note still lower in the scale and quite rasping; that the Blackburnian and parula warblers tilt about far up in the tree-tops, as if they scorned the ground; that the black-throats and creepers dance airily about in the bushes or lower branches of the trees, come confidingly near you, a tiny interrogation point dangling from every eyelash, ask you what you are about, what you do when you are at home, whether you have just come from the hospital that you look so pale, and, having decided that you are a harmless monomaniac, to say the worst, go about their playful toil of capturing insects, apparently unmindful of your presence. But when your heart is jolly and full of nature love, all these simple facts, proving the large diversity of temperament in bird-land's denizens, are a source of joy to you; you note them, are glad on account of them, though you scarcely know why.

—Leander S. Keyser, *In Bird Land*, 1897

One man may take a walk and scarcely see a bird; another, with him, sees or hears, perhaps, five and twenty species.

—A. J. R. Roberts, *The Bird Book*, 1903

There is a fascination about the quest for the largest list of birds in a day which is not equalled even by the search for new species in a region which one has worked for years. The limits of time, strength, and territory possible to cover furnish the incentive for a sort of field study which is wholly out of accord with any accepted method. One cannot tarry long in any place and wait for the birds to come to him; he must search out the birds. Nor will time permit him to study the individuals without sacrificing the purpose of the day's work. A species once recorded must be put aside as finished for the day and the quest for those not yet seen carried forward vigorously. It may very well be true that this nervous activity which forbids the usual method of field work—the calm waiting for the birds to appear— make us overlook some species; but if so, it certainly discovers to us many that would not be likely to come within our ken. It is an exhausting work, both on account of the length of the day and the energy which must be thrown into it. One may well pause to ask if it pays, or if the results justify the outlay. We think they do.

—Lynds Jones, *Wilson Bulletin*, 1902

If life is, as some hold it to be, a vast melancholy ocean over which ships more or less sorrow-laden continually pass, yet there lie here and there upon it isles of consolation on to which we may step out and for a time forget the winds and waves. One of these we may call Bird-isle—the island of watching and being entertained by the habits and humours of birds—and upon this one, for with the others I have here nothing to do, I will straightaway land, inviting such as may care to, to follow me.

—Edmund Selous, *Bird Watching*, 1901

In walking under a hot sun the head may be sensibly protected by green leaves or grass in the hat; they may be advantageously moistened, but not enough to drop about the ears. Under such circumstances the slightest giddiness, dimness of sight, or confusion of ideas, should be taken as a warning of possible sunstroke, instantly demanding rest, and shelter if practicable. Hunger and Fatigue are more closely related than they might seem to be: one is a sign that the fuel is out, and the other asks for it. Extreme fatigue, indeed, destroys appetite; this simply means, temporary incapacity for digestion. But even far short of this, food is more easily digested and better relished after a little preparation of the furnace. On coming home tired it is much better to make a leisurely and reasonably nice toilet than to eat at once, or to lie still thinking how tired you are; after a change and a wash you will feel like a "new man," and go to table in capital state. Whatever dietetic irregularities a high state of civilization may demand or render practicable a normally healthy person is inconvenienced almost as soon as his regular meal-time passes without food; and few can work comfortably or profitably fasting over six or eight hours. Eat before starting; if for a day's tramp, take a lunch; the most frugal meal will appease if it do not satisfy hunger, and so postpone its urgency. As a small scrap of practical wisdom, I would add, keep the remnants of the lunch, if there are any; for you cannot always be sure of getting in to supper. . . .

The three golden rules here are—never drink before breakfast, never drink alone, and never drink bad liquor; their observance may make even the abuse of alcohol tolerable. Serious objections for a naturalist, at least, are that science, viewed through a glass, seems distant and uncertain, while the joys of rum are immediate and unquestionable; and that intemperance being an attempt to defy certain physical laws, is therefore eminently unscientific.

—Elliott Coues, *Field Ornithology*, 1874

I suppose that all growing boys tend to be grubby; but the ornithological small boy, or indeed the boy with a taste for natural history of any kind, is generally the very grubbiest of all.

—Theodore Roosevelt, *Theodore Roosevelt: An Autobiography*, 1920

When you begin to study the warblers you will probably conclude that you know nothing about birds, and can never learn. But if you begin by recognizing their common traits, and then study a few of the easiest, and those that nest in your locality, you will be less

discouraged; and when the flocks come back at the next migration
you will be able to master the oddities of a larger number.

—Florence Merriam, *Birds Through an Opera Glass*, 1889

Travelers in the Sierra forests usually complain of the want
of life. "The trees," they say, "are fine, but the empty stillness is
deadly; there are no animals to be seen, no birds. We have not heard
a song in all the woods." And no wonder! They go in large parties
with mules and horse; they make a great noise; they are dressed in
outlandish, unnatural colors: every animal shuns them. Even the
frightened pines would run away if they could. But Nature lovers,
devout, silent, open-eyed, looking and listening with love, find no
lack of inhabitants in these mountain mansions, and they come to
them gladly. Not to mention the large animals or the small insect
people, every waterfall has its ouzel and every tree its squirrel or
tamias or bird: tiny nuthatch threading the furrows of the bark,
cheerily whispering to itself as it deftly pries off loose scales and
examines the furled edges of lichens; or Clarke crow or jay examining the cones; or some singer—oriole, tanager, warbler—resting,
feeding, attending to domestic affairs. Hawks and eagle sail overhead, grouse walk in happy flocks below, and song sparrows sing in
every bed of chaparral. These is no crowding, to be sure. Unlike the
low Eastern trees, those in the Sierra in the main forest belt average
nearly two hundred feet in height, and of course many birds are
required to make much show in them and many voices to fill them.
Nevertheless, the whole range from foothills to snowy summits is
shaken into every summer; and though low and thin in the winter,
the music never ceases.

—John Muir, *Among the Birds of the Yosemite*, 1898

When one thinks of a bird, one fancies a soft, swift, aimless,
joyous thing, full of nervous energy and arrowy motions,—a song
with wings. So remote from ours their mode of existence, they seem
accidental exiles from an unknown globe, banished where none
can understand their language; and men only stare at their darting

inexplicable ways, as at the gyrations of the circus. Watch their little traits for hours, and it only tantalizes curiosity.

—T. W. Higginson, *The Life of Birds*, 1862

I think that if our common birds were minutely and patiently watched, we might trace here and there in their actions the beginnings of some of those more wonderful ones, which obtain amongst birds far away.

—Edmund Selous, *Bird Watching*, 1901

If a walk is taken for mental as well as bodily exercise, it is most unwise to ignore familiar objects, or refuse the ramble because there is nothing to see. When once the impression of nothing to see gains possession of a person, he is in a bad way, as he is deprived of one great source of pleasure, and must acquire his knowledge at second hand or not at all. Not that I think little of book-knowledge of Nature, for I read many books with delight; but the best book is that which sends us out-of-doors, in search of information, rather than to the library.

—Charles C. Abbott, *A Naturalist's Rambles About Home*, 1885

From John Clare's Bird List of 1825–26

Sky Lark—
a bird that is as of much use in poetry as the Nightingale account of
one kept tame by a publican at Tallington

Field Lark—

Grass hopper lark—
think this is our Cricket bird

Tree lark—
I have seen no such thing

Wood lark—
builds its nest in the woods on the ground under a stoven with long
dead grass & lines it with horse hair & roots lays 6 eggs of a dirty
white thickly swarmed all over with dusky spots it has an odd way of
singing as it flyes from tree to tree dropping down a little way & then
rising up with a jerk & when they fly up they are silent singing every
time they drop trembling their wings till they jerk up agen & when
they are weary they either stuntly drop on the ground or settle on a
tree where their song ceases till they are agen on the wing

Tit lark—
I dont know it

Red Lark—
never seen it

Great Lark—
dont know it

Migration

The migration of birds has been, and still is, quite a mystery. It is undoubtably a matter of instinct, and also of example from older to younger birds. That these birds have any idea of the exact time of an advancing season is not to be accepted.

—Anonymous correspondent, *Scientific Digest*, 1899

If the Emperor Napoleon, when on the road to Moscow with his army in 1811, had condescended to observe the flights of storks and cranes passing over his fated battalions, subsequent events in the politics of Europe might have been very different. These storks and cranes knew of the coming on of a great and terrible winter, the birds hastened towards the south, Napoleon and his army towards the North.

—Frank Buckland, in George C. Bompas's *Life of Frank Buckland*, 1885

At particular times of the year most birds remove from one county to another, or from the more inland districts toward the shores: The times of these migrations or flittings are observed with the most astonishing order and punctuality; but the secrecy of their departure and the suddenness of their re-appearance have involved the subject of migration in general in great difficulties. . . .

Without the means of conveying themselves with great swiftness from one place to another, birds could not easily subsist: The food which Nature has so bountifully provided for them is so irregularly distributed, that they are obliged to take long journies to distant parts in order to gain the necessary supplies; at one time it is given in great abundance; at another it is administered with very sparing hand; and this is one cause of those migrations so peculiar to the feathered tribe.

—Thomas Bewick, *The History of English Birds*, 1797

The natural history of the Rail, or, as it is called in Virginia, the Sora, and in South Carolina, the Coot, is, to the most of our sportsmen, involved in profound and inexplicable mystery. It comes, they know not whence; and goes, they know not where. No one can detect their first moment of arrival; yet all at once the reedy shores and grassy marshes of our large rivers swarm with them, thousands being sometimes found within the space of a few acres. These, when they do venture on wing, seem to fly so feebly, and in such short flut-tering flights among the reeds, as to render it highly improbable to most people that they could possibly make their way over an exten-sive tract of the country. Yet, on the first smart frost that occurs, the whole suddenly disappear, as if they had never been.

To account for these extraordinary phenomena, it has been sup-posed by some that they bury themselves in the mud; but as this is every year dug into by ditchers, and people employed in repairing the banks, without any of those sleepers being found, where but a few weeks before these birds were innumerable, this theory has been generally abandoned. And here their researches into this mysterious matter generally end in the common exclamation of "What can become of them!"

—Alexander Wilson, *American Ornithology*, 1826

There remains something yet more difficult to be cleared up in Relation to the Passage of some Birds; I mean several of the short-winged Water-Fowl, that, during the Summer Months, inhabit the Northern Island of Europe; such as the Danish Islands of Faroo, and Iceland, and many other farther North, even on the Coast of Greenland. Amongst these, the most remarkable for its short Wings, is my Northern Penguin ... which is a Bird never supposed to be capable of any Flight at all, not even so much as to free itself from the Water. There are several others with short Wings, and of such short Flight, that they cannot fly to the Places where they breed, on high Rocks, without making several Stages, by flying from one Ridge to another, and so mounting at last to their Nests and roosting Places. Amongst these are the Razor-Bill, the Gillemot, and the Coulterneb. . . . All these Birds, with some others of the same Genus, disappear in the Winter, and it is not conceivable that they should take long Flights in order to change their Situation, especially the Penguin, who certainly cannot fly at all.

It remains to consider what should become of these Birds, during their Absence from the Sight of the Inhabitants of those Islands: There must be some providential Means to preserve them unseen, in that Part of the World where they appear only in the Summer Months; for in the Spring they are said to appear all at once, in as great Numbers as if they had never been absent. I think the most rational Conjecture, of the Manner of their hiding themselves, and being preserved during the long and cold Winters of those Climates, is, that there are Sub-marine Caverns in the rocky Shores of those Islands, the Mouths of which Caverns, though they be under Water, may lead to Hollows, so rising within Side as to afford a convenient dry Harbour, fit to preserve these Birds in a kind of torpid State during the Winter. The Sea lying before the Mouths of such Caverns and they having a vast Depth of Mountain over them, their inward Capacity must be defended from any rigid Cold, which may be a Means to preserve these Fowls; and late in the Spring (about May) the Time of the Appearance of these Birds, the outward Warmth of the Air, and the returning strong Sun Beams on the Water, near the

Mouth of the Cavern, may, by a small Degree of Heat and Light, re-animate, as it were, these Animals, and bring them from their State of Forgetfulness, by Degrees, to the Use of Life and Motion, till at last they are emboldened to launch forth for another Summer, seek their Prey in the Ocean, and propagate their Species on the neigh-boring Rocks.

I humbly beg Pardon for troubling the Reader with Conjectures so new and uncommon, but as I cannot solve the Disappearance of these Birds any other Way, I hope the Hint may put some Person of a more acute Penetration, upon searching out the true Place of their Winter Habitation, or at least produce some more probable Conjecture.

—George Edwards, *A Natural History of Birds*, 1750

What, for example, is that wonderful power by which migratory birds and fishes are capable of steering with the precision of the expertest mariner from climate to climate, and from coast to coast; and which, if possessed by man, might, perhaps, render superfluous the use of the magnet, and considerably infringe upon the science of logarithms? Whence comes it that the field-fare and red-wing, that pass their summers in Norway, or the wild-duck and merganser, that in like manner summer in the woods and lakes of Lapland, are able to track the pathless void of the atmosphere with the utmost nicety, and arrive on our own coast uniformly in the beginning of October?

—John Mason Good, *The Book of Nature*, 1839

On the last day of August, 1902, at about five o'clock p.m., I noticed a flight of night hawks going south. From the porch of our home in Chicago I watched their flight as they came scattered along restlessly pursuing their way. The open view from where I stood would allow a vision of about a one-mile stretch, looking east. At 5:26 p.m. I took note with watch in hand and counted all the individual twilight birds that passed the line of vision. In four min-utes one hundred had passed the line, the time then being five-thirty. Still continuing counting, another hundred birds passed just at 5.37 ½ p.m., or in four minutes. If this was a fair computation, one thousand five hundred birds would pass in an hour. Allowing only six miles as the width of the city, nine thousand birds would pass over the line drawn across the city at a given point in an hour. As a matter of fact, the birds fly in scattered flocks over a large area, and while these flocks come periodically, lasting into the night, there are quiescent spells when almost no birds are seen in the sky for a space of a minute to several minutes at a time. A fair estimate would indicate that eighteen thousand birds pass over the city in a single night in this migration the last of August. The birds seemed much more plentiful fifteen years ago, when similar timing gave a larger percentage during these migrations.

—Joseph Lane Hancock, *Nature Sketches in Temperate America*, 1911

The Prophet Jeremiah has an allusion to the wandering of the swallow, which he includes among other migratory birds: "Yea, the stork in the heavens knoweth her appointed times, and the turtle, and the crane, and the swallow observe the time of their coming; but my people know not the judgment of the Lord." (Jer. viii.7.) Indeed, it is but just to the common sense of man to say that the obvious fact of the migration of those swift-winged birds seems only to have been doubted during a century or so; and among the achievements of our own age may be numbered that of a return to the simple truth of this point of ornithology. We hear nothing nowadays of the mud or cave theories.

—Susan Fenimore Cooper, *Rural Hours*, 1850

Having mentioned most of the animals in these parts of America, which are most remarkable or useful, there remains however yet some observations on birds, which by some may be thought not impertinent.

There are but few that have fallen under my observation but have been mentioned by the zoologists, and most of them very well figured in Catesby's, or Edwards's works.

But these authors have done very little towards illucidating the subject on the migration of birds, or accounting for the annual appearance and disappearance, and vanishing of these beautiful and entertaining beings, who visit us at certain stated seasons; Catesby has said very little on this curious subject, but Edwards more, and perhaps all, or as much as could be said in truth, by the most able and ingenious, who had not the advantage and opportunity of ocular observation, which can only be acquired by travelling, and residing a whole year at least in the various climates from north to south to the full extent of their peregrinations, or minutely examining the tracts and observations of curious and industrious travellers who have published their memoirs on this subject. There may perhaps be some persons who consider this enquiry not to be productive of any real benefit to mankind, and pronounce such attention to natural history merely speculative, and only fit to amuse and entertain the idle virtuoso; however, the ancients thought otherwise, for with them, the knowledge of the passage of birds was the study of their priests and philosophers, and was considered a matter of real and indispensable use to the state, next to astronomy, as we find their system and practice of agriculture was in a great degree regulated by the arrival and disappearance of birds of passage, and perhaps a calender under such a regulation at this time, might be useful to the husbandman and gardener.

But however attentive and observant the ancients were on this branch of science, they seem to have been very ignorant, or erroneous in their conjectures concerning what became of birds, after their disappearance, until their return again. In the southern and temperate climates some imagined they went to the moon: in the northern regions they supposed that they retired to caves and hollow trees, for shelter and security, where they remained in a dormant state during the cold seasons; and even at this day, very celebrated men have asserted that swallows (*hirundo*) at the approach of winter, voluntarily plunge into lakes and rivers, descend to the bottom, and there creep into the mud and slime, where they continue overwhelmed by ice in a torpid state until the returning summer warms them again into life, when they rise, return to the surface of the water, immediately take wing, and again people the air. This notion, though the latest, seems the most difficult to reconcile to reason or common sense; that a bird so swift of flight that can with ease and pleasure move through the air even swifter than the winds, and in a few hours time shift themselves twenty degrees from north or south, even from frozen regions to climes where frost is never seen, and where the air and plains are replenished with flying insects of infinite variety, their favourite and only food.

Pennsylvania and Virginia appear to me to be the climates in North America, where the greatest variety and abundance of these winged emigrants choose to celebrate their nuptials, and rear their offspring, which they annually return with, to their winter habitations in the southern regions of N. America; and most of these beautiful creatures who annually people and harmonize our forests and groves in the spring and summer seasons, are birds of passage from the southward.

—William Bartram, *Travels*, 1791

White-Throated Sparrow

The first intimation I had of their return this fall was in the clearing one day, when I found two of them sitting atilt of a blackberry bush in front of me. As one of them sat facing me and the other had his back to me and only turned to look over his shoulder, I had a chance to note not only the white chine and ash-gray breast but the black striped chestnut back and the pretty five-striped crown, whose central grayish line is enclosed by two black lines, bounded in turn by the whitish line over the eyes. While I was watching them their attention was diverted by the barking of a gray squirrel in the woods, but they seemed to listen to him as they had to me, with quiet interest, little more.

—Florence Merriam, *Birds Through an Opera Glass*, 1889

The flight of the Wild Goose is heavy and laborious, generally in a straight line, or in two lines approximating to a point, thus, >; in both cases, the van is led by an old gander, who, every now and then pipes his well-known *honk*, as if to ask how they come on, and the honk of "All's well" is generally returned by some of the party. Their course is in a straight line, with the exception of the undulations of their flight. When bewildered in foggy weather, they appear sometimes to be in great distress, flying about in an irregular manner, and for a considerable time over the same quarter, making a great clamor. On these occasions, should they approach the earth and alight, which they sometimes do, to rest and recollect themselves, the only hospitality they meet with is death and destruction from a whole neighborhood already in arms for their ruin.

—Alexander Wilson, *American Ornithology*, 1826

October, 1885

We have had a perfect storm of gold crests, poor little souls! perching on the ledges of the window-panes of the lighthouse, preening their feathers in the glare of the lamps. On the 29th all the island swarmed with them, filling the gardens and all over the cliff—hundreds of thousands. By 9 a.m. most of them had passed on again.

—Heinrich Gatke, *Heligoland as an Ornithological Observatory*, 1895

In spring they come, jubilant, noisy, triumphant, from the South, the winter conquered and the long journey done. In autumn, they come timidly from the North, and, pausing on their anxious retreat, lurk within the fading copses and twitter snatches of song as fading. Others fly as openly as ever, but gather in flocks, as the Robins, most piteous of all birds this season,—thin, faded, ragged, their bold note sunk to a feeble quaver, and their manner a mere caricature of that inexpressible military smartness with which they held up their heads in May.

—T. W. Higginson, *The Life of Birds*, 1862

No sooner does the snow disappear from a sunny and sheltered spot than a flush of green overspreads it, and the typical colors of winter and summer are now alternating, over all the fields and woods, in picturesque patchwork. Snow-birds are becoming numerous, and on the morning of the 16th [March] appeared the first true migrant of the season—a flock of fox sparrows, having evidently arrived during the preceding night. This is the largest and handsomest of all the sparrows, and distinctly different in plumage, which is a rich, rusty-red above, and white beneath streaked with reddish. Being about seven inches long, to the casual observer they are not unlike a diminutive wood thrush. On the first day after arrival, perhaps being especially hungry, they were searching with unusual vigor for food among the dead leaves, and were less shy than usual at one's approach. It is quite noticeable that in spring birds are much more approachable than at any other time.

—Howard E. Parkhurst, *The Birds' Calendar*, 1894

On Grackles

The lower parts of Virginia, North and South Carolina, and Georgia are the winter residences of these flocks. Here numerous bodies, collecting together from all quarters of the interior and northern districts, and darkening the air with their numbers sometimes form one congregated multitude of many hundred thousands. A few miles from the banks of the Roanoke, on the 20th of January, I met with one of those prodigious armies of Grakles. They rose from the surrounding fields with a noise like thunder, and, descending on the length of road before me, covered it and the fences completely with black; and when they again rose, and, after a few evolutions descended on the skirts of the high-timbered wood, at that time destitute of leaves, they produced a most singular and striking effect; the whole trees for a considerable extent, from the top to the lowest branches, seemed as if hung in mourning; their notes and screaming the meanwhile resembling the distant sound of a great cataract, but in more musical cadence, swelling and dying away on the ear, according to the fluctuation of the breeze.

—Alexander Wilson, *American Ornithology*, 1826

There is a decided pleasure that savors not at all of spring time enthusiasm, in observing the autumn and winter migrants. A quiet content seems to permeate their life and movements that tends to impress one with the similarity between their characteristics and emotions, and our own. They, like us, seem imbued with a consciousness of the sadness of the season that precedes the bitter days of ice and snow. The enthusiasm of love and courtship has passed away, and the content of accomplishment is upon them, the peace of the aftermath as it were. Their gregariousness is a strong evidence of their freedom from the individual interests that so absorbs them during the season of parental cares, and now they are willing to quietly enjoy the rest and pleasure of friendly association with their kind.

Only the other day I met a flock of migrants consorting as merrily as a party of human pleasure seekers out for a holiday. There were white-throated and white-crowned sparrows, and by the way, there is no more stylish, dapper young dandy in bird society than your white-crowned sparrow, whose every movement betokens a supercilious vanity quite in keeping with his human prototype. Junco in abundance were with the party and also a few groundsels— a gold finch or two—and I heard though I did not see, a bluebird "with a bit of blue sky for a back," but there was no mistaking his autumnal song note of "cheery-up" and "through-wort." And by the way, I had an opportunity this fall while crossing Lake Huron on a steamer, of associating intimately for several hours with a number of these migrants. After a heavy gale on the previous night which doubtless blew the migrating birds out of their course seaward, our boat was boarded by juncos, white-throated sparrows, pine warblers, yellow warblers, a pair of wrens, a grackle, a Blackburnian warbler, and a black-throated blue warbler, and exhaustion and hunger had rendered them so tame that they hopped about our steamer chairs like pet chickens, picking up the numerous insects that swarmed about the deck. It was a truly delightful experience to a bird lover, this intimate association with birds naturally so shy and timid.

—Alberta A. Field, in *American Ornithology for the Home and School*, Volume 1, 1905

That birds of a feather flock together, even in migration, is evident enough every spring. When in the morning you see one of a
kind, you may confidently look for many more. When, in early May,
I see one myrtle warbler, I presently see dozens of them in the trees
and bushes all about me; or, if I see one redpoll on the ground, with
its sharp chirp and nervous behavior, I look for more. Yesterday, out
the kitchen window, I saw three speckled Canada warblers on the
ground in the garden. How choice and rare they looked on the dull
surface! In my neighbor's garden or dooryard I should probably
have seen more of them, and in his trees and shrubbery as many
magnolia and bay-breasted and black-throated warblers as in my
own; and about his neighbor's place, and his, and his, throughout the
township, and on west throughout the county, and throughout
the State, and the adjoining State, on west to the Mississippi and
beyond, I should have found in every bushy tangle and roadside and
orchard and grove and wood and brookside, the same advancing line
of migrating birds—warblers, flycatchers, finches, thrushes, sparrows, and so on—that I found here. I should have found high-holes
calling and drumming, robins and phoebes nesting, swallows skim-
ming, orioles piping, oven-birds demurely tripping over the leaves
in the woods, tanagers and grosbeaks in the ploughed fields, purple
finches in the cherry-trees, and white-throats and white-crowned
sparrows in the hedges.

One sees the passing bird procession in his own grounds and
neighborhood without pausing to think that in every man's grounds
and in every neighborhood throughout the State, and throughout a
long, broad belt of States, about several millions of homes, and over
several millions of farms, the same flood-tide of bird-life is creeping
and eddying or sweeping over the land. When the mating or nesting
high-holes are awakening you in the early morning by their insistent
calling and drumming on your metal roof or gutters or ridge-boards,
they are doing the same to your neighbors, near by, and to your
fellow countrymen fifty, a hundred, a thousand miles away. Think of
the myriads of dooryards where the "chippies" are just arriving; of
the blooming orchards where the passing many-colored warblers are

eagerly inspecting the buds and leaves; of the woods and woody streams where the oven-birds and water-thrushes are searching out their old haunts; of the secluded bushy fields and tangles where the chewinks, the brown thrashers, the chats, the catbirds, are once more preparing to begin life anew—think of all this and more, and you may get some idea of the extent and importance of our bird-life.

—John Burroughs, *Wake Robin*, 1893

Early of a winter's morning at Nantasket I once saw a flock of geese, many hundreds in number, coming in from the Bay to cross the land in their line of migration. They advanced with a vast, irregular front extending far along the horizon, their multitudinous honking softened into music by the distance. As they neared the beach the clamor increased and the line broke up in apparent confusion, circling round and round for some minutes in what seemed aimless uncertainty. Gradually the cloud of birds resolved itself into a number of open triangles, each of which with its deeper-voiced leader took its way inland; as if they trusted to their general sense of direction while flying over the water, but on coming to encounter the dangers of the land, preferred to delegate the responsibility.

—T. W. Higginson, *Our Birds, and Their Ways*, 1857

It is amusing to find pieces of newspaper bedizening the house of the wood-thrushes so frequently, though it cannot be said that they showed the highest literary taste in their selections; for one or two of the fragments contained accounts of political caucuses.

—Leander S. Keyser, *In Bird Land*, 1897

Perhaps it is no more fair to judge of the family life and customs of night herons from a trip below the trees in which they are nesting, than it would be to judge of the customs of the Parisians by a journey through their sewers. Be this as it may, the noise and the stench of a large heronry remain long in the memory.

—Charles Wendell Townsend, *Sand Dunes and Salt Marshes*, 1913

June 7, 1853

Visited my nighthawk on her nest. Could hardly believe my eyes when I stood within seven feet and beheld her sitting on her eggs, her head to me. She looked so Saturnian, so one with the earth, so sphinx-like, a relict of the reign of Saturn which Jupiter did not destroy, a riddle that might well cause a man to go dash his head against a stone. It was not an actual living creature, far less a winged creature of the air, but a figure in stone or bronze, a fanciful production of art, like the gryphon or phoenix. In fact, with its breast toward me, and owing to its color or size no bill perceptible, it looked like the end of a brand, such are common in a clearing, its breast mottled or alternately waved with dark brown and gray, its flat, grayish, weather-beaten crown, its eyes nearly closed, purposely, lest those bright beads should betray it, with the stony cunning of the Sphinx. A fanciful work in bronze to ornament a mantel. It was enough to fill one with awe. The sight of this creature sitting on its eggs impressed me with the venerableness of the globe. There was nothing novel about it. All the while, this seemingly sleeping bronze sphinx, as motionless as the earth, was watching me with intense anxiety through those narrow slits in its eyelids. Another step, and it fluttered down the hill close to the ground, with a wabbling motion, as if touching the ground now with the tip of one wing, now with the other, so ten rods to the water, which it skimmed close over a few rods, then rose and soared in the air above me. Wonderful creature, which sits motionless on its eggs on the barest, most exposed hills, through pelting storms of rain or hail, as if it were a rock or a part of the earth itself, the outside of the glove, with its eyes shut and wings folded, and, after the two days' storm, when you think it has become a fit symbol of the rheumatism, it suddenly rises into the air a bird, one of the most aerial, supple, and graceful of creatures, without stiffness in its wings or joints! It was a fit prelude to meeting Prometheus bound to his rock on Caucasus.

—Henry David Thoreau, journal

It is not as a singer that the reed warbler shines, but as an architect. As the kingfisher is unrivalled among the regular water birds in the splendour of its appearance, so the reed warbler is easily first in the art of nest building. The nest is nearly described by Meyer as being "like a stocking in the process of knitting, hanging among its many pins." It is woven round the reed stems, which sway with almost every gust of wind and sometimes are swept down almost to the surface of the water. To provide against the constant danger of the eggs or young being rolled out, the reed warbler builds for its size a very long nest composed outwardly of strong dry grasses and fibres and inwardly of finer grasses and horsehair. For weaving purposes this bird, like the chaffinch and the goldcrest, is fond of using cobwebs, and sometimes a little moss is skillfully worked in. The reed warbler's nest is one of the most dainty objects to my mind in nature—that is, when it is left where it is found; but the dried and "preserved" nest of the collector is as inferior to the same nest in its natural position as a battered purple emperor is to the glorious perfect specimen. There are some things which can be preserved more or less in their original beauty; a bird's nest is not among them.

—George A. B. Dewar, *The Angler's Birds*, 1898

I doubt the cuckoo's alleged total indifference to her young. They certainly linger in the neighbourhood of the nest which they have selected to deposit their eggs in. On another occasion a cuckoo used a wagtail's nest in a different part of the garden here—in some ivy that had grown round the decaying stump of an old fir tree. This bird was watched, but not interfered with; she came repeatedly, and was seen on the nest, and the egg observed. Afterwards a cuckoo sang continuously day after day on an ash tree close to the garden.

—Richard Jeffries, *Wild Life in a Southern County*, 1881

A certain amount of moisture is of vital moment to the landrail, or corncrake as the bird is generally called. One small meadow of about two acres, which I have passed twice every day during April, May, June, and July, is usually a sure spot where they may be found. On both sides and in front of it run roads, well-used ones too, and a railway is at the back of it—and yet here they come in preference to places that might be considered far more suitable for them; but the birds know best about that. As the field is small, the owner has it mown, not cut with a machine, and the nesting birds are spared, if possible, for a small tuft is left for them; in fact, the mowers cut round them and pass on. But this year the rail is absent.

This bird, when sitting, has no fear, for although the haymakers were tossing the grass up in all directions, spreading it out to dry, and coming now and again to have a look at her as she sat on her nest, the bird never moved. Between three and four in the afternoon, when she hatched out, she went off with her little black mouse-like brood, just like a farmyard hen.

—Jordan Denham, *From Spring to Fall*, 1894

The Yellow Warbler seems to be one of the few birds, and represents perhaps the only species, which resent and often defeat the Cowbird's parasitic practice of laying its eggs in the nests of other birds and of unloading upon them its parental responsibilities. This the bird does by building a flooring over its eggs among which a Cowbird has deposited one of her own. That the bird does this deliberately, and with the definite purpose of avoiding the hatching and rearing of the ugly and voracious foundling, is shown by the fact that the intended victim of the Cowbird frequently repeats the floor-building operation twice or even three times, to forestall as many of the parasite's attempts to make it a foster parent. Why the Yellow Warbler should be apparently capable of this discernment, and should resent and defeat the intended imposition, while other Warblers, not to mention various Vireos and Sparrows, evidently not only make no effort to get rid of the egg, but feed the young Cowbird as solicitously as they feed their own young, is one of Nature's riddles of which there appears to be no solution.

—George Gladden, *Birds of America*, 1917

Pewits or lapwings not only pack in the winter, but may almost be said to pass the nesting-time together.... Upon approaching, the old bird flies up, circles round, and comes so near as almost to be within reach, whistling "pee-wit, pee-wit," over your head. He seems to tumble in the air as if wounded and scarcely able to fly; and those who are not aware of this intention may be tempted to pursue, thinking to catch him. But so soon as you are leaving the nest behind he mounts higher, and wheels off to a distant corner of the field, uttering an ironical "pee-wit" as he goes. If you neglect his invitation to catch him if you can, and search for the nest or stand still, he gets greatly excited and comes much closer, and in a few minutes is joined by his mate, who also circles round; while several of their friends fly at a safer distance, whistling in sympathy.

—Richard Jeffries, *Wild Life in a Southern County*, 1881

June 3d 1870

found 6 nests three with birds the others old. The last I took. I made hay and strolled with Mr. Garison and had a splendid time.

June 6th 1870

We began to build a hut and had a nice time and found a birds nest with 3 eggs (but we did not take them).

—Theodore Roosevelt, age 12

It is well known that certain birds usually select a particular kind of tree for their nests. For instance, goldfinches breed in maples oftener than in all other trees put together; so does the warbling vireo. Baltimore orioles prefer elms. Brown thrashers select thorny shrubs. Many birds are not particular so long as they have a good cover.

Between food and nest habits, he who would plant trees can select such varieties as to fill his grounds with beauty and song. Let him set a few maples. Vireos will peer and sing in them all summer long, and very often leave their pendent nests as a reminder of summer days, when the branches are bare and cold winds go moaning through them. goldfinches are sure to come in August.

Robins and cedar-birds frequently reside there, and when the pine-finch comes down from the North on its winter visit, the buds and seeds of the maple are certain to receive a call.

—Anonymous, *Birds in Their Relations to Man*, 1903

The nightingale is one of the birds whose habit of returning every year to the same spot can hardly be overlooked by anyone. Hawthorn and Hazel are supposed to attract them: I doubt it strongly. If there is a hawthorn bush near their favourite nesting-place they will frequent it by choice, but of itself it will not bring nightingales.

—Richard Jeffries, *Wild Life in a Southern County*, 1881

Though called a Golden-crowned Thrush our subject is really not a Thrush at all, but a member of the Warbler family. He gets his most familiar name, Oven-bird, from the way he has of building his nest, which is placed on the ground and domed like an old-fashioned oven. Oven-bird, though very common in Albany County, is probably unfamiliar to any one except the bird student. He is more often heard than seen, and when one has learned to recognize his ringing, up-and-down notes he will be recognized in about every thicket or wood one penetrates. He also has a very beautiful song, but few people have heard it.

Oven-bird figured in one of my earliest and most startling ornithological experiences. I was a small boy then, and, attracted and even alarmed by the frantic cries and up-standing feathers of two of the birds, which greeted me as I passed through a quiet wood, I began a search for the nest. I supposed that it was my presence that had disturbed the parent birds, therefore when I discovered the domed structure I plunged my hand into the side entrance with boy-like curiosity, with the object of discovering what treasures the nest contained. I found out all too soon. My fingers came in contact with the cold, slimy folds of a snake.

I jumped probably about a rod. The frenzy of the birds was redoubled. They followed me, screaming and crying. There was a pathetic note of appeal in their voices. Yes, I understood, now. They were begging, imploring me to save their offspring. My fancy, you say? Not at all. Those birds begged me as clearly as human beings could have done to come to their relief. Having quickly got over my fright I approached and with a stout stick pried the horrid reptile out of the nest. He had one baby bird in his jaws and a lump in his middle which told the tale of the fate of another. One blow of my stick paralyzed His Snakeship and caused him to drop the bird from his mouth. It was not badly injured and was able to run back into the nest, where I found three other fledglings resting comfortable and unaware of the danger in which they had been. I then pounded the snake to death and threw it far away.

What a peace suddenly fell over that bird household! The parents ceased their cries and with little purring notes of gratitude returned to the nest, although I stood near at hand. I don't believe birds can count and, as the nestling that had gone down the throat of the snake was not missed, the parents, finding order apparently restored, resumed their ordinary duties as though nothing tragic had occurred.

—Wilbur Webster Judd, *The Birds of Albany County*, 1907

On Flamingos

They build their nests in shallow ponds where there is much mud, which they scrape together, making little hillocks, like small islands, appearing out of the water a foot and a half high from the bottom. They make the foundation of these hillocks broad, bringing them up tapering to the top, where they leave a small, hollow pit to lay their eggs in; and when they either lay their eggs or hatch them, they stand all the while not on the hillock, but close by it with their legs on the ground and in the water, resting themselves against the hillock and covering the hollow nest upon it with their rumps. For their legs are very long, and building thus as they do upon the ground, they could neither draw their legs conveniently into their nests nor sit down upon them otherwize than by resting their whole bodies there, to the prejudices of their eggs or their young, were it not for this admirable contrivance.

—William Dampier, *New Voyage*, 1697

Flamingos

It would be gratifying certainly to know just how this bird disposes of its legs when nesting.

—Charles C. Abbott, *Young Folks' Cyclopedia of Natural History*, 1899

Rooks

The couple in the branch above are the worst. Their plan of building is the most extravagant, the most absurd, I ever heard of. They hoist up ten times as much material as they can possibly use; you might think they were going to build a block and let it out in flats to the other rooks. Then what they don't want they fling down again. Suppose we built on such a principle. Suppose a human husband and wife were to start erecting their house in Piccadilly Circus, let us say; and suppose the man spent all the day steadily carrying bricks up the ladder while his wife laid them, never asking her how many she wanted, whether she didn't think he had brought up sufficient, but just accumulating bricks in a senseless fashion, bringing up every brick he could find. And then suppose, when evening came, and looking round they found they had some twenty cartloads of bricks lying unused upon the scaffold, they were to begin flinging them down into Waterloo Place. They would get themselves into trouble; somebody would be sure to speak to them about it. Yet that is precisely what those birds do, and nobody says a word to them.

—Jerome K. Jerome, *Second Thoughts of an Idle Fellow*, 1890

Birds have a Feng-shui of their own—an unwritten and occult science of the healthy and unhealthy places of residence—and seem to select localities in accordance with the laws of this magical interpretation of nature.

—Richard Jeffries, *Wild Life in a Southern County*, 1881

A Peculiar Nesting Site
Greensburg, Indiana
January 1889—

While digging a gas-well in this city, the workmen broke some part of the machinery and had to quit work for a few days. During that time, a pair of Bluebirds built a nest and laid two eggs in the sand pump. After the nest was removed and work commenced again, the birds remained on the derrick for nearly two days.

—Jas. S. Zoller, *The Ornithologists' and Oologists' Semi-Annual*

I found a few days ago an egg of the Quail, lying on the bare ground in the midst of the public road; it was pure white, very sharp at the small end, almost conical. Though it generally makes a large nest, well covered over, I am told that it is not uncommon for it to drop its eggs on the ground, without any nest.

—Philip Henry Gosse, *Letters from Alabama
Chiefly Relating to Natural History*, 1859

Robin

When the children make their debut, they are more strikingly homely than their parents; possibly because we have known the old birds until, like some of our dearest friends, their plainness has become beautiful to us. In any case, the eminently speckled young gentlemen that come out with their new tight-fitting suits and awkward ways do not meet their father's share of favor.

Perhaps the nest they come from accounts for their lack of polish. It is compact and strong, built to last, and to keep out the rain; but with no thought of beauty. In building their houses the robins do not follow our plan, but begin with the frame and work in. When the twigs and weed stems are securely placed they put on the plaster—a thick layer of mud that the bird moulds with her breast till it is as hard and smooth as a plaster cast. And inside of all, for cleanliness and comfort, they lay a soft lining of dried grass.

—Florence Merriam, *Birds Through an Opera Glass*, 1889

On the whole, there seems to be a system of Women's Rights prevailing among the birds, which, contemplated from the standpoint of the male, is quite admirable. In almost all cases of joint interest, the female bird is the most active. She determines the site of the nest, and is usually the most absorbed in its construction. Generally, she is more vigilant in caring for the young, and manifests the most concern when danger threatens. Hour after hour I have seen the mother of a brood of blue grossbeaks pass from the nearest meadow to the tree that held her nest, with a cricket or grasshopper in her bill, while her better-dressed half was singing serenely on a distant tree or pursuing his pleasure amid the branches.

—John Burroughs, *Wake Robin*, 1893

The cock was a fraud. You know how some persons make a great show of passing things to you at luncheon time. Actually they do nothing—they let it go. But each time you reach for the salt, they wave a hand after it as though a magic wand. The cock snow-bunting had learned this trick well. Very assiduous, very fussy, he accompanied his wife up and down. He waited upon her while she hunted up fibres; he flew back with her and watched while she worked at the nest—a perfect example of a despot lord. I do not believe he gathered a solitary thing himself; I never saw him do it.

—Aubyn Trevor-Battye, *Ice-Bound on Kolguev: A Chapter in the Exploration of Arctic Europe*, 1895

A bird's nest is a bedroom, dining-room, sitting-room, parlor, and nursery all in one; for there the young birds sleep, eat, rest, entertain their guests (if they ever have any), and receive their earliest training.

—Leander S. Keyser, *In Bird Land*, 1897

How alert and vigilant the birds are, even when absorbed in building their nests! In an open space in the woods, I see a pair of cedar-birds collecting moss from the top of a dead tree. Following the direction in which they fly, I soon discover the nest placed in the fork of a small soft-maple, which stands amid a thick growth of wild-cherry trees and young beeches. Carefully concealing myself beneath it, without any fear that the workmen will hit me with a chip or let fall a tool, I await the return of the busy pair. Presently I hear the well-known note, and the female sweeps down and settles unsuspectingly into the half-finished structure. Hardly have her wings rested, before her eye has penetrated my screen, and with a hurried movement of alarm, she darts away. In a moment, the male, with a tuft of wool in his beak (for there is a sheep pasture near), joins her, and the two reconnoitre the premises from the surrounding bushes. With their beaks still loaded, they move around with a frightened look, and refuse to approach the nest till I have moved off and laid down behind a log. Then one of them ventures to alight upon the nest, but, still suspecting all is not right, quickly darts away again. Then they both together come, and after much peeping and spying about and apparently much anxious consultation, cautiously proceeded to work. In less than half an hour, it would seem that wool enough has been brought to supply the whole family, real and prospective, with socks, if needles and fingers could be found fine enough to knit it up. In less than a week, the female has begun to deposit her eggs,—four of them in as many days,—white tinged with purple, with black spots on the larger end. After two weeks of incubation, the young are out.

—John Burroughs, *Wake Robin*, 1893

> They'll come again to the apple tree,—
> Robin and all the rest,—
> When the orchard branches are fair to see
> In the snow of blossoms dressed,
> And the prettiest thing in the world will be
> The building of the nest.
>
> —Mrs. M. E. Sangster, *Bird World*, 1898

The baby orioles were dumpy little yellowish things, much like a young chicken in color, and the most persistent cry-babies I ever saw among birds. The young robin generally sits on his branch motionless, seldom opens his mouth for a call, and makes demonstrations only when food is in sight; the baby thrush is patience and silence itself,—indeed how otherwise could be a thrush? Even the little blackbird, though restless and fussy, does not cry much; but those oriole infants simply bawled (there's no other word) every instant. The cry was very peculiar, four or five loud notes on an ascending scale, rapidly and constantly repeated, like "chr-r-r."

I should think the parents of these clamorous creatures would have been driven wild, and they did appear nearly so; almost every moment one or the other brought food to the two bawlers, who were on different trees.

—Olive Thorne Miller, *Bird-Ways*, 1885

One morning I was hurrying noisily through the underbrush of a clearing to get home in time for breakfast, when, suddenly, I came face to face with a pair of chickadees. Even then they did not stir, but sat eying me calmly for several seconds. I suspected a nest, and when they had flown off, I discovered the opening in a decayed stub close by my side. The stub was a small one, being perhaps eight or ten inches in diameter and four and half feet high. The entrance was about a foot from the top, and the nest itself a foot or more below this. What a tasteful little structure it was! Although out of sight, it was far prettier than most bird-houses on exhibition in the forest. Bits of fresh green moss gave it a dainty air, and brought out the dark gray of the squirrel or rabbit hair that made it snug and warm. I was tempted to wonder where the fur came from—had this innocent chickadee tweaked it out of the back of some preoccupied animal? Perhaps the demure little recluse has a spice of wickedness after all, and its satisfaction in its secure retreat has something of exultant mischief in it!

—Florence Merriam, *Birds Through an Opera Glass*, 1889

We believe that in every case of nest decoration apparently prompted by a taste for the beautiful, it will invariably and without exception be found that the primary, we may even say the exclusive, motive is that of concealment; an effort to evade discovery by harmonising the exterior of the nest with surrounding objects, either by an assimilation or blending of colour, or a collection of similar material to that near which the nest is built. Let it be clearly understood, however, that these remarks are in no way intended to convey the idea that birds have no taste for the beautiful. On the contrary, birds as a group have perhaps this aesthetic taste more highly developed than any other living creatures, man alone excepted.

—Charles Dixon, *Birds' Nests*, 1902

Let me not forget to mention the nest under the mountain ledge, the nest of the common pewee, a modest mossy structure, with four pearl-white eggs, looking out upon some wild scene and overhung by beetling crags. After all has been said about the elaborate, high-hung structures, few nests, perhaps, awaken more pleasant emotions in the mind of the beholder than this of the pewee,—the gray, silent rocks, with caverns and dens where the fox and the wolf lurk, and just out of their reach, in a little niche, as if it grew there, the mossy tenement!

—John Burroughs, *Wake Robin*, 1893

Many writers write sermons on that peculiar & as they imagine invariable instinct in birds of the same kind using the same materials in building their nests but a closer observation of nature will show that it tis not invariable—in some places it varies for want of those materials which they most prefer & in such cases they use the things nearest to their habitations & make up for the loss of those they want as well as they can—but it is often found that where the things which they use in common are found in greatest plenty that the same kind of birds will use different materials in the construction of their nests & I have observed for years that all the nests of Blackbirds or nearly all that are built first or earliest in the spring use grass both within & without their nests & those built later in the season are composed of moss without & grass & leaves within wether this be the different tastes of the different species I cannot tell—but when ever I caught a black bird at work earlily in spring when they are built of grass it was always the cock-bird which was building it & when later & composed of moss the hen bird was invariably the builder which I could easily distinguish by her dun coloured bill & rich umber coloured breast.

—John Clare, journal, 1820s

Some time ago, as I sat smoking a contemplative pipe in my piazza, I saw with amazement a remarkable instance of selfishness displayed on a very small bird, which I had hitherto respected for its inoffensiveness. Three nests were placed almost contiguous to each other in my piazza; that of a swallow was affixed in the corner next to the house, that of a phebe in the other, a wren possessed a little box which I had made on purpose, and hung between. Be not surprised at their tameness, all my family had long been taught to respect them as well as myself. The wren had shown before signs of dislike to the box which I had given it, but I knew not on what account; at last it resolved, small as it was, to drive the swallow from its own habitation, and to my very great surprise it succeeded. Impudence often gets the better of modesty, and this exploit was no sooner performed, than the signs of triumph appeared very visible, it fluttered its wings with uncommon velocity, an universal joy was perceivable in all its movements. Where did this little bird learn that spirit of injustice? It was not endowed with what we term reason! Here then is a proof that both those gifts border very near on one another; for we see the perfection of the one fixing with the errors of the other! The peaceable swallow, like the passive Quaker, meekly sat at a small distance and never offered the least resistance; but no sooner was the plunder carried away, than the injured bird went to work with unabated ardour, and in a few days the depredations were repaired. To prevent however a repetition of the same violence, I removed the wren's box to another part of the house.

—Crèvecoeur, *Letters from an American Farmer*, 1782

A bird's nest is the most graphic mirror of a bird's mind. It is the most palpable example of those reasoning, thinking qualities with which these creatures are unquestionably very highly endowed.

Evidence of this reasoning power confronts the student of Birds' Nests as he gazes upon each procreant cradle, no matter how crude on the one hand, or how elaborate on the other it may chance to be for each type of home represents the best possible harmony with the conditions under which reproduction may take place.

—Charles Dixon, *Birds' Nests*, 1902

Night

the Night-hawk is singing his
frog-like tune,
Twirling his watchman's rattle
about

—William Wordsworth

Nightingale, Cock, Hen and Egg.

The evening was magnifi-
cent; the lake, in deep repose,
did not have a single ripple on
its surface; the murmuring river
bathed our peninsula, which
was decorated by false ebony
trees still covered with leaves;
the bird called the Carolina cuckoo repeated its monotonous
call; we would hear it close at
times, at others farther away, as
the bird changed the place from which it uttered its love calls.

—Chateaubriand, *Voyages en Amerique*, 1836

What, then, is the meaning of this dancing, of these strange little
sudden gusts of excitement arising each day at about the same time
and lasting till the birds fly away? We have here a social display as
distinct from a nuptial or sexual one, for it is in the autumn that these
assemblages of the great plovers take place, after the breeding is all
over; the deportment of the courting or paired birds towards each
other—their nuptial antics—is of a different character. With birds,

as with men, all outward action must be the outcome of some mental state. What kind of mental excitement is it which causes the stone-curlews to behave every evening in this mad, frantic way? I believe that it is one of expectancy and making ready, that these odd antics—the mad running and leaping and waving of the wings—give expression to the anticipation of going and desire to be gone which begins to possess the birds as evening falls. They are the prelude to, and they end in, flight. The two, in fact, merge into each other, for short flights grow out of the tumblings over the ground, and it is impossible to say when one of these may not be continued into the full flight of departure. They are a part of the dance, and, as such, the birds may almost be said to dance off. Surely in actions which lead directly up to any event there must be an idea, an anticipation of it, nor can the idea of departure exist in a bird's mind (hardly, perhaps, in a man's) except in connection with what it is departing for—food, in this case, a banquet. So when I say that these birds "think the joys of the night" need this be merely a figure? May it not be true that they do so and dance forth each night, to their joy?

—Edmund Selous, *Bird Watching*, 1901

The last thing every night, when the house was dark and still, I would lean out of my window to listen to the nightingales singing, widely scattered, some near and loud, some at a distance, scarcely audible. At such times the dark earth, spread out before me, and the wide sky above, each through a different sense—one with melody of hidden birds, the other with glitter of stars—seemed to produce a similar effect of the mind: for just as the stars, some large, intensely bright, others small and pale, burned and sparkled in the dusky blue of heaven, so did the birds, far and near, scattered over that darker under-sky, each in his place, shine and sparkle in their melody.

—W. H. Hudson, *London Birds*, 1899

As late as 7.20 p.m., one evening, I heard the Maryland yellow-throat singing beside the country road. At the same time the chimney-swift was also seen flitting high in space. The voices of the birds were quieting down before the advent of night, but still I could hear the mournful coo of the dove. These notes in the quiet of the evening, when the afterglow is lighting the landscape, are most enjoyable. A robin seems to want his voice heard, and stationed on a fence post he gives out a varied song as late as half-past seven. Even the barn swallow is making his last rapid flight through space. Then, finally, the Maryland yellow-throat comes forth again with the last song of the parting day, mounts into the air almost perpendicularly for about a hundred feet, then as suddenly drops toward the earth. As he takes his farewell evening flight, he has not lost the opportunity to assert his last cheery song, "Be-with-you—be-with-you—be with-you!"

—Joseph Lane Hancock, *Nature Sketches in Temperate America*, 1911

September—

While the inhabitants of this great city are fast asleep, during the dark nights that occur generally about this period of September, many wonderful events are going on high up in the air, far above our heads. Of the nature and cause of these phenomena the general public are little aware. The noises proceeding from the numerous creatures, that are passing over our towns in mid-air, during the darkness of the night, would in former days have probably been put down to the supernatural agency of ghosts and goblins. Observation however, has taught us that the mysterious forms, shadows and cries proceed from flocks of migratory birds, passing from one part of the earth's surface to another. More especially when the clear and frosty nights come on, may be heard in the sky the rush of the wings, and the wild cries of various water-birds, such as wild duck, wild geese and other water-fowl, as they are passing from the northern to the more southern regions.

—Frank Buckland, in George C. Bompas's *Life of Frank Buckland*, 1885

Usually it is not until the gold begins to pass that I notice the nighthawk, though he may have been circling and crying "peent,

peent" all the afternoon. If you can catch sight of him before the light fades too much you will see the white bar which crosses each wing beneath and looks exactly like a hole, as if the bird had transparencies in his pinions as has the polyphemus moth.

—Winthrop Packard, *Old Plymouth Trails*, 1920

As I sit in the cool of the evening, at the backdoor of the house where I am residing, I have an opportunity of witnessing those singular evolutions of the Chimney Swallows (Hirundo pelasgia), which are the prelude to their nightly repose. There is a tall chimney rising from the smithy a few rods distant, round the summit of which some hundreds of swallows assemble every evening, about sunset. They come one by one from all parts, trooping to the common lodging at the same hour; and as soon as each is arrived, he begins to wheel round and round in the air above the chimney-top. In a few minutes a large number are collected, which sweep round in a great circle, twittering and chirping; others continuing to arrive every moment, which immediately take their part in the circumvolution. By and by, one and another, and another, drop, as it were, into the chimney, as the circle passes over it, until they pour down in a stream, with a roaring sound, which, when heard from within the building, sounds like the sullen boom of a distant cataract. At length, when objects begin to be dim and indiscernible, all have entered and taken up their places within the shaft, where they remain for the night. In the morning, near sunrise, they emerge in a dense stream, pouring out like bees, make a few wide revolutions, and disperse on their daily occupation.

—Philip Henry Gosse, *Letters from Alabama Chiefly Relating to Natural History*, 1859

At sunset all the whistlers leave the marshes, where they have been feeding during the day, and fly out to sea to spend the night. It would be manifestly unsafe for ducks to sleep on the surface of the narrow creeks, for they would either be carried by the wind or tide against the banks or stranded on the flats, whereas on the surface of the ocean they can rest undisturbed. In the daytime I have noticed that sleeping ducks, with their bills buried in the feathers of the back, head up into the wind, and that they paddle gently so as to keep in the same place. Sometimes, with one leg tucked under a wing, the bird paddles with the other, so that it revolves in a circle.

The black duck has a different outlook on life, for he prefers to feed by night, and when the whistler goes to sleep on the sea, he arises from his daytime slumbers in the same region and repairs to the marshes. . . . I have seen great flocks of black ducks floating in a long line off the beach in the bright sunlight, most of them fast asleep. They are alert birds, however, and cannot be caught napping, for there are always some on the watch, and even the sleepiest awake from time to time, stretch their wings and yawn, as they look about before settling down for another nap.

—Charles Wendell Townsend, *Sand Dunes and Salt Marshes*, 1913

The nighthawk's cry, falling from the high gold of the waning sunset to dusky pasture glades, has no notes of melancholy but a soothing sleepiness about it that makes it a lullaby of contentment. I rarely hear him after dark. I fancy he goes higher and higher to keep in the soft radiance of the fading glow. Only once have I ever seen one sky-coasting, falling like a dark star from a height where he seemed but a mote in the gold . . .

It was as if his wings had lost their hold on the thinner air of this remote height. He half shut them to his body and dived head fore-most on a perilous slant. Then, just as he must be dashed to pieces on the gray rock of the ledge on which I sat, he spread them wide, caught the air that sang through the wide-spread primaries with a clear, deep-toned note, and rose again; and in his "peent, peent" was a quaint note of self-satisfaction and praise.

It is customary to ascribe actions of this sort on the part of a bird to a desire to please and astound the mate who is supposed to look on with fervent admiration. Sometimes this may be the case, but I think more often the bird, like my nighthawk, does it to please himself. There was no mate in sight when this nighthawk did his sky coasting, nor did any appear afterward. It was after the mating season and I think the bird did it in just pure joy in his own dare-deviltry. He liked to see how near he could come to breaking his neck without actually doing it. In the same way a male woodcock will keep up his shadow-dancing antics long after the nesting season is over, and the partridge drums more or less the year around. The other bird may have much admiration for these actions if she sees them, but never half so much as the bird who performs. Nothing could equal that.

—Winthrop Packard, *Old Plymouth Trails*, 1920

The nightjars, in pairs or small parties of four or five birds, could be heard reeling on all sides; and some of them, spying my motionless figure, and curious to know what manner of creature I was, would come to me and act in the most fantastical manner—now wheeling round and round my head like huge moths, anon tossing themselves up and down like shuttlecocks; in the meantime uttering their loud, rattling, castanet notes, and smiting their wings violently over their backs, producing a sound like the crack of a whiplash.

—W. H. Hudson, *London Birds*, 1899

The night heron, half as large again as the green heron, is a familiar bird in these regions. Although, as its name would imply, it is largely a bird of the night, yet, when it has insatiable young in the nest clamoring for food, it must needs work by day. Indeed at all seasons it is commonly seen by day, but, when the young shift for themselves, it generally spends the hours of light in slothful ease, dozing in companies on the tops of bushes or trees. At dusk it is all alert, and flies to the beach and the marshes, squawking as it goes. It delights most in the lowest tides, for then it can fish in the pools and meandering streams of the sand flats. As one pushes a canoe along the winding creek in the darkness and silence of the night, there is nothing more startling than the uncanny cries with which these birds suddenly pierce the gloom.

—Charles Wendell Townsend, *Sand Dunes and Salt Marshes*, 1913

The Bobolink has a call not unlike that of any other American bird, a rich chink which is often heard from the sky in the clear autumn nights. Who knows what the Bobolink is doing up there in darkness instead of sleeping in the long grass?

—J. H. Stickney, *Bird World*, 1898

The herald of the moon is the whippoor-will. I do not recall hearing him sing on pitch black nights. Starshine is enough for him, but I am convinced that he is only half nocturnal and that he watches for signs of moonlight as eagerly as I do. Last night I saw the glint of it in the upper sky an hour before the moon rose, a silvery shine which did not touch the lower atmosphere, but shot athwart the higher stars like a ghost of aurora. The whippoor-will saw it, too, and began his call, which I do not find a melancholy plaint, but rather an eager asking. It was a voice of shrill longing, sounding out of luminous loneliness after the moon began to silver all things.

Three hours later the moon had slipped down from the zenith into cushions of velvety, violet black, low in the western sky. Its bright white glow was lost in part and it was haloed with a yellow nimbus of its own fog distillation. Over on the margin of the pines the little screech owl, now full of field mice and having time to worry, voiced his trouble about it in little sorrowful whinnies. Down in the pasture a fox barked distinctly and a coon answered the plaint of the screech owl in a voice not unlike his. It always seems to me that the night hunters of pasture and woodland bewail the passing of such a night as much as I do. The whippoor-will began to voice his petulant wistfulness again. He had been silent for hours, feasting I dare say on myriad moths and unable to call with his mouth full. The whippoor-will chants matins as querulously as he does vespers. Far in the east the stars that had been gleaming brighter as the moon descended paled again. The night in all its perfect beauty was over, for into the shrill eagerness of the whippoor-will's call cut the joyous carol of a dawn-worshipping robin.

—Winthrop Packard, *Old Plymouth Trails*, 1920

From Gilbert White's Journal, 1769

Jan. 25. Soft day. Bunting sings. A snipe appears on the high downs among the wheat. Royston crow. Skylark sings.

Jan. 31. Sowed the meadows with ashes.

Feb. 4. Fog, rain, sun, grey. Hedge sparrows sing vehemently.

March 6. The cock swan at two year's old.

March 7. Green woodpecker begins to laugh. Last night I hear that short quick note of birds flying in the dark: if this should be the voice of Oedicnemus [stone curlew], as is supposed: then that bird, which is not seen in the dead of winter, is returned. Blood-worms appear in the water: they are gnats in one state.

March 10. Oats are sown. Crows build: rooks build. Ewes & lambs are turned into the wheat to eat it down.

March 11. Made the bearing cucumber-bed for four lights with seven loads of dung. the bed was much wetted in making by the snow.

March 12. Gold-crested wren, regulus cristatus, sings. His voice is as minute as his body.

Birds of Western America

About the only bird having no representative on the Atlantic coast is the "chaparral-cock," "road-runner," or paisano, as the native Californians call it. It looks much like a cross between a hawk and a hern-shaw; long-geared, long-tailed, swift of foot, white, gray, and blue, with a bluish topknot and long bill. Though generally deemed unfit to eat, it really is one

of the fattest and finest-flavored birds we have, in spite of its diet of centipedes, lizards, and scorpions. It is an interesting bird, easily tamed, and may be made a great pet. It is quite harmless, and is rarely shot, except by foolish tourists who think it the proper thing to murder everything they see. The common story about its killing rattlesnakes by surrounding them with lobes of prickly-pear, or putting balls of cactus in their coil, so that in striking them they strike themselves, I have found, upon most diligent inquiry among Indians and Mexicans, to rest upon about the same foundation as the old story about raccoons catching crabs by dipping their tails in the water, and when they got a bite jerking them out before the crabs could let go.

—Theodore S. Van Dyke, *Southern California: Its Valleys, Hills, and Streams; Its Animals, Birds, and Fishes; Its Gardens, Farms, and Climate*, 1886

The white-crowns in the Georgetown valley seemed to be excessively shy, and their singing was a little too reserved to be thoroughly enjoyable, for which I reason I am disposed to think that mating and nesting had not yet begun, or I should have found evidences of it, as their grassy cots on the ground and in the bushes are readily discovered. Other birds that were seen in this afternoon's ramble were Wilson's and Audubon's warblers, the spotted sandpiper, and that past-master in the art of whining, the kildeer. Another warbler's trill was heard in the thicket, but I was unable to identify the singer that evening, for he kept himself conscientiously hidden in the tanglewood. A few days later it turned out to be one of the most beautiful feathered midgets of the Rockies, Macgillivray's warbler, which was seen in a number of places, usually on bushy slopes. He and his mate often set up a great to-do by chirping and flitting about, and I spent hours in trying to find their nests, but with no other result than to wear out my patience and rubber boots. I can recall no other Colorado bird, either large or small, except the mountain jay, that made so much ado about nothing, so far as I could discover. But I love them still, on account of the beauty of their plumage and the gentle rhythm of their trills.

—Leander S. Keyser, *Birds of the Rockies*, 1902

We hear the Inca [Dove] before we saw him. We did not have to listen; we could not help hearing him from dawn till dark. Of all wooing birds, this Dove is the most constant. A pair of lovers will sit on the telephone wire by the hour and keep up a mournful cooing, that to some people is positively disconcerting. But all the world should love a lover. The song is really more suggestive of a funeral procession than of a wedding journey.

—William L. Finley, *Birds of America*, 1917

Go as far as you dare in the heart of a lonely land, you cannot go so far that life and death are not before you. Painted lizards slip in and out of rock crevices, and pant on the white hot sands. Birds, humming-birds even, nest in the cactus scrub; woodpeckers befriend the demoniac yuccas; out of the stark, treeless waste rings the music of the night-singing mocking-bird. If it be summer and the sun well down, there will be a burrowing owl to call. Strange, furry, tricksy things dart across the open places, or sit motionless in the conning towers of the creosote. The poet may have "named all the birds without a gun," but not the fairy-footed, ground-inhabiting, furtive, small folk of the rainless regions. They are too many and too swift; how many you would not believe without seeing the footprint tracings in the sand. They are nearly all night workers, finding the days too hot and white. In mid-desert where there are no cattle, there are no birds of carrion, but if you go far in that direction the chances are that you will find yourself shadowed by their tilted winds. Nothing so large as a man can move unspied upon in that country, and they know well how the land deals with strangers. There are hints to be had here of the way in which a land forces new habits on its dwellers. The quick increase of suns at the end of spring sometimes overtakes birds in their nesting and effects a reversal of the ordinary manner of incubation. It becomes necessary to keep eggs cool rather than warm. One hot, stifling spring in the Little Antelope I had occasion to pass and repass frequently the nest of a pair of meadow larks, located unhappily in the shelter of a very slender weed. I never caught them setting except near night, but at midday they stood, or drooped above it, half fainting with pitifully parted bills, between their treasure and the sun. Sometimes both of them together with wings spread and half lifted continued a spot of shade in a temperature that constrained me at last in a fellow feeling to spare them a bit of canvas for permanent shelter.

There was a fence in that country shutting in a cattle range, and along its fifteen miles of posts one could be sure of finding a bird or two in every strip of shadow; sometimes the sparrow and the hawk, with wings trailed and beaks parted, drooping in the white truce of noon.

—Mary Austin, *Land of Little Rain*, 1903

On the alkali plains of the Southwest, where only yuccas, sagebrush, and cacti grow, is the home-land of Bell's Sparrow and its variants, the Sage Sparrow (*Amphispiza nevadensis nevadensis*),

Gray Sage Sparrow (Amphispiza nevadensis cinerea), and the California Sage Sparrow (Amphispiza nevadensis canescens). Here, amid the dreary wastes of hot sands, these grayish brown or brownish gray little mites cheerfully go about the duties of their lives, preaching sermons on patience, courage, and the joy of life to all their human friends.

—Unattributed, *Birds of America*, 1917

The condor, which is quite often called "vulture," is generally seen only in the high mountains, though it used often to be seen in the lowlands before their settlement. In shape and appearance it is much like the common buzzard, but is nearly black. The gray band on the under side of the wing is on the opposite side from that of the buzzard. It is the largest bird in North America, "rivaling in size the condor of the Andes," according to Dr. Coues. Its spread of wing is as wide as ten and a half feet, and it weighs from forty to eighty pounds, according to the time of weighing—before or after dinner. Like the condor of the Andes, it sometimes gorges itself to such an extent that it can hardly fly; and in days gone by, when not too wild to approach near enough, it has been lassoed by a sudden dash with a good horse. A friend who had a tame one that had been caught in this way told me it averaged a sheep a day. It is quite certain, however, that they can go many days without anything to eat. The condor is the most graceful sailor of all american birds; far more so than even the frigate-bird. In the high thin air above the highest mountains, it spends hours with outstretched wings without making the slightest motion that can be detected, even by the strongest glass, and it probably spends the whole day without resting upon the earth or flapping its wings in the sky.

—Theodore S. Van Dyke, *Southern California: Its Valleys, Hills, and Streams; Its Animals, Birds, and Fishes; Its Garden, Farms, and Climate*, 1886

One bright morning in early June, on the way from Fyffe to Slippery Ford on the Lake Tahoe state route, we flushed a Plumed Partridge from the roadside, and my companion remarked that he had flushed a partridge from that place two days before. A search for a nest began among the manzanita bushes and "mountain misery," which latter was thick, nearly ten inches high. After a short hunt we discovered the treasure hidden well at the base of a tall cedar and guarded by the pretty white blossoms and green leaves of Chamaebatia. It was made of leaves and stems of this plant and lined with feathers, and in it lay ten eggs of the Plumed Partridge. They were nearly ready to hatch,—how ready I did not guess,—and with a hope that no one would molest them in the meantime, we departed, resolving to come back the next day. But I reckoned without my host, for having eaten luncheon and rested, I stole back alone for a last peep at them, and two had pipped the shells while a third was cuddled down in the split halves of his erstwhile covering. The distress of the mother was pitiful, and I had not the heart to torture the beautiful creature needlessly; so going off a little way, I lay down flat along the "misery," regardless of the discomfort, and awaited developments. Before I could focus my glasses she was on the nest, her anxious eyes still regarding my suspiciously. In less time than it takes to tell it, the two were out and the mother cuddled them in her fluffed-out feathers. This was too interesting to be left. Even at the risk of being too late to reach my destination, I must see the outcome. Two hours later every egg had hatched and a row of tiny heads poked out from beneath the mother's breast. I started toward her and she flew almost into my face, so closely did she pass me. Then by many wiles she tried in vain to coax me to go another way. I was curious and therefore merciless. Moreover, I had come all the way from the East for just such hours as this. But once more a surprise awaited me. There was the nest, there were the broken shells; but where were the young partridges? Only one of all that ten could I find. For so closely did they blend in coloring with the shadows on the pine needles under the leaves of the "misery" that although I knew they were there, and dared not step for fear of crushing them, I was not sharp enough to discover them. No doubt a thorough search would have been successful, but this a dread of injuring them forbade me to make.

So picking up the one which had crouched motionless beside a leaf and which was really not much larger than my thumb, I contented myself with trying to solve the mystery of how so much bird ever grew in that small shell, half of which would scarcely cover his head. Once fairly in my hand, he cuddled down perfectly contented to let me fit the empty shell to his fat little body, as if he knew he was out of that for good. He was a funny little ball of fluffy down, with a dark strip down his back and a lesser one on each side of that. Meanwhile the adult bird had disappeared, and there was no choice but to put the youngster back in the nest and go on my way. But I had learned two things,—that affairs move rapidly in the partridge household, and that human eyes are seldom a match for a bird's instinct.

—Irene Grosvenor Wheelock, *Birds of California*, 1912

Loveland, Colorado

One of the handsomest of our western waders is Wilson's Phalarope *Phalaropus lobatus*, and for activity while swimming it surpasses all others, and on land it has but few peers. Its beautiful shade of chestnut and red are so blended and artistic that one cannot but admire it if they possess the least admiration for the beautiful.

One peculiarity, differing from all migratory birds that I am acquainted with, is that the female arrives here several days in advance of the male, which is about the first week in May. She is by far the brightest hued and seems to shun the company of the more sober colored males; but as soon as they arrive they begin to talk business to their proud mistresses and after considerable persuasion coax them to lead a more retired life. They mutually select a place to start housekeeping, scratch a slight depression in the ground and make a rude nest of dead grass, usually on the shady side of a bunch of weeds; but often in full view.

After depositing the eggs, the female pays very little or no attention to them; but again joins her more dressy companions and leaves her mate to bear the whole of the cares and responsibility to hatch out the chicks, which he is not loth to do, and even after they are hatched she cares but very little for her offsprings. Though she may materially assist in feeding them, I am afraid they would go to sleep hungry if it was not for their provident papa.

—William G. Smith, *The Ornithologists' and Oologists' Semi-Annual*, 1889

Unless you have hard the Cactus Wren sing, you will wonder at the science that classes him with the wrens. But when you listen to the rich, ringing, wren-like song, and come upon the singer sitting on a thorny twig in the exact attitude of the thrashers, with lifted bill and tail curved downward, you are satisfied to leave his name among the wren family. He sings constantly as well as sweetly. His clear notes are the first to waken the weary camper in the morning, and oftentimes they alone break the death-like hush of evening. The Leconte thrasher runs him a close race in this, but, I believe, is always a little short of winning. A spirit brave enough to sing in all the dreary waste and scorching heat wins your honest admiration, and you try to imagine what the parched and silent desert would be without these two birds.

—Irene Grosvenor Wheelock, *Birds of California*, 1912

Of all the desert plants, the cholla cactus is the most treacherous. I shall never forget my first experience. It is a favorite nesting place of the Cactus Wren. When I first saw a Cactus Wren's nest, I was anxious to find out what it contained. It was a gourd-shaped bundle of fibers and grasses with a hallway running in from the side. I couldn't look in, so I tried to feel. I ran my hand in as far as I could till the thorns about the entrance pricked into my flesh. I started to pull back. The more I pulled, the tighter the thorns clung and the deeper they pricked. I was in a trap. I reached for my knife to cut some of the thorns off, but had to cringe and let some of the others tear out. I looked at them, but could see no barbs. Yet when they once enter the flesh, one can readily tell they have tiny barbs, for it tears the flesh to get them out.

The Cactus Wren, as a rule, selects the thorniest place in a cholla cactus, although he sometimes nests in a mesquite or palo verde. Like the Tule Wren or Winter Wren, this bird often builds nests that are not used. These are called "cock nests," and are probably built by the male while the female is incubating. It is a question whether they are built from the standpoint of protection, that is having several unused nests about as a ruse, or whether the bird merely builds homes until the pair gets a nest that suits them exactly.

—William L. Finley, *Birds of America*, 1917

The Dotted Cañon Wren is a fairly common resident in certain parts of the Sierra Nevada, chiefly along the west slope. He may be seen darting in and out on the steep sides of rocky cañons, and, but for his white throat, looking much like a big brown bug. A nearer view with field glasses reveals the tiny black and white polka-dots of his brown coat. He is a handsome little fellow and a fine singer, making the cool depths of the cañon ring with his jubilant song. "The Bugler" some one has called him, and one thinks of the name whenever listening to the song. He is a rather shy bird, creeping in and out among the rocks, pausing a moment to eye the intruder curiously, tilt his tail, and scurry off again. The busy search in every crack of the hard stone for possible insects so absorbs him that he has not time to speculate on what business the intruder may have there. Enough for him if he can place a boulder between himself and observing eyes while he gathers food for his mate or his brood. His long bill probes every moss-covered crevice and tiny hole, and often you may see him jerk a worm out of its hiding place and scramble up the cañon wall to his nest with it. A tiny hole is the entrance to his nesting site, sometimes under a boulder, sometimes far up the face of a cliff. He will fly down from it, or rather drop down with closed wings like a stone, but I have never seen him fly all the way up to it. Sometimes he ascends by a series of short flights, but oftener by hops and fluttering scrambles. He loves those bare bleak rocks and sits upon them to sing, rather than upon any vegetation there may be, hiding behind them or on them, much as the lizards do.

—Irene Grosvenor Wheelock, *Birds of California*, 1912

The bird music of Colorado, though not so abundant as one could wish, is singularly rich in quality, and remarkable for its volume. At the threshold of the State the traveler is struck by this peculiarity. As the train thunders by, the Western meadow-lark mounts a telegraph pole and pours out such a peal of melody that it is distinctly heard above the uproar of the iron wheels. . . .

Another unique singer of the highlands is the horned lark. One morning in June a lively carriage party passing along the mountain side, on a road so bare and bleak that it seemed nothing could live there, was startled by a small gray bird, who suddenly dashed out of the sand beside the wheels, ran across the path, and flew to a fence on the other side. Undisturbed, perhaps even stimulated, by the clatter of two horses and a rattling mountain wagon, undaunted by the laughing and talking load, the little creature at once burst into song, so loud as to be heard above the noisy procession, and so sweet that it silenced every tongue.

"How exquisite! What is it?" we asked each other, at the end of the little aria.

"It's the gray sand bird," answered the native driver.

"Otherwise the horned lark," added the young naturalist, from his broncho behind the carriage.

Let not his name mislead: this pretty fellow, in soft, gray-tinted plumage, is not deformed by "horns;" it is only two little tufts of feathers, which give a certain piquant, wide-awake expression to his head, that have fastened upon him a title so incongruous. The nest of the desert-lover is a slight depression in the barren earth, nothing more; and the eggs harmonize with their surroundings in color. The whole is concealed by its very openness, and as hard to find, as the bobolink's cradle in the trackless grass of the meadow.

—Olive Thorne Miller, *A Bird-Lover in the West*, 1900

Clarke Crow

Everybody notices him, and nobody at first knows what to make of him. One guesses that he must be a woodpecker, another a crow or some sort of jay, another a magpie. He seems to be a pretty thoroughly mixed and fermented compound of all these birds, has all their strength, cunning, shyness, thievishness, and wary, suspicious curiosity combined and condensed. He flies like a woodpecker, hammers dead limbs for insects, digs big holes in pine cones to get at the seeds, cracks nuts held between his toes, cries like a crow or Steller jay,—but in a far louder, harsher, and more forbidding tone of voice,—and besides his crow caws and screams, has a great variety of small chatter talk, mostly uttered in a fault-finding tone. Like the magpie, he steals articles that can be of no use to him. Once when I made my camp in a grove at Cathedral Lake, I chanced to leave a cake of soap where I had been washing, and a few minutes afterward I saw my soap flying past me through the grove, pushed by a Clarke crow.

—John Muir, *Among the Birds of the Yosemite*, 1898

What drew us first to the pasture—which we came to at last—was our search for a magpie's nest. The home of this knowing fellow is the Rocky Mountain region, and naturally, he was the first bird we thought of looking for. There would be no difficulty in finding nests, we thought, for we came upon magpies everywhere in our walks. Now one alighted on a fence-post approach, tilting upward his long, expressive tail, the black of his plumage shining with brilliant blue reflections, and the white fairly dazzling the eyes. Again we caught glimpses of two or three of the beautiful birds walking about on the ground, holding their precious tails well up from the earth and gleaning industriously the insect life of the horse pasture. At one moment we were saluted from the top of a tall tree, or shrieked at by one passing over our heads, looking like an immense dragonfly against the sky. Magpie voices were heard from morning till night; strange, loud calls of "mag! mag!" were ever in our ears. "Oh, yes," we had said, "we must surely go out some morning and find a nest." . . .

Selecting a favorable-looking clump of oak-brush, we attempted to get in without using the open horse paths, where we should be in plain sight. Melancholy was the result; hats pulled off, hair disheveled, garments torn, feet tripped, and wounds and scratches innumerable. Several minutes of hard work and stubborn endurance enabled us to penetrate not more than half a dozen feet, when we managed, in some sort of fashion to sit down, on opposite sides of the grove. Then, relying upon our "protective coloring" (not evolved, but carefully selected in the shops), we subsided into silence, hoping not to be observed when the birds came home, for there was the nest before us.

A wise and canny builder is Madam Mag, for though her home must be large to accommodate her size, and conspicuous because of the shallowness of the foliage above her, it is, in a way, a fortress, to despoil which the marauder must encounter a weapon not to be despised,—a stout beak, animated and impelled by indignant motherhood. The structure was made of sticks, and enormous in size; a half-bushel measure would hardly hold it. It was covered, as if to protect her, and it had two openings under the cover, toward either of which she could turn her face. It looked like a big, coarsely woven basket resting in a crotch up under the leaves, with a nearly closed cover supported by a small branch above. The sitting bird could draw herself down out of sight, or she could defend herself and her brood, at either entrance.

In my retreat, I had noted all these points before any sign of life appeared in the brush. Then there came a low cry of "mag! mag!" and the bird entered near the ground. She alighted on a dead branch, which swung back and forth, while she kept her balance with her beautiful tail. She did not appear to look around; apparently she had no suspicions and did not notice us, sitting motionless and breathless in our respective places. Her head was turned to the nest, and by easy stages and with many pauses, she made her way to it. I could not see that she had a companion, for I dared not stir so much as a finger; but while she moved about near the nest there came to the eager listeners on the ground low and tender utterances in the sweetest of voices,—whether one or two I know not,—and at last a song, a true melody, of a yearning, thrilling quality that

few song-birds, if any, can excel. I was astounded! Who would sus-
pect the harsh-voiced, screaming magpie of such notes! I am certain that the bird or birds had no suspicion of listeners to home
talk and song, for after we were discovered, we heard nothing of
the sort.

This little episode ended, madam slipped into her nest, and
all became silent, she in her place and I in mine. If this state of
things could only remain; if she would only accept me as a tree-
trunk or a misshapen boulder, and pay no attention to me, what
a beautiful study I should have! Half an hour, perhaps more, passed
without a sound, and then the silence was broken by magpie
calls from without. The sitting bird left the nest and flew out of
the grove, quite near the ground; I heard much talk and chatter
in low tones outside, and they flew. I slipped out as quickly as
possible, wishing indeed that I had wings as she had, and went
home, encouraged to think I should really be able to study the
magpie.

But I did not know my bird. The next day, before I knew she was
about, she discovered me, though it was plain that she hoped I had
not discovered her. Instantly she became silent and wary, coming to
her nest over the top of the trees, so quietly that I should not have
known it except for her shadow on the leaves. No talk or song
now fell upon my ear; calls outside were few and subdued. Everything was different from the natural unconsciousness of the previous
day; the birds were on guard, and henceforth I should be under
surveillance.

From this moment I lost my pleasure in the study, for I feel little
interest in the actions of a bird under the constraint of an unwelcome
presence, or in the shadow of constant fear and dread. What I care to
see is the natural life, the free, unstudied ways of birds who do not
notice or are not disturbed by spectators. Nor have I any pleasure in
going about the country staring into every tree, and poking into
every bush, thrusting irreverent hands into the mysteries of other
lives, and rudely tearing away the veils that others have drawn
around their private affairs. That they are only birds does not signify

to me; for me they are fellow-creatures; they have rights, which I am bound to respect.

—Olive Thorne Miller, *A Bird-Lover in the West*, 1900

Pasadena will rest in memory as a bird paradise. Here no less than thirty-eight of the eighty-three species recorded were new to my life list, while twenty-eight species were seen here and nowhere else during the entire trip. But this is not all. Birds are everywhere in Pasadena. Mockingbirds greet you from every house-top at all times of day and night. Goldfinches, towhees, and hummingbirds of several kinds are everywhere. Brewer's Blackbird adds tone by contrast to the tropical splendor all about. But I cannot begin to tell—you must go and see for yourself.

—Lynds Jones, *Wilson Bulletin*, 1900

Valley Quail

Four or five pairs rear their young around our cottage every spring. One year a pair nested in a straw pile within four or five feet of the stable door, and did not leave the eggs when the men led the horses back and forth within a foot or two. For many seasons a pair nested in a tuft of pampas grass in the garden; another pair in an ivy vine on the cottage roof, and when the young were hatched, it was interesting to see the parents getting the fluffy dots down. They were greatly excited, and their anxious calls and directions to their many babes attracted our attention. They had no great difficulty in persuading the young birds to pitch themselves from the main roof to the porch roof among the ivy, but to get them safely down from the latter to the ground, a distance of ten feet, was most distressing. It seemed impossible the frail soft things could avoid being killed. The anxious parents led them to a point above a spireaea bush, that reached nearly to the eaves, which they seemed to know would break the fall. Anyhow they led their chicks to this point, and with infinite coaxing and encouragement got them to tumble themselves off. Down they rolled and twisted through the soft leaves and panicles to the pavement, and, strange to say, all got away unhurt except one that lay as if dead for a few minutes. When it revived, the joyful parents, with their brood fairly launched on the journey of life, proudly led them down the cottage hill, through the garden, and along an osage orange hedge into the cherry orchard.

—John Muir, *Among the Birds of the Yosemite*, 1898

Before the orange-colored glare of the poppy begins to pale along the meadow, before the indigo of the larkspur extinguishes the light of violet and bell-flower, and the gold of the primrose is lost beneath the phacelia's wealth of blue, the large flocks of the valley quail whose roaring wings have all winter resounded in the valleys of California begin to break up, and over the spangled slopes where the first of the pink flowers of the alfileria and the yellow heads of the clover are fading, quail in pairs may be seen trotting about in all directions.

—Theodore S. Van Dyke, *Southern California: Its Valleys, Hills, and Streams;*
Its Animals, Birds, and Fishes; Its Gardens, Farms, and Climate, 1886

At Portland, Ore., on July 16, there was time between trains to climb the hill west of the city where Streaked Horned Lark, Gambel's Sparrow and Russet-backed Thrush were added to the list. It was on this height that the lifting clouds revealed the ice cap of St. Helens. It was not until the Columbia river was behind us that I even suspected the presence of other snow-clad peaks, because not until now did the clouds break away. I feel certain of being forgiven for the break in the bird record after Adams and Ranier joined St. Helens to form as matchless a company of snow-clads as anywhere graces a landscape. As we wound around now toward them, now away they were always changing, revealing some hidden grandeur or beauty. It was a glorious interlude.

Portland, Oregon, July 16

Great Blue Heron. Belted Kingfisher. Gairdner's Woodpecker. Western Wood Pewee Streaked Horned Lark American Crow American Goldfinch Gambel's Sparrow Western Chipping Sparrow Tree Swallow Violet Green Swallow Cliff Swallow Bank Swallow Louisiana Tanager Cassin's Vireo Yellow Warbler Russet-backed Thrush Western Robin

A water sprite spirited me away from Seattle, landing me at Everett in the dead of night. It was miserably cold, and nowhere could even so much as a cot be found at that time of night. Those three miserable hours stretched out into weeks. But with the dawn came the birds and some degree of comfort physically. . . . The hill overlooking the bay and town had given up its secrets. No less than thirteen species added themselves to my list of personal acquaintances. Chief among these were Pileolated and Macgillivray's Warblers, Redbreasted Sapsucker and Oregon Towhee. They seemed anxious to know who and what I was, and they sang for me by the half hour.

—Lynds Jones, *Wilson Bulletin*, 1900

The first bird I noticed in the quiet Mormon village where I settled myself to study was a little beauty in blue. I knew him instantly, for I had met him before in Colorado. He was dining luxuriously on the feathery seeds of a dandelion when I discovered him, and at no great distance was his olive-clad mate, similarly engaged. . . .

The lazuli-painted finch should be called the blue-headed finch, for the exquisite blueness of his whole head, including throat, breast, and shoulders, as if he had been dipped so far into blue dye, is his distinguishing feature. The bluebird wears heaven's color; so does the jay, and likewise the indigo bird; but not one can boast the lovely and indescribable shade, with its silvery reflections, that adorns the lazuli. Across the breast, under the blue, is a broad band of chestnut, like the breast color of our bluebird, and back of that is white, while the wings and tail are dark. Altogether, he is charming to look upon. Who would not prefer him about the yard to the squawking house sparrow, or even the squabbling chippy?

—Olive Thorne Miller, *A Bird-Lover in the West*, 1900

On the thirtieth of June my companion and I were riding slowly down the mountainside a few miles below Gray's Peak, which we had scaled two days before. My ear was struck by a flicker's call above us, so I dismounted from my burro, and began to clamber up the hillside. Presently I heard a song that seemed one moment to be near at hand, the next far away, now to the right, now to the left, and anon directly above me. To my ear it was a new kind of bird minstrelsy. I climbed higher and higher, and yet the song seemed to be no nearer. It had a grosbeak-like quality, I fancied, and I hoped to find either the pine or the evening grosbeak, for both of which I had been making anxious search. The shifting of the song from point to point struck me as odd, and it was very mystifying.

Higher and higher I climbed, the mountain side being so steep that my breath came in gasps, and I was often compelled to throw myself on the ground to recover strength. At length a bird darted out from the pines several hundred feet above me, rose high into the air, circled and swung this way and that for a long time, breaking at intervals into a song which sifted down to me faintly through the blue distance. How long it remained on the wing I do not know, but it was too long for my eyes to endure the strain of watching it. Through my glass a large part of the wings showed white or yellowish-white, and seemed to be almost translucent in the blaze of the sunlight. What could this wonderful haunter of the sky be? It was scarcely possible that so roly-poly a bird as a grosbeak could perform so marvelous an exploit on the wing.

I never worked harder to earn my salary than I did to climb that steep and rugged mountain side; but at last I reached and penetrated over the zone of pines, and finally, in an area covered with dead timber, standing and fallen, two feathered strangers sprang in sight, now flitting among the lower branches, now sweeping to the ground. They were not grosbeaks, that was sure; their bills were quite slender, their bodies lithe and graceful, and their tails of well-proportioned length. Same in color, they presented a decidedly thrush-like appearance, and their manners were also thrush-like.

Indeed, the colors and marking puzzled me not a little. The upper parts were brownish-gray of various shades, the wings and tail for the most part dusky, the wing coverts, tertials, and some of the quills bordered and tipped with white, also the tail. The white of both wings and tail became quite conspicuous when they were spread. This was the feathered conundrum that flitted about before me. The birds were about the size of the hermit thrushes, but lithe and suppler. They ambled about gracefully, and did not seem to be very shy, and presently one of them broke into a song—the song that I had previously heard, only it was loud and ringing and well-articulated, now that I was near the singer. Again and again they lifted their rich voices in song. When they wandered a little distance from each other, they called in affectionate tones, giving their "All's well."

Then one of them, no doubt the male, darted from a pine branch obliquely into the air, and mounted up and up and up, in a series of graceful leaps, until he was a mere speck against the blue dome, gyrating to and fro in zigzag lines, or wheeling in graceful circles, his song dribbling faintly down to me at frequent intervals. A thing of buoyancy and grace, more angel than bird, that wonderful winged creature floated about in the cerulean sky; how long I do not know, whether five minutes, or ten, or twenty, but so long that at last I flung myself upon my back and watched him until my eyes ached. He kept his wings in constant motion, the white portions making them appear filmy as the sun shone upon them. Suddenly he bent his head, partly folded his wings, and swept down almost vertically like an arrow, alighting safe somewhere among the pines. I have seen other birds performing aerial evolutions accompanied with song, but have never known one to continue so long on the wing.

What was this wonderful bird? It was Townsend's solitaire (Myadestes towsendiis)—a bird which is peculiar to the West, especially to the Rocky Mountains, and which belongs to the same family as the thrushes and bluebirds. No literature in my possession contains any reference to this bird's astonishing aerial flight and song, and I cannot help wondering whether other bird-students have witnessed the interesting exploit.

—Leander S. Keyser, *Birds of the Rockies*, 1902

On the Long-Crested or Steller's Jay

All jays make their share of noise in the world; they fret and scold about trifles, quarrel over anything, and keep everything in a ferment when they are about. The particular kind we are now talking about is nowise behind his fellows in these respects—a stranger to modesty and forbearance, and the many gentle qualities that charm us in some little birds and endear them to us; he is a regular filibuster, ready for any sort of adventure that promises sport or spoil, even if spiced with danger. Sometimes he prowls about alone, but oftener has a band of choice spirits with him, who keep each other in countenance (for our jay is a coward at heart, like other bullies) and share the plunder on the usual terms in such cases, of each one taking all he can get. Once I had a chance of seeing a band of these guerrillas on a raid; they went at it in good style ... A vagabond troop made a descent upon a bush-clump, where, probably, they expected to find eggs to suck, or at any rate a chance for mischief and amusement. To their intense joy, they surprised a little owl quietly digesting his grasshoppers with both eyes shut. Here was a lark, and a chance to wipe out a large part of the score that the jays keep against owls for injuries received time out of mind. In the tumult that ensued, the little birds scurried off, the woodpeckers overhead stopped tapping to look on, and a snake that was basking in a sunny spot concluded to crawl into his hole. The jays lunged furiously at their enemy, who sat helpless, bewildered by the sudden onslaught, trying to look as big as possible, with his wings set for bucklers and his bill snapping; meanwhile twisting his head till I though he would wring it off, trying to look all ways at once. They jays, emboldened by partial success, grew more impudent, till their victim made a break through their ranks and flapped into the heart of a neighboring juniper, hoping to be protected by the tough, thick foliage. The jays went trooping after.

—Elliott Coues, *Birds of the Northwest: A Handbook of the Ornithology of the Region Drained by the Missouri River and Its Tributaries,* 1874

Water Ouzel

Though not a water bird in structure, he gets his living in the water, and is never seen away from the immediate margin of streams. He dives fearlessly into rough, boiling eddies and rapids to feed at the bottom, flying under water seemingly as easily as in the air. He has the oddest, neatest manners imaginable, and all his gestures as he flits about in the wild, dashing waters bespeak the utmost cheerfulness and confidence. He sings both winter and summer, in all sorts of weather,—a sweet, fluty melody, rather low, and much less keen and accentuated than from the brisk vigor of his movements one would be led to expect.

How romantic and beautiful is the life of this brave little singer on the wild mountain streams, building his round bossy nest of moss by the side of a rapid or fall, where it is sprinkled and kept fresh and green by the spray! No wonder he sings well, since all the air about him is music; every breath he draws is part of a song, and he gets his first music lessons before he is born; for the eggs vibrate in time with the tomes of the waterfalls. Bird and stream are inseparable, songful and wild, gentle and strong,—the bird ever in danger in the midst of the stream's mad whirlpools, yet seeming immortal. And so I might go on, writing words, words, words; but to what purpose? Go see him and love him, and through him as through a window look into Nature's warm heart.

—John Muir, *Among the Birds of the Yosemite,* 1898

When I first visited California, it was my good fortune to see the "big trees," the Sequoias, and then to travel down into the Yosemite, with John Muir . . . [who] met me with a couple of packers and two mules to carry our tent, bedding, and food for a three days' trip. The first night was clear, and we lay down in the darkening aisles of the great Sequoia grove. The majestic trunks, pillars of a mightier cathedral than ever was conceived even by the fervor of the Middle ages. Hermit thrushes sang beautifully in the evening, and again, with a burst of wonderful music in the dawn. I was interested and a little surprised to find that, unlike John Burroughs, John Muir cared little for birds or bird songs, and knew little about them. The hermit thrushes meant nothing to him, the trees and the flowers and the cliffs everything. The only birds he noticed or cared for were some that were very conspicuous, such as the water-ousels—always particular favorites of mine too.

—Theodore Roosevelt, *Theodore Roosevelt: An Autobiography*, 1920

The present-day resident of the canyon that I discovered with the greatest surprise and pleasure in the hot desert bottom was our little friend of cold mountain streams, the gray short-tailed water ouzel or dipper. Here it was keeping cool by standing characteristically on a rock in the middle of the creek. Who can say which of all the many prized western birds is his favorite, the one he would be most glad to see after years of absence from their home? This little fellow, so brave, so cheery, such an exuberant songster, associated with such pure secluded mountain streams, is surely one of the most heart-warming.

While standing spellbound I watched my Bright Angel dipper walk down a streak of sunlit water, after which it came up and stood on a stone dipping true to form. Here, after years of waiting in the East, my water ouzel has come to me, the gift of the Bright Angel. Farther up the singing stream I found it again, this time preening itself on a stone in the shade of the willows. Then, with its familiar and undeniably rather tinny rattling cry, it flew down over the water.

—Florence Merriam Bailey, *Among the Birds in the Grand Canyon Country*, 1939

Fort Pierre, Missouri. Just above Tetons river on Little Missouri
June 1st 1843

Johnny would have enjoyed this trip well, for he would have
seen many new things, and would have been surprised to see many
of the Water Birds found along our shores, such as blackheaded
Gulls, Willets, Curlews, spotted Sandpipers, Rails, Woodcocks,
Whippoorwills, rosebreasted Grosbeaks, Cowbirds, Cedar birds and
more house Wrens than I ever thought could be found *in the woods.*
Cliff Swallows, roughed winged & Sand Martins and probably all
the Woodpeckers and Sylvia that inhabit the Eastward.

—John James Audubon, from a letter to his wife

Sage Cock

It is only in the broad, dry, half-desert sage that they are quite at
home, where the weather is blazing hot in summer, cold in winter. If
any one passes through a flock, all squat and hold their heads low,
hoping to escape observation; but when approached within a rod or
so, they rise with a magnificent burst of wing-beats, looking about as
big as turkeys and making a noise like a whirlwind.

—John Muir, *Among the Birds of the Yosemite*, 1898

Hummingbirds

After all that has been written, the first sight of a living humming-bird, so unlike in its beauty all other beautiful things, comes like a revelation to the mind . . . The minute exquisite form, when the bird hovers on misty wings, probing the flowers with its coral spear, the fan-like tail expanded, and poising motionless, exhibits the feathers shot with many hues; and the next moment vanishes, or all but vanishes, then reappears at another flower only to vanish again, and so on successively, showing its splendours not continuously, but like the intermitted flashes of the firefly—this forms a picture of airy grace and loveliness that baffles description.

—W. H. Hudson, *The Naturalist in La Plata*, 1895

One is admiring some brilliant and beautiful flower, when between the blossom and one's eye suddenly appears a small dark object, suspended as it were between four short black threads meeting each other in a cross. For an instant it shows in front of the flower; again another instant, and emitting a momentary flash of emerald and sapphire light, it is vanishing, lessening in the distance, as it shoots away, to a speck that the eye cannot take note of.

—Alfred Newton, mid-1800s, in A. R. Wallace's *Humming-Birds*

The name we usually give to the birds of this family is derived from the sound of their rapidly-moving wings, a sound which is produced by the largest as well as by the smallest member of the family. The Creoles of Guiana similarly call them Courdons or hummers. The French term, Oiseau-mouche, refers to their small size; while Colibri is a native name which has come down from the Carib inhabitants of the West Indies. The Spaniards and Portuguese call them by more poetical names, such as Flower-peckers, Flower-kissers, myrtle-suckers,—while the Mexican and Peruvian names showed a still higher appreciation of their beauties, their meaning being rays of the sun, tresses of the day-star, and other such appellations. Even our modern naturalists, while studying the structure and noting the peculiarities of these living gems, have been so struck by their inimitable beauties that they have endeavoured to invent appropriate English names for the more beautiful and remarkable genera. Hence we find in common use such terms as Sun-gems, Sun-stars, Hill-stars, Wood-stars, Sun-angels, Star-throats, Comets, Coquettes, Flame-bearers, Sylphs, and fairies; together with many others derived from the character of the tail or the crests.

—Alfred Russel Wallace, *Humming-Birds*, 1877

The Ruby-throat Humming-bird (Trochilus colubris) delights to visit these flowers; their deep capacious tubes are just the thing for him. We may sometimes see half-a-dozen at once round a single bush, quite in their glory, humming and buzzing from one flower to another, as if too impatient to feed; now burying themselves to the very wings in the deep corolla, sipping the nectar, or snapping up the multitudes of little flies entangled in the tube; now rushing off in a straight line like a shooting star, now returning as swiftly, while their brilliant plumage gleams in the sun like gold and precious stones.

—Philip Henry Gosse, *Letters from Alabama*
Chiefly Relating to Natural History, 1859

At Phantom Ranch, where we saw perhaps the last covey of quail in the region, on the stony slopes above the tent house, the hot desert feeling of the bottom of the canyon was given by a variety of cacti, a small barrel form, large pincushion kinds, and, most conspicuous, the pale-green tuni pads, flat ovals with large silken yellow or deep-pink blossoms. These were tightly closed during the long sunless hours of morning. For when the sun had risen so high above the South Rim that it illumined the pale vertical cliffs of the Kaibab on the opposite North Rim, Bright Angel Canyon thousands of feet below, a narrow slit between enclosing rock walls, still slumbered in darkness. But though the dark nights were long in the bottom, breaks in the walls of Bright Angel let in the slanting rays of the rising and setting sun, touching up the tops of the highest crags and pinnacles. Once as the morning hours passed and the sunlight finally reached the floor of the canyon the yellow cactus flowers, whose slow opening was being registered by a patient photographer from Nature Magazine, became gorgeous with the light full on their wide-spread satiny saucers. Then the hummingbirds gathered as if invited to a feast and swung around the shining blossoms eagerly probing for insects and honey.

The pretty little black-chinned hummingbirds with white collars and violet neckbands were common early in May together with much larger green hummers, probably migrating broad-tailed Rocky Mountain birds, many of which have been found on both rims of the canyon . . . One of the green females that I watched near our tent house sat on the edge of a silky yellow petal, her tiny claws tightly gripped as she leaned forward probing deep into the middle of the flower.

Hummingbirds were attracted not only by the tuni cactus blossoms but also by the creamy yellow flower spikes of the tall agave or mescal with its dagger-like basal leaves, in full bloom at the time and the most spectacular plant of the region, individuals standing like solitary sentinels stationed at their posts from the bottom to the top of Bright Angel Canyon. One posted on the far bank of the white-foamed creek caught the full sun on its long yellow spike, on its green stalk, and on the tips of its basal daggers. So many black forms of big Carpenter Bees, moths, other insects, and hummingbirds buzzed around the creamy flowers that at a little distance I often asked myself, "Is it bird or insect?"

—Florence Merriam Bailey, *Among the Birds in the Grand Canyon Country*, 1939

We saw but few birds on our journey; woodpeckers of several sorts, a handsome yellow bird, something like a goldfinch, a few crows, and some small birds, much like tom-tits. As my youngest daughter was carrying some flowers in her hand, a humming bird settled on them, it made her start, thinking it was a large insect; it was not larger than a chafer, but a beautiful bird.

—John Woods, *Two Years' Residence in the Settlement
on the English Prairie in the Illinois Country, United States*, 1822

Saw a number of humming-birds. They are particularly partial to the evening hours. One is sure to find them now towards sunset, fluttering about their favorite plants. Often there are several together among the flowers of the same bush, betraying themselves, though unseen, by the trembling of the leaves and blossoms. They are extremely fond of the Missouri currant—of all the early flowers, it is the greatest favorite with them; they are fond of the lilacs also, but do not care much for the syringa; to the columbine they are partial, to the bee larkspur also, with the wild bergamot or Oswego tea, the speckled jewels, scarlet trumpet-flower, red-clover, honeysuckle, and the lychnic stribe. There is something in the form of these tube-shape blossoms, whether small or great, which suits their long, slender bills, and possibly, for the same reason, the bees cannot find such easy access to the honey and leave more in these than in open flowers.

—Susan Fenimore Cooper, *Rural Hours*, 1850

When engaging in collecting its accustomed sweets, in all the energy of life, it seemed like a breathing gem, a magic carbuncle of flaming fire, stretching out its glorious ruff as if to emulate the sun itself in splendour.

—Thomas Nuttall, *Manual of the Ornithology
of the United States and Canada*, 1834

He seems like some exiled pygmy prince, banished, but still regal, and doomed to wings. Did gems turn to flowers, flowers to feathers, in that long-past dynasty of Humming-Birds? It is strange to come upon his tiny nest, in some gray and tangled swamp, with this brilliant atom perched disconsolately near it, upon some mossy twig; it is like visiting Cinderella among her ashes.

—T. W. Higginson, *The Life of Birds*, 1862

When on the Amazon I once had a nest brought me containing two little unfledged humming-birds, apparently not long hatched. Their beaks were not at all like those of their parents, but short, triangular, and broad at the base, just as the form of the beak of a swallow or swift slightly lengthened. Thinking (erroneously) that the young birds were fed by their parents on honey, I tried to feed them with a syrup made of honey and water, but though they kept their mouths constantly open as if ravenously hungry, they would not swallow the liquid, but threw it out again and sometimes nearly choked themselves in the effort. At length I caught some minute flies, and on dropping one of these into the open mouth, it instantly closed, the fly was gulped down, and the mouth opened again for more; and each took in this way fifteen or twenty little flies in succession before it was satisfied. They lived thus three or four days, but required more constant care than I could give them.

—Alfred Russel Wallace, *Humming-Birds*, 1877

From John Clare's Bird List of 1825–26

Marsh Titmouse or Black cap—
this is what we call the little black cap it haunts woods & Ozier holts
& builds in the neglected holes of the small Woodpecker it keeps
constantly in motion hopping among the oak tops & pecking
uttering a double tootling note at the same time.

Bearded Titmouse—
I know nothing of this bird

Chimney swallow—
they come about the middle of april & I observe on their first visit
that they follow the course of brooks & rivers I have observed this
for years & always found them invariably pursuing their first flights
up the brinks of the meadow streams & I have always observed that
they come eastward they build their nests in chimneys of dust straw
& feathers generally chusing the side were the chimneys of smoke is
the strongest they lay 5 eggs of a dirty white freckled with pink spots
they often make their nest under brig arches in barns & out houses
under the rig trees entering thrg a hole in the walls or door way &
when i was a boy I found one yearly under a low arch that overstrid
a dyke at the entrance to wood croft house—they collect together in
the autumn & learn their young to flye who at first take short circuits
& then flye on their chimneys to rest when the old ones come & feed
them when more used to flye they venture wider circuits & leave the
place were they was bred altogether chusing the bartlements of the
church as a place of rest—they genneraly haunt rivers & brooks
before they start & may be seen settling 4 or 5 together on twigs of
Osiers beside the stream that bend with them till they nearly touch
the water—they make westward when they start & often return
again resting by flocks on churches & trees in the village as if they
were making attempts before they started for good

Sand Martin—

We have none of these in our neeghbourhood but they are very numerous about the upland neighbourhood & a man with whom I burnt lyme said they build their nests by scores on the side of a quarry were he worked near Northampton.

City Birds

SWALLOWS.

In early spring it was pretty to see the wood-pigeons in flocks on the leafless willows and poplar devouring the catkins; they also fed on the tender young leaves of the hawthorn and a few other trees, and on the blossoms of the almond tree. Year by year the changes in the habits of our town race become more marked. Thus, during the last summer, numbers of wood-pigeons could be seen constantly flying to and alighting on roofs and chimney-pots on the tallest houses. Many of these birds were no doubt breeding on houses—a new habit which we first observed only two years ago. Tamer than they now are these birds can never be. One morning in September I saw a man sitting on a bench at the side of Rotten Tow with a wood-pigeon perched on his wrist feeding on bread from his hand. I asked him if the pigeons knew him—if he was accustomed to feed them at that spot? He replied that it was the first time he had brought bread for the birds; that as soon as he began to throw crumbs to the sparrows, the dove to his surprise flew down from the tree and alighted on his arm.

—W. H. Hudson, *London Birds*, 1899

A large Eagle some years ago made an attack upon a little boy about seven years of age, residing near the city of New York, who, with a younger brother was amusing himself with attempting to reap, during the absence of their parents. The bird sailed slowly over them, and with a sudden swoop endeavored to seize the child, but luckily missed him.

—William L. Baily, *Our Own Birds*, 1869

The sparrow is, to paraphrase Bacon, a wise thing for itself, but a shrewd thing for everybody else. Bold, active, and vivacious, its distribution is as wide as that of the Englishman. Patronising art, science, and law, the sparrow broods and breeds in the temples dedicated to their shrines, and in one European capital has unwittingly attempted to destroy the balance of justice by constructing her nest in one of the pans held by the blind emblem of that inestimable virtue.

—Anonymous, *Winter Birds*, 1889

The most picturesque view in the famous Central Park is to be had from the foot-bridge over the lake at its upper extremity. On one side of the bridge is the tip-end of the lake, forming a secluded basin with steep, rocky embankments, hedged about by overarching trees and luxuriant shrubbery, and enriched in the season with purple and pink masses of wistaria and azalea, while on the other side the eye ranges over the whole expanse of the irregular lake, flanked on the right by the massive and turreted "Dakota," its farther shore revealing a majestic row of poplars and cypresses, and beyond them a line of lofty buildings looming up like castle walls for a solid background, and with the two white spires of the Cathedral pricking the sky in the blue distance. A pair of large night herons, coursing hither and thither over the water, give the requisite and poetic touch of animation.

—Howard E. Parkhurst, *The Birds' Calendar*, 1894

Many a summer afternoon I have seen nighthawks circling erratically above Boston Common, and there their cry has sounded like a plaint. No doubt these birds fly there by choice and bring up their young on the tops of Back Bay buildings because they prefer the place, but this has not prevented a tinge of melancholy in their voices. Like many another city dweller they may take habit for preference, but the longing for the freedom of the woods, thought unconscious, will voice itself some way.

—Winthrop Packard, *Old Plymouth Trails*, 1920

All migratory birds appear to be found in the suburbs, or within a radius of ten miles of London, earlier than in any other part of the country. Londoners, therefore, have no excuse for not knowing the notes of birds, having every opportunity of listening to their song.

—Frank Buckland, in George C. Bompas's *Life of Frank Buckland*, 1885

Hermit Thrush

This elegant bird, attractive in voice and personality, occasionally spends the Summer in Washington Park. In vocal powers he is regarded by many writers as the Nightingale of America, and while the migrating individuals seen about Albany are silent, those that remain to breed sing freely. Mr. Horace G. Young informs me that one sang gloriously near the Albany Country Club late into June, 1907. As its name implies, the Hermit is extremely retiring, preferring well grown woods for an abiding place; still, one will occasionally approach the farmhouse, or even enter the city. A fine male spent the first two weeks of April, 1907, in the rear yard of the house where I have my lodgings on High Street. This yard is directly in the rear of the old home of the Albany Institute and Historical and Art Society. The bird did not mind the presence of the laundress hanging out clothes, but calmly surveyed the scene from the branches of a small peach tree. Hermit spent most of the time on the ground in the fence corners grubbing for worms. He was absolutely silent. One morning while observing the bird from my room with a glass I discovered near him two White-crowned Sparrows feeding on the ground.

—Wilbur Webster Judd, *The Birds of Albany County*, 1907

Kingfishers are very abundant this autumn, and may now be seen about the brooks, ponds, and lakes in the neighbourhood of London. This is the time of year that these beautiful birds take their flight from their breeding places and fishbone-made nests in the holes of water-side banks. A kingfisher was lately seen on the Serpentine, and it is not at all improbable that when the parks are quiet, and people are not moving about, they may be observed about the Kensington Gardens waters, at the northern end of the Serpentine.

—Frank Buckland, in George C. Bompas's *Life of Frank Buckland*, 1885

All parks and public grounds about the city are full of blackbirds. They are especially plentiful in the trees about the White House, breeding there and waging war on all other birds. The occupants of one of the offices in the west wing of the Treasury one day had their attention attracted by some object striking violently against one of the window-panes. Looking up, they beheld a crow-blackbird pausing in mid-air, a few feet from the window. On the broad stone window-sill lay the quivering form of a purple finch. The little tragedy was easily read. The blackbird had pursued the finch with such murderous violence, that the latter, in its desperate efforts to escape, had sought refuge in the Treasury. The force of the concussion against the heavy plate-glass of the window had killed the poor thing instantly. The pursuer, no doubt astonished at the sudden and novel termination of the career of its victim, hovered a moment, as if to be sure of what had happened, and made off. . . .

The Capitol grounds, with their fine large trees of many varieties, draw many kind of birds. In the rear of the building, the extensive grounds are peculiarly attractive, being a gentle slope, warm and protected and quite thickly wooded. Here in early spring I go to hear the robins, cat-birds, blackbirds, wrens, etc. In March the white-throated and white-crowned sparrows may be seen, hopping about on the flower-beds, or peering slyly from the evergreens. The robin hops about freely on the grass, notwithstanding the keeper's large-lettered warning, and at intervals, and especially at sunset, carols from the tree-tops his loud, hearty strain.

—John Burroughs, *Wake Robin*, 1893

Along with my five flights goes a piece of roof, flat, with a wooden floor, a fence, and a million acres of sky. I couldn't possibly use another acre of sky, except along the eastern horizon, where the top floors of some twelve-story buildings intercept the dawn.

With such a roof and such a sky, when I must, I can, with effort, get well out of the city. I have never fished nor botanized here, but I have been a-birding many time.

Stone walls do not a prison make, nor city streets a cage—if one have a roof.

—Dallas Lore Sharp, *Roof and Meadow*, 1904

All winter long, from the most crowded thoroughfares of the city, any one, who has leisure enough to raise his eyes over the level of the roofs to the tranquil air above, may see the gulls passing to and fro between the harbor and the flats at the mouth of Charles River. The gulls, and particularly that cosmopolite, the herring gull, are met with in this neighborhood throughout the year, though in summer most of them go farther north to breed. On a still, sunny day in winter, you may see them high in the air over the river, calmly soaring in wide circles, a hundred perhaps at a time, or plying themselves leisurely on the edge of a hole in the ice. When the wind is violent from the west, they come in over the the city from the bay outside, strong-winged and undaunted, breasting the gale, now high, now low, but always working to windward, until they reach the shelter of the inland waters.

—T. W. Higginson, *Our Birds, and Their Ways*, 1857

1901

About three o'clock in the afternoon of a bright sunshiny day in June, I was taking a pleasure ride on my wheel in Garfield Park, one of the Cleveland public parks. I was riding along the main driveway which is lined with tall oaks, cedars and maples when I heard a loud screeching from overhead.

I got off my wheel and looked about to see where it came from, when suddenly I saw a large crow fly upwards from a tall oak, whirl about and dart down at something in the top of tree. Its mate soon did the same.

I tried to discover the cause for this funny performance by walking around the tree and peering through the places where the foliage was scarce. Near the top of the tree I could see a nest which the crows seemed to be trying to guard against some intruder, but could see no cause for their funny performance and making such a racket.

I was just going to get on my wheel and ride off, when I saw the crows fly downward from the top of the tree and pick at something which seemed to be coming down the tree. I now thought it must be a snake as I had often heard of snakes climbing trees to get birds eggs. I waited a minute and a large fox squirrel came running down the side of the tree and stopped on one of the lower branches which was about thirty feet from the ground.

I now found out that cause of the crows acting so. The squirrel had been after the eggs in the nest and the crows had been trying to defend their nest from him.

The crows not satisfied with driving the squirrel from their nest came darting at him again. The squirrel in trying to defend himself from their attack lost his balance and fell to the ground.

I thought he must be hurt so I ran toward the spot where he lay to see if I could catch him and see how badly the crows had hurt him. I got within about seven feet of him when he jumped up and ran to a nearby tree. I got near enough to see that the crows had in several places pierced through his skin and pulled off quite a bit of his fur. The place on which he fell on the ground was a spot of blood from the wounds the crows had given him.

—J. F. Goss, letter, in *American Ornithology
for the Home and School*, Volume 1, 1905

Nighthawk

On summer mornings, between the hours of four and five o'clock, when day is just breaking, the harsh peet of the Nighthawk is a familiar sound over Albany. So shrill and penetrating is the bird's cry that it can be heard over the hum of the trolley cars and the rattle of the early-going milk-carts. Persons who never give any sort of bird a thought, frequently are seen to turn their gaze upward in questioning wonder, as though they would like to know what this bold, aerial marauder might be. Sometimes the birds swoop down close to the tops of the buildings, but straightaway sweep rapidly upward, sometimes to a great height. In the early evening the birds are just as common over the City, though their presence is not so noticeable, for the noise of the city is greater.

—Wilbur Webster Judd, *The Birds of Albany County*, 1907

In autumn the birds, as their habit is, fell upon and devoured the acorns and most of the wild fruit in the parks, as it ripened. On the island at the east end of St. James's Park there is a good-sized well-grown Beam Tree (Pyrus), which was laden with clusters of beautiful orange-coloured fruit. The wood-pigeons have discovered that this fruit is very nice, and they flocked to the tree in numbers to feast on it; but the long slender boughs bent down with the weight of the terminal bunches of fruit, made it impossible for them to perch in the usual way to feed; and they were forced to suspend themselves heads down, like parrots or tits, while picking the berries. A prettier or stranger sight than this tree, laden with its brilliantly coloured fruit and a score or two of dove-acrobats clinging to its drooping branches could not well be imagined.

—W. H. Hudson, *London Birds*, 1899

Birds of Woodland and Meadow

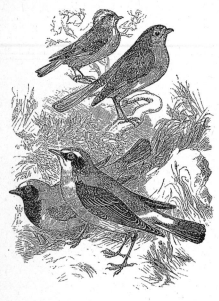

I know of no more strongly marked character than the wood thrush. First to be noticed is his love of quiet. Not only does he prefer the solitary parts of the woods, but he especially avoids the neighborhood of his social cousin, the robin. The chattering, the constant noise, the curiosity, the general fussiness, of that garrulous bird are intolerable to his more reposeful relative. He may be found living harmoniously among many varieties of smaller birds, and he even shows no dislike of the catbird; but come into a robin haunt, and you may look in vain for a wood thrush.

Then his gravity. When a thrush has nothing to do, he does nothing. He scorns to amuse himself with senseless chatter, or aimless flitting from twig to twig. When he wants a worm, he seeks a worm, and eats it leisurely; and then he stands quietly till he wants another, or something else. Even in the nest the baby thrush is dignified. No clamor comes from this youngster when his parent approaches with food. On such occasions the young robin calls vociferously, jerks himself about, flutters his wings, and in every way shows the impatience of his disposition. The young thrush sits silent, quivering with expectation, while the parent, slightly lifting the wings, pops the sweet morsel into the waiting mouth; but no impatience and no cries.

—Olive Thorne Miller, *Bird-Ways*, 1885

Robin

How admirable the constitution and temper of this cheery, graceful bird, keeping glad health over so vast and varied a range. In all America he is at home, flying from plains to mountains up and down, north and south, away and back, with the seasons and supply of food. Oftentimes, in the High Sierra, as you wander through the solemn woods, awe-stricken and silent, you will hear the reassuring voice of this fellow wanderer ringing out sweet and clear as if saying, "Fear not, fear not. Only love is here." In the severest solitudes he seems as happy as in gardens and apple orchards.

—John Muir, *Among the Birds of the Yosemite*, 1898

I shall not ask pardon of those critics who are always canting about genius—and who would probably deny this gift to the Robin, because he cannot cry like a chicken or squall like a cat, and because with his charming strains he does not mingle all sorts of discords and incongruous sounds—for assigning to the Robin the highest rank as a singing-bird. Let them say of him, in the cant of modern criticism, that his performances cannot be great, because they are faultless; it is enough for me, that his mellow notes, heard at the earliest flush of morning, in the more busy hour of noon, or the quiet lull of evening, come upon the ear in a stream of unqualified melody, as if he had learned to sing under the direct instruction of that beautiful Dryad who taught the Lark and the Nightingale.

—T. W. Higginson, *Birds of the Garden and Orchard*, 1858

Green Grosbeak

This is a well-known bird: the general colour yellowish green, palest on the rump and breast, and inclining to white on the belly: the quills are edged with yellow, and the four outer tail feathers are yellow from the middle to the base; the bill is pale brown, and stout; and the legs flesh colour.

The female inclines more to brown.

The Greenfinch is pretty common in *Great Britain*, and makes the nest in some low bush or hedge, composed of dry grass, and lined with hair, wool, &c. laying five or six greenish eggs, marked at the larger end with red brown.

—John Latham, *A General Synopsis of Birds*, 1781

Catbird

Like some people, he seems to give up his time to the pleasure of hearing himself talk . . . With lazy self-indulgence he sits by the hour with relaxed muscles, and listlessly drooping wings and tail. If he were a man you feel confident that he would sit in shirt sleeves at home and go on the street without a collar.

—Florence Merriam, *Birds Through an Opera Glass*, 1889

Catesby in his history of Carolina, speaking of the cat-bird says, "They have but one note, which resemble the mewing of a cat;" a mistake very injurious to the fame of that bird. He, in reality, being one of our most eminent songsters, little inferior to the philomela or mock-bird; and in some remarkable instance, perhaps, exceeds them both, in particular as a buffoon or mimick; he endeavours to imitate every bird and animal, and in many attempts does not ill succeed, even in rehearsing the songs, which he attentively listens to, from shepherdess and rural swain, and will endeavour and succeed to admiration, in repeating the melodious and variable airs from instrumental music, and this in his wild state of nature.

—William Bartram, *Travels*, 1791

Scarlet Tanager

Among all the birds that inhabit our woods, there is none that strikes the eye of a stranger, or even a native, with so much brilliancy as this. Seen among the green leaves, with the light falling strongly on his plumage, he really appears beautiful. If he has little of melody in his notes to charm us, he has nothing in them to disgust. His manners are modest, easy, and inoffensive. He commits no depredations on the property of the husbandman, but rather benefits him by the daily destruction, in spring, of many noxious insects; and, when winter approaches, he is no plundering dependent, but seeks, in a distant country, for that sustenance which the severity of the season denies to his industry in this. He is a striking ornament to our rural scenery, and none of the meanest of our rural songsters. Such being the true traits of his character, we shall always with pleasure welcome this beautiful, inoffensive stranger to our orchards, groves, and forests.

—Alexander Wilson, *American Ornithology*, 1826

The tanager flies through the green foliage as if it would ignite the leaves.

—Henry David Thoreau, journal

But how could Madam tanager ever live with such a fiery husband if her eyes did not find relief in her own greens? Even then it would seem that she had to become accustomed to him by degrees, for in his youth her gay cavalier is relieved by green, yellow, and black. Perhaps even his own eyes get tired, for like the bobolink and goldfinch in the fall he gets out his old clothes and flies away south in as plain a garb as his lady's.

—Florence Merriam, *Birds Through an Opera Glass*, 1889

To speak candidly, [the] Tanager is usually a rather stupid and lifeless bird in its action. It moves about with an air of being dull-witted or dazed, or, perhaps, bored. Also, it has a characteristic trick of peering, with its head cocked first to one side and then to the other, as though it were in doubt about something. But perhaps it realizes that it doesn't have to perform or cut capers in order to attract attention, which indeed is the case. On the other hand, it is only fair to add that the bird not only does comparatively little posing in plain sight, but spends much of his time in the tree-tops where he gives the observer only exasperatingly brief glimpses of his radiant apparel.

—T. Gilbert Pearson, *Birds of America*, 1917

Kingbird, or Bee Martin

In eastern Pennsylvania it is a common migrant. It reaches this latitude during the latter part of April, usually from the 15th or the 30th. For a short time after its arrival, it seems to have a decided predilection for waste fields and pasture-grounds, where it may often be seen in pairs, constantly on the alert for winged insects. But as the season advances, and the mating period draws near, the foregoing localities are deserted for the more congenial habitations of man. Its busy life, unsuspicious nature, and friendly disposition at these times, are highly commendable, and should naturally waken in the bosoms of its most inveterate persecutors, a generous sympathy in its behalf. It pursues the even tenor of its life without the slightest manifestation of that ugly jealous tempter, which amatory influences are wont to excite.

During the breeding-season, it displays a pugnacity of disposition, truly remarkable. The audacious boldness with which it will attack superior strength, the pertinacity with which it will maintain the unequal struggle, should command our admiration. The appellation of Kingbird is given to it, on the supposition that it is superior to all other birds, in these contests. Its attacks are mostly confined to the larger birds, and are prompted by an instinctive desire of self-preservation. Hens, Owls, Eagles, Crows, Grakles, Jays, and others, are the ordinary objects of its vengeance. The smaller birds, many of which are exceedingly mischievous, have either profited by bitter experience not to molest the subject of the present sketch, or else have taken warning from the fate of others.

We have often watched these attacks, and have been surprised at the intrepidity with which a single individual would pounce upon and harass a vastly superior enemy. Ever on the alert, they are not slow to perceive an enemy's approach, even daring to rush out, as if courting an encounter. In these attacks, they will fly above their antagonist, pounce down upon his back, which they speedily forsake for his more exposed flanks, and only leaving them, to repeat the same manoeuvres, with the most determined animosity. In all these encounters, the Kingbird comes off victorious.

—Thomas G. Gentry, *Life-Histories of the Birds of Eastern Pennsylvania*, 1877

Redheaded Woodpecker
Vermilion, South Dakota, *1878*

One of them, which had its headquarters near my house, was observed making frequent visits to an old oak post, and on examining it I found a large crack where the woodpecker had inserted about 100 grasshoppers of all sizes (for future use, as later observation proved), which were put in without killing them, but they were so firmly wedged in the crack that they in vain tried to get free. I told this to a couple of farmers, and found that they had also seen the same thing, and showed me posts which were used for the same purpose. Later in the season the woodpecker whose station was near my house commenced to use his stores, and to-day (February 10) there are only a few shriveled-up grasshoppers left.

—Dr. G. S. Agersborg in F. E. L. Beal's *Food of the Woodpeckers of the United States*, 1911

Blackbirds

They assemble by thousands in the corn fields and exact a heavy tax. They are very bold, for when they are disturbed they only go and settle in another part of the field. In that manner they always pass from one end of the field to the other, and do not leave it till they are satisfied. They fly in incredibly large flocks in autumn; and it can hardly be conceived whence such large numbers of them can come. When they rise in the air they darken the sky, and make it look almost black. They are then in such great numbers and so close together, that it is surprising how they find room to move their wings.

—Peter Kalm, *Travels into North America*, 1770

If birds have no conception of manners, how does it happen that half a dozen Cedar Waxwings, sitting close together on a limb—which they often do—will pass a cherry along from one to another, down to the end of the line and back again, none of the birds making the slightest attempt to eat even part of the fruit?

—George Gladden, *Birds of America*, 1917

Pinnated Grouse
New York,
Sept. 19, 1810

Dear Sir,—It gives me much pleasure to reply to your letter of the 12th instant, asking of me information concerning the Grouse of Long Island.

The birds which are known there emphatically by the name of Grouse, inhabit chiefly the forest range. This district of the island may be estimated as being between forty and fifty miles in length, extending from Bethpage, in Queen's County, to the neighborhood of the Court-House, in Suffolk. Its breadth is not more than six or seven. For, although the island is bounded by the Sound, separating it from Connecticut on the north, and by the Atlantic Ocean on the south, there is a margin of several miles, on each side, in the actual possession of human beings.

The region in which these birds reside, lies mostly within the towns of Oysterbay, Huntington, Islip, Smithtown, and Brookhaven; though it would be incorrect to say that they were not to be met with sometimes in Riverhead and Southampton. Their territory has been defined by some sportsmen, as situated between Hampstead Plain on the West, and Shinnecock Plain on the east.

The most popular name for them is Heath-Hens. By this they are designated in the act of our legislature for the preservation of them and of other game. I well remember the passing of this law. The bill was introduced by Cornelius J. Bogert, Esq., a member of the Assembly from the city of New York. It was in the month of February, 1791, the year when, as a representative from my native county of Queens, I sat for the first time in a legislature.

—Samuel L. Mitchell, in *Wilson's American Orinthology with Additions Including the Birds Described by Audubon, Bonaparte, Nuttall, & Richardson*, 1854

Whiskey-Jack

This inelegant but familiar Jay inhabits the woody districts from latitude 65 deg. to Canada, and in the winter time makes its appearance in the northern sections of the United States. Scarcely has the winter traveller in the fur-countries chosen a suitable place of repose in the forest, cleared away the snow, lighted his fire, and prepared his bivouac, when the Whiskey-Jack pays him a visit, and boldly descends into the circle to pick up any crumbs of frozen fish or morsels of pemmican that have escaped the mouths of the hungry and weary sledge-dogs. This confidence compensates for the want of many of those qualities which endear others of the feathered tribes to man. There is nothing pleasing in the voice, plumage, form, or attitudes of the Whiskey-Jack; but it is the only inhabitant of those silent and pathless forests which, trusting in the generosity of man, fearlessly approaches him; and its visits were, therefore, always hailed by us with satisfaction.

—William Swainson, *Fauna Boreali-Americana of the Zoology of the Northern Parts of British America*, 1831

In these days every bird has his apologist, but I should rather not be the advocate to defend Whiskey John. He is the worst thief, the greatest scoundrel, the most consummate hypocrite abroad in feathers, with his Quaker clothes, his hoary head, his look of patriarchal saintliness. He is a thief, a thief, a thief!

—Fannie Hardy Eckstrom, *Bird-Lore*, 1902

Scissor-Tailed Flycatcher

This is one of the most picturesque and graceful of American birds; and he has individuality, too, which would make him conspicuous without these physical peculiarities. His picturesqueness is due chiefly to his long and strikingly marked tail, which he is likely to open and shut when he is excited about anything. This ornament also serves to accentuate the grace or the erratic character of the bird's aerial gyrations, many of which apparently are indulged in simply for the fun of the thing. One of these is a rapidly executed series of ascents and dives, the bizarre effect of which is heightened by the spreading and closing of the streaming tail-feathers, the performance being accompanied by harsh screams emphasized at each crest of the flight wave. Again and for no apparent reason he will interrupt a slow and decorous straight-line flight by suddenly darting upward, uttering at the same time an ear-piercing shriek. Altogether there is something rather uncanny about much of this bird's conduct; and perhaps its unusual ways are responsible for the Mexican peasants' belief that its food is the brains of other birds, which of course, is a hideous slander.

—Unattributed, *Birds of America*, 1917

Greater Northern Shrike

Birds of this genus have the habit of spitting insects on a thorn, as a butcher would skewer a piece of meat, whence their appellation of "Butcher-birds;" but no instance of this fell under my notice . . . Like the other species of this genus and of Tyrannus, this Shrike attacks the Eagles, Crows, and other large birds, when they approach its haunts, and, by its fierceness and perseverance, drives them away.

—William Swainson, *Fauna Boreali-Americana of the Zoology of the Northern Parts of British America*, 1831

Paul Smith's
August 12th, 1871

I also observed several red bellied nuthatches (Sitta canadensis) picking insects from the bark of the dead trees. They appeared to be perfectly indifferent as to whether they were on the upper or the lower side of a branch and I at first thought they were small woodpeckers.

—Theodore Roosevelt, age 13

I had not taken a hundred paces when I saw a flock of turkeys busy eating the berries of ferns and the fruits of the service tree. These birds are rather different from those of their race domesticated in Europe: they are larger; their plumage is slate colored, tipped at the neck, on the back, and at the extremity of the wings with a copper red color; with the proper lighting this plumage shines like burnished gold. The wild turkeys often gather in great flocks. In the evening they perch on the tops of the highest branches. In the morning they let their repeated cry be heard from the tops of the trees; a little after sunrise their clamors cease, and they descend into the forests.

—Chateaubriand, *Voyage en Amerique*, 1836

The bald eagle is the national emblem of the United States. It was well remarked by Dr. Franklin that the wild turkey would have answered the purpose better, being exclusively indigenous to North America, and having an innate and violent antipathy to red coats.

—Godfrey T. Vigne, *Six Months in America*, 1832

Magpies, for instance, are really most beautiful objects when seen on the lawn in front of a house: their tints of purple, green, velvety black and blue, flash and show lights, like those on the feathers of the Impeyan pheasant—these tints being brought out and relieved by the pure white of the rest of the bird's plumage. The bald terms of black and white, which are generally used in speaking of the magpie, do not really give a correct idea of it. Quite independently of the flashing tones of colour I have mentioned, the white portions of the plumage show pearly greys as the bird, in its ever-active movements, causes the white edges to overlap the dark parts of the feathering.

—Jordan Denham, *From Spring to Fall*, 1894

There was a half-dead walnut tree standing alone near our home where many birds congregated during the summer. In July I often saw nut-hatches, downy, hairy, and red-headed woodpeckers, who made frequent excursions on the bark. The latter species was especially delighted after discovering some corn which I threw into a cavernous opening low down in the trunk of a tree. The corn was thrust into the hole more with a view to feeding and taming some young red squirrels that played about the grounds, than to feed the birds. It was something of a surprise one day when I found the red-headed woodpecker a more persistent visitor to the hole in the tree than the chickadees. I not only learned by this that yellow field corn was a choice diet for these woodpeckers, but I also acquired a knowledge of its feeding habits, that gave me much pleasure to observe.

On a large, outstretched, dead branch free from bark, near the top of the tree, the woodpeckers found a suitable spot to rest. Here the parent birds came to feed two almost fully grown young in July. As I remember the young, they differed from the parents principally in that their heads were dark instead of red, and were thus easily distinguished. One of the parent birds would fly down to the hole, step inside, and seize a kernel of corn in its bill, then, flying to the dead branch, as I have depicted in the illustration on the foregoing page, it placed the kernel in a little hollow pit. Then the bird would drive the corn into the bottom with several determined strokes of its bill. There were several of these pits which the birds used as mortars. The corn, on being placed in the bottom of them, was then cracked into bits with the chisel-like tip of the bird's beak. Then, removing the pieces they had thus made, piecemeal, they were fed one fragment at a time into the opened mouths of the young, who had, in the meantime, expectantly awaited the parent's action. These young birds would always stand by watching their parents during the process of breaking the corn within the pits, and they often fought each other for positions of advantage.

—Joseph Lane Hancock, *Nature Sketches in Temperate America*, 1911

Now we are going through a belt of stunted pine woods, mixed, however, with some hard-wood trees of slender growth: here the beautiful Cardinal grosbeak (*Fringilla cardinalis*) delights to haunt. We hear its singular whistle on each side of us—"whit, wit, whit, whit," and there we catch sight of its brilliant plumage. Is he not a charming fellow? Look at his bright scarlet body, wings, and tail, his coal-black face and read beak, and his fine conical crest, now erect, and now lying flat: with what vivacity he hops from bough to bough, his glowing colour flashing out like a coal of fire among the sombre pine shades, then again hidden from sight; he cannot be still an instant.

—Philip Henry Gosse, *Letters from Alabama*
Chiefly Relating to Natural History, 1859

On the Rose-Breasted Grosbeak

An efficient, resourceful, and viril American
—Unattributed, *Birds of America*, 1917

If one were to ask what tree was the most attractive to birds, almost the first thought is the mulberry tree. Aside from the apple orchard, the presence of one or more of these valuable trees is a great invitation in fruiting time to the birds and squirrels. One summer a kingbird passed back and forth before our veranda, making constant visits to the mulberry tree. Here was often gathered an assemblage of birds from every quarter of the grounds. The branches were fairly weighed down by the avian visitors as they got out on the small branches to pick the luscious berries from the stems. To enumerate the species witnessed one day: Besides the kingbird, there were four goldfinches, the first in point of numbers; two robins, three catbirds, and two waxwings. The kingbird remained long enough to partake of a few berries to satisfy his hunger, then, selecting a choice one in his bill, he flew to his nest in a nearby elm tree to feed his young. The bluebirds were also seen feeding on these berries and a pair on our grounds made frequent journeys to one of these trees, carrying the berries off to their young, who lived in a box provided for them.

—Joseph Lane Hancock, *Nature Sketches in Temperate America*, 1911

King-Bird or Tyrant-Flycatcher

The habits of royalty or tyranny I have never been able to perceive,—only a democratic habit of resistance to tyrants; but this bird always impresses me as a perfectly well-dressed and well-mannered person, who amid a very talkative society prefers to listen, and shows his character by action only.

—T. W. Higginson, *The Life of Birds*, 1862

The Tyrant

The Courage of this little Bird is singular. He pursues and puts to Flight all kinds of Birds that come near his Station, from the smallest to the largest, none escaping his Fury; nor did I ever see any that dar'd to oppose him while flying; for he does not offer to attack them when sitting. I have seen one of them fix on the Back of an Eagle, and persecute him so, that he has turned on his Back into various Postures in the Air, in order to get rid of him, and at last was forc'd to alight on the Top of the next Tree, from whence he dared not move, till the little Tyrant was tired, or thought fit to leave him.

—Mark Catesby, *The Natural History of Carolina,
Florida, and the Bahama Islands*, 1818

I have been looked over several times by Chickadees. I generally approach as close as possible to them and then stand or sit motion-less. This sudden turn of affairs attracts their attention and they approach gradually. It has been claimed that they will alight on one's shoulder or head, but none has ever honored me to that extent. I have had them come within three or four feet of me and then, evidently finding me too commonplace to warrant further attention, they have uttered a mellow chick-a-dee-de-de-de-dede, and gone their way.

—Wilbur Webster Judd, *The Birds of Albany County*, 1907

August 8th. 1871

Today we went into the woods. Our party consisted of Father and his guide Godfrey in one boat; Uncle Hill and his guide Moses Sawyer in another one and we three boys and our guide Jake Hayes in another one. We first rode through the lower St. Regis for about three miles and then put our boats on sleds drawn by horses and made a portage of 5 miles through the woods. We finally arrived at a small stream where we were about to launch our boats, when a thunder shower coming up, forced us to turn them upside down and get under them. While in the lake St. Regis we saw other kinds of wild ducks (Aythya americana?) loons (Colymbus torquatus) and a great blue heron (Ardea herodias). While going down stream we saw numerous tracks of deer and occasionally of wolves and bears. I also saw a kingfisher (beryle alcyon) dive for a fish and a mink (Putorius vison) swam across the stream while covys of quail (Ortyx virginianus) and grouse (Bonasa umbellus) rose from the banks . . . After supper Father read aloud to us from "The Last of the Mohicans". In the middle of the reading I fell asleep. Father read by the light of the campfire.

—Theodore Roosevelt, age 13

Strawberries are considered luscious morsels by the Baltimore oriole. There is no sight more beautiful to the eyes than the brilliant orange-colored male oriole with a crimson strawberry in his mouth, passing in midair, back and forth from the berry patch to his exquisitely hanging nest. The bird lover may well sacrifice some of these berries for the privilege of viewing this beautiful sight.

—Joseph Lane Hancock, *Nature Sketches in Temperate America*, 1911

Alabama Towhee

The Alabama race of the towhee, only recently distinguished as a subspecies, occurs nearly throughout the State, both summer and winter, breeding locally in moderate numbers. . . . The resident form of the towhee has red eyes, like the northern bird, but differs from it in having less white on the tail feathers and (in the females) grayer colors on the back. The songs and call notes are noticeably different from those of the northern race and the call note—jo-ree— is rendered practically as one syllable.

—Arthur H. Howell, *Birds of Alabama*, 1924

Yellowhammers have a habit of sitting on a rail or bough with their shoulders humped so that they seem to have no neck. In that attitude they will remain a long time, uttering their monotonous chant; most other birds stretch themselves and stand upright to sing.

—Richard Jeffries, *Wild Life in a Southern County*, 1881

But I was going to tell you of my bird-seeking expedition yesterday at dawn of day. Besides the vultures, I was surprised to meet with very few birds indeed. I had supposed that at such an hour I should meet with very many; but perhaps I was wrong in going into the woods, instead of keeping near the edges. We by-and-by discovered, however, what I thought well worth my trouble, a pair of those splendid birds, the Ivory-billed Woodpeckers (Picus principalus). They were engaged in rapping some tall dead pines, in a dense part of the forest, which rang with their loud notes. These were not at all like the loud laugh of the Pileated (P. pileatus), nor the cackle of the smaller species, but a single cry frequently repeated, like the clang of a trumpet. As it hung on the perpendicular trunk in full view, digging away with great force and effect, I thought this a very magnificent bird. It is the largest of all the tribe, being twenty inches in length, of a glossy black, broadly marked with pure white. The neck is long and slender, the head is crowned with a tall conical crest of the most splendid crimson, the eye is bright yellow; but the beak is his chief distinction. This is four inches in length, and a full inch in diameter at the base; it tapers to a sharp point, which is wedge-shaped. You would suppose it made of the finest ivory, highly polished, of great hardness, and beautifully grooved or fluted through its whole length. This is the male; the female exactly resembles it, except that her crest is of the same glossy black as the body.

—Philip Henry Gosse, *Letters from Alabama*
Chiefly Relating to Natural History, 1859

Though jays indulge themselves in the luxuries of our garden, they eat acorns, (whence their trivial name, Glandarius,) and beech mast and other seeds. There is something of pertness and importance in a Jay, when he rears the feathers of his head and looks about him, as if he supposed himself to be a bird of considerable consequence, and was conscious of his beauty.

—Charlotte Smith, *A Natural History of Birds Intended*
Chiefly for Young People, 1819

Monticello, Apr. 7, 05

Sir

I received here yesterday your favor of March 18, with the elegant drawings of the new birds you found on your tour to Niagara, for which I pray you to accept my thanks. The Jay is quite unnknown to me, from my observations while in Europe, on the birds & quadrupeds of that quarter, I am of opinion there is not in our continent a single bird or quadruped which is not sufficiently unlike all the members of it's family there to be considered as specifically different. On this general observation I conclude with confidence that your Jay is not a European bird.

—Thomas Jefferson, from a letter to Alexander Wilson

When Nature made the blue jay she must have done it as an object-lesson, to show how greatly good looks will always be discounted by ill-manners.

—Howard E. Parkhurst, *The Birds' Calendar*, 1894

The kingdom of ornithology is divided into two departments—birds and english sparrows. English sparrows are not real birds, they are little beasts.

—Henry van Dyke, *American Ornithology for the Home and School*, Volume 1, 1905

In Utah, as everywhere, the English sparrows are sharp-witted rogues, and they have discovered and taken possession of the most comfortable place for bird quarters to be found, for protection from the terrible heat of summer, and the wind and snow of winter; it is between the roof and the stone or adobe walls of the houses. Wherever the inequalities of the stones or the shrinkage of the wood has left an opening, and made penetration possible, there an English sparrow has established a permanent abode.

—Olive Thorne Miller, *A Bird-Lover in the West*, 1900

Rooks

Though even more gregarious than the Starlings, they believe in giving each other plenty of elbow-room, and extend in open order all over the field; each bird stalking solemnly about on its own quest, and signifying its success by an occasional "caw." How corporate a community is the Rookery, and how highly organized! The birds nest together in a few neighbouring trees, and become so attached to their home, that only the most persistent persecution will drive them away. They adjourn to a field to feed together, and even post sentries on the nearest trees to give warning of any approaching danger. If we could only understand their language, what might we not learn? True, it is unmistakable enough when we ascend the trees to their nests, but if we could only hear the talk that goes on as they return in the evening and hold a parliament before settling down to roost! . . .

To most people rook is a "Crow," I suppose on account of his blackness, but there is no real difficulty in distinguishing the one from the other. The difference in size—for the crow is the larger bird—is not, indeed sufficiently great to be readily appreciable, even if the birds are together, but the greyish white patch of bare skin at the base of the beak at once reveals the Rook's identity. If another guide to recognition is required, it may be found in the fact that, while the rook is gregarious, the Crow is usually found hunting in couples, for it probably pairs for life.

—A. J. R. Roberts, *The Bird Book*, 1903

The crow is sometimes looked upon as a mere marauder; but this description also is much too narrow for him. He is anxious only for his dinner, and swallows seed-corn and noxious grubs with perfect impartiality. He is not a mere pirate, living by plunder alone, but rather like the old Phoenician sea-farer, indifferently honest or robber as occasion serves,—and robber not from fierceness of disposition, but merely from utter unscrupulousness as to means.

—T. W. Higginson, *Our Birds, and Their Ways*, 1857

Guy Emerson of Duxbury, Mass., reports seeing a partly Albino Robin, the tail, wings and head being nearly a pure white, while the body was the usual robin color. It was with several other robins and was last seen on July 19th.

—Albert C. Reed, *American Ornithology for the Home and School*, Volume 2, 1905

I saw here a remarkably large turkey of the native wild breed: his head was above three feet from the ground when he stood erect; he was a stately beautiful bird, of a very dark dusky brown colour, the tips of the feathers of his neck, breast, back, and shoulders, edged with a copper colour, which in a certain exposure looked like burnished gold, and he seemed not insensible of the splendid appearance he made . . .

Our turkey of America is a very different species from the mileagris of Asia and Europe; they are nearly thrise their size and weight.

I have seen several that have weighed between twenty and thirty pounds, and some have been killed that weighed near forty. They are taller, and have a much longer neck proportionally, and likewise longer legs, and stand more erect; they are also very different in colour. Ours are all, male and female, of a dark brown colour, not having a black feather on them; but the male exceedingly splendid, with changeable colours. In other particulars they differ not.

—William Bartram, *Travels*, 1791

I am amused with the golden-crowned thrush,—which, however, is no thrush at all, but a warbler, like the nightingale. He walks on the ground ahead of me with such an easy, gliding motion, and with such an unconscious, preoccupied air, jerking his head like a hen or a partridge, now hurrying, now slackening his pace, that I pause to observe him. If I sit down, he pauses to observe me, and extends his pretty ramblings on all sides, apparently very much engrossed with his own affairs, but never losing sight of me. But few of the birds are walkers, most being hoppers like the robin.

Satisfied that I have no hostile intentions, the pretty pedestrian mounts a limb a few feet from the ground, and gives me the benefit of one of his musical performances, a sort of accelerating chant. Commencing in a very low key, which makes him seem at a very uncertain distance, he grows louder and louder, till his body quakes and his chant runs into a shriek, ringing in my ear with a peculiar sharpness. This lay may be represented thus: "Teacher, teacher, TEACHER, TEACHER, TEACHER!"—the accent on the first syllable and each word uttered with increased force and shrillness.

—John Burroughs, *Wake Robin*, 1893

Goatsucker of Carolina

They are very numerous in Virginia and Carolina, and are called there *East India* Bats. In the evening they appear most, and especially in cloudy weather: before rain, the air is full of them, pursuing and dodging after Flies and Beetles. Their Note is only a screek; but by their precipitating and swiftly mounting again to recover themselves from the ground, they make a hollow and surprizing noise; which to Strangers is very observable, especially at dusk of the evening, when the cause is not to be seen. This noise is like that made by the wind blowing into a hollow vessel; wherefore I conceive it is occasion'd by their wide mouth forcibly opposing the air, when they swiftly pursue and catch their prey, which are flies, Beetles, &c.

—Mark Catesby, *The Natural History of Carolina,
Florida, and the Bahama Islands,* 1818

Gold-Winged Woodpecker

Inhabits *Virginia, Carolina,* and Canada, and is plenty in *New Jersey,* and about *New York,* where it is called by some *Hittock* or *Pint,* and by others *High-hole.* Both the first names have some relation to its note; and perhaps the latter, from the situation of the nest. It is almost continually on the ground, and is not observed to climb on the trees, like others of the genus. It lives chiefly on insects, and is commonly very fat . . .

Forster in *Philosophical Transactions* . . . observes that it is a bird of passage in the *northern parts of America,* visiting the neighbourhood of *Albany Fort* in *April,* and leaving it in *September;* that it lays from four to six eggs, in hollow trees, and feeds on *worms,* and other *insects.* Called by the natives *Ou-thee-quan now.*

—John Latham, *A General Synopsis of Birds,* 1781

The Wren is a very active bird, and one of the most restless of the feathered tribe. He is continually in motion, and even when singing he is always flitting about and changing his position. We see him in almost all places, as it were, at the same moment of time,— now warbling in ecstasy from the roof of a shed, then, with his wings spread and feathers ruffled, scolding furiously at a Blue-bird or a Swallow that has alighted on his box, or driving a Robin from a cherry-tree that stands hear his habitation. The next instant we observe him running along on a stone wall, and diving down and in and out, from one side to the other, through the openings between the stories, with all the nimbleness of a squirrel. He is on the ridge of the barn-roof, he is peeping into the dove-cote, he is in the garden under the currant-bushes, or chasing a spider or a moth under a cabbage-leaf; again he is on the roof of the shed, warbling vociferously; and all these manouvres and peregrinations have occupied hardly a minute, so rapid and incessant is he in his motions.

—T. W. Higginson *Birds of the Garden and Orchard*, 1858

Cardinal

The Hen is brown; yet has a tincture of red on her Wings, Bill and other parts . . . These Birds are common in all parts of *America*, from *new-England* to the *Capes* of *Florida*, and probably much more South. They are seldom seen above three or four together. They have a very great Strength with their Bill, with which they will break the hardest Grain of *maiz* with much facility. It is a hardy and familiar Bird . . . having some Notes not unlike our Nightingale, which in *England* seems to have caused its name of the *Virginia-Nightingale*, though in those Countries they call it the *Red-Bird*.

—Mark Catesby, *The Natural History of Carolina,*
Florida, and the Bahama Islands, 1818

The bluebird carries the sky on his back.

—Henry David Thoreau, journal

When Nature made the bluebird she wished to propitiate both the sky and the earth, so she gave him the color of the one on his back and the hue of the other on his breast, and ordained that his appearance in spring should denote that the strife and war between those two elements was at an end. He is the peace-harbinger; in him the celestial and terrestrial strike hands and are fast friends. He means the furrow and he means the warmth; he means all the soft, wooing influence of the spring on the one hand, and the retreating footsteps of winter on the other.

—John Burroughs, *Wake Robin*, 1893

When rosy plumelets tuft the larch,
And rarely pipes the mounted thrush;
Or underneath the barren bush
Flits by the sea-blue bird of March.

—Tennyson, *In Memoriam*, 1850

In the spring about the middle of May, the black pied rice bird (which is called the male) appear in Pennsylvania; at that time the great yellow ephemera, called May fly, and a species of locusta appear in incredible multitudes, the favourite delicious food of these birds, when they are sprightly, vociferous, and pleasingly tuneful.

When I was at St. Augustine, in E. Florida, in the beginning of April, the same species of grasshoppers were in multitudes on the fields and commons about the town, when great flights of these male rice birds suddenly arrived from the South, who by feeding on these insects became extremely fat and delicious, they continued here two or three weeks, until their food became scarce, when they disappeared I suppose pursuing their journey North after the locusta and ephemera; there were a few of the yellow kind, or true rice bird, to be seen amongst them. Now these pied rice birds seem to observe the same order and time in their migrations Northerly, with the other spring birds of passage, and are undoubtedly on their way to their breeding place; but then there are no females with them, at least not one to ten thousand of the male colour, which cannot be supposed are a sufficient number to pair and breed by. Being in Charleston in the month of June, I observed at a gentleman's door, a cage full of rice birds, that is of the yellow or female colour, who were very merry and vociferous, having the same variable music with the pied or male kind, which I thought extraordinary, and observing it to the gentleman, he assured me that they were all of the male kind, taken the preceding spring, but had changed their colour, and would be next spring of the colour of the pied, thus changing colour with the seasons of the year. If this is really the case, it appears they are both of the same species intermixt, spring and fall. In the spring they are gay, vociferous and tuneful birds.

—William Bartram, *Travels*, 1791

Purple Martin

Is larger than our common Martin. The whole Bird is of a dark shining Purple; the Wings and Tail being more dusky and inclining to Brown. They breed like Pigeons in Lockers prepared for them against Houses, and in Gourds hung on Poles for them to build in, they being of great Use about Houses and Yards for pursuing and chasing away Crows, Hawks and other Vermin from the Poultry. They retire at the Approach of Winter, and return in the Spring to *Virginia* and *Carolina*.

—Mark Catesby, *The Natural History of Carolina,*
Florida, and the Bahama Islands, 1818

I know no prettier sight than a bevy of these bright little creatures, met from a dozen different farm-houses to picnic at a wayside pool, splashing and fluttering, with their long wings expanded like butterflies, keeping poised by a constant hovering motion, just tilting in upon their feet, which scarcely touch the moist ground. You will seldom see them actually perch on anything less airy than some telegraphic wire; but, when they do alight, each will make chatter enough for a dozen, as if all the rushing hurry of the wings had passed into the tongue.

—T. W. Higginson, *The Life of Birds*, 1862

From Gilbert White's Journals, 1779

Apr. 28. Five *long-legged plovers, charadrius himantopus,* were shot at Frinsham-pond. there were three brace in all. these are the most rare of all British birds. their legs are marvellously long for the bulk of their bodies. To be in proportion of weight for inches the legs of the *Flamingo* should be more than 10 feet in length.

Apr. 30. Two swifts seen at Puttenham in Surrey. Bank-martins on the heaths all the way to london.

May 1. A pair of Creepers (Certhia) build at one end of the parsonage-house at Greatham, behind some loose plaster. It is very amusing to see them run creeping up the walls with the agility of a mouse. They take great delight in climbing up steep surfaces, & support themselves in their progress with their tails, which are long, & stiff & inclined downwards.

May 3. Shower of snow. The snow lay but a small time. Began to turn my horses into my field lain down last year with rye-grass & dutch-clover. Wheat look wretchedly.

May 5. The swifts which dashed-by on saturday last have not appeared since; & were therefore probably on their passage.

May 8. A good crop of rye-grass in the field sown last year; but the white clover takes only in patches. Sowed 4 pound more of white clover & a willow basket of hay-seeds. the white clover since is spread all over the field.

May 22. Nightingales have eggs. They build a very inartificial nest with dead leaves, & dry stalks. Their eggs are of a dull olive colour. A boy took my nest with five eggs: but the cock continues to sing: so probably they will build again

May 24. Fiery lily blows: orange lily blows.

May 26. The nightingale continues to sing; & therefore is probably building again

May 28. Young pheasants!

Bird History

Birds, then, may be roughly described as reptiles with feathers . . .
It must be remembered, of course, that all the other characters which
we always have in our mind as part of the abstract idea of the bird are
either not constant or not peculiar to birds alone. For instance, we
usually think of a bird as a flying animal; but then on the one hand,
many birds, such as the ostriches, kiwis, penguins, and dodos, do not
or did not fly at all; and on the other hand many other creatures, such
as the bats, flying squirrels, flying lemurs, pterodactyls, dragon-
lizards, and butterflies, do or did once fly just as much as the birds.
So with their other peculiarities: their habit of laying eggs descends
to them from fish and reptiles; their nest-building propensities,
which are wanting in some birds, are found in the Australian water-
mole, in field-mice, and even in stickleback; and their horny bill,
which is almost confined to them, nevertheless occurs again in the
ornithorhyncus and in many turtles. In short, every other apparently
distinctive point about birds except the possession of feathers either
breaks down on examination or else descends to them directly from
early unbirdlike ancestors. And the first feathered creature of which
we know anything, archaeopteryx, was at least as much of a reptile
as of a bird.

—Grant Allen, *The Ancestry of Birds*, 1884

From the crocodile to the crow is a far cry, yet there was time in the remote past when ancestors of both these creatures were so much alike that it would have required a careful naturalist, had he lived then, and a thorough examination of bones and articulations, to decide whether the said ancestors were birds or reptiles. The presence of teeth do not make the reptile, nor the absence of them the bird, anymore than the presence of wings make the bird, and their absence the reptile.

—Charles Wendell Townsend, *Sand Dunes and Salt Marshes*, 1913

A moulted feather, an eagle feather!
Well, I forget the rest.

—Robert Browning, "Memorabilia," 1842

The older folk still retain some faint superstitions about swallows, looking upon them as semi-consecrated and not to be killed or interfered with. They will not have their nests knocked down. If they do not return to the eaves but desert their nests it is a sign of misfortune impending over the household. So, too, if the rooks quit the rookery . . . If at night a bird flutters against the window-pane in the darkness—as they will sometimes in a great storm of wind, driven, perhaps, from their roosting-places by the breaking of the boughs, and attracted by a light within—the knocking of their wings betokens that something sad is about to happen. If an invalid asks for a pigeon—taking a fancy to a dish of pigeons to eat—it is a sign either of coming dissolution or of extreme illness.

—Richard Jeffries, *Wild Life in a Southern County*, 1881

I do not wonder to find that Birds, who breed on the Sea Shores, and make long Flights over the Sea in the Northern Parts, should be, indifferently, Inhabitants both of the New and Old Worlds, because we know that toward the North Pole the Continents of Europe and America are very near to one another, and may, for ought we know, join near the Pole. We must suppose that these Birds have passed from America to Europe, or from Europe to America; or that there were created, at first, Birds of the self-same Species in both these

Parts of the World, which, according to my Way of Reasoning, cannot be supposed. Most of the World agree, that each Species sprung from an original single Pair: But it seems more easy to conceive how the Northern Water-Fowl should inhabit the Northern Parts of the World, than to imagine how small Land Birds, and some greater Fowls of short Flight, such as the white Partridge, should be able from one and the same Original to propagate itself in Europe and America.

—George Edwards, *A Natural History of Birds*, 1750

Monday, January 29th

The Crows are airing themselves this mild day; they are out in large flocks sailing slowly over the valley, and just rising above the crest of the hills as they come and go; they never seem to soar far above the woods. This afternoon a large flock alighted on the naked trees of a meadow south of the village; there were probably a hundred or two of them, for three large trees were quite black with them. The country people say it is a sign of pestilence, when the crows show themselves in large flocks in winter; but if this were so, we should have but an unhealthy climate, for they are often seen here during the winter.

—Susan Fenimore Cooper, *Rural Hours*, 1850

When Columbus was making that eventful voyage which led to the discovery of the New World, he was cheered by the sight of small birds that appeared beside his ship, telling him of his approach to land. And ever since then these children of the air have been of interest to the white people who have come to America, as they had been for untold ages before to the red men who roamed over the continent. The early New England settlers were troubled by some birds against which they declared war, and cheered by others to which they extended the offering of friendship. And even in those early days there were some men who found in the study of birds a source of delight to which they gladly gave their time.

—Clarence M. Weed and Ned Dearborn, *Birds in Their Relations to Man*, 1903

From the integument of the skin originates also that beautiful PLUMAGE which peculiarly characterizes the class of birds, and the colours of which are probably a result of the same delicate pigment that produces, as we have already remarked, the varying colours of the skin itself; though, from the minuteness with which it is employed, the hand of chemistry has not been able to separate it from the exquisitely fine membrane in which it is involved. But it is impossible to follow up this ornamental attire through all its wonderful features of graceful curve and iridescent colouring,—of downy delicacy and majestic strength,—from the tiny rainbow that plays on the neck of the humming-bird, to the beds of azure, emerald, and hyacinth, that tesselate the wings of the parrot tribe, or the ever-shifting eyes that dazzle in the tail of the peacock;—from the splendour and taper elegance of the feathers of the bird of para- dise, to the giant quills of the crested eagle or the condor—that crested eagle, which in size is as large as a sheep, and is said to be able to cleave a man's skull at a stroke; and that condor which, extending its enormous wings to a range of sixteen feet in length, has been known to fly off with children of ten or twelve years of age.

—John Mason Good, *The Book of Nature*, 1839

Indeed, what would be more interesting than the history of our birds for the last two or three centuries? There can be no doubt that the presence of man has exerted a very marked and friendly influ- ence upon them, since they so multiply in his society. The birds of California, it is said, were mostly silent till after its settlement, and I doubt if the Indians hear the wood-thrush as we hear him. Where did the bobolink disport himself before there were meadows in the North and rice fields in the South? Was he the same blithe, merry- hearted being then as now? And the sparrow, the lark, and the goldfinch, birds that seem so indigenous to the open fields and so averse to the woods—we cannot conceive of their existence in a vast wilderness and without man.

—John Burroughs, *Wake Robin*, 1893

The European house-sparrow, familiarly known to Americans as the English sparrow, was first introduced into the United States in 1850, when eight pairs were brought from England to Brooklyn, New York. These did not thrive, and two years later a large lot of the birds were brought to the same city and liberated during the spring of 1853 in Greenwood Cemetery. During the next twenty years extensive importations were made, the birds being brought from England and Germany and liberated in Maine, Rhode Island, Massachusetts, Connecticut, New York, Pennsylvania, Ohio, and Texas. The largest consignment was that received in Philadelphia, where one thousand birds were set free. After the sparrows had become established in these various centers, misguided men assisted their migrations by carrying them to towns and cities in which they were not yet found. Everywhere they were petted and watched over; in some States special laws were enacted to protect them: the people fostered an evil that is not now easily subdued. Even when kindly Nature sent the great northern shrike to check the sparrow's increase on Boston Common, the authorities hired a man to shoot the shrikes and save the sparrows,—a reversal of the wiser process.

—Clarence M. Weed and Ned Dearborn, *Birds in Their Relations to Man*, 1903

Bird Physiology

A study of bills would be as suggestive as interesting . . . The form is modified to suit the needs of the birds—the woodpeckers have long strong bills for hammering and excavating; the sparrows short stout cones for seed cracking; the vireos long slender bills for holding worms; and the flycatchers bills hooked at the end for holding insects; but perhaps the most extreme case of adaptation are to be found in those of the kingfisher, hummingbird, crossbill, and nighthawk. In the night-hawk and whippoorwill the enormous fish-trap of the kingfisher is exchanged for—almost no bill at all, merely a hook and eye for a wide gaping mouth.

—Florence Merriam, *Birds Through an Opera Glass*, 1889

The beak is hardest in those Birds which tear their prey, as Eagle and Falcons; in those which bruise hard seeds and fruits, as Parrots and Grosbeaks; and in those which pierce the barks of trees, as Woodpeckers, in the larger species of which the beak absolutely acquires the density of ivory. The hardness of the covering of the beak gradually diminishes in those Birds which take less solid nourishment, or which swallow their food entire; and it changes at last to a soft skin in those which feed on tender substances, or which have occasion to probe for their food in muddy or sandy soils, or at the bottom of the water, as Ducks, Snipes, Woodcocks, etc.

—Richard Owen, *On the Anatomy of Vertebrates, Volume 2,*
Birds and Mammals, 1866

If any one were to ask me why birds should have been provided with an organ of flight of such extraordinary complexity as a wing composed of feathers, instead of the relatively simple arrangement of a membrane stretched upon the digits of a bat or the exceedingly effective meshed wing of a dragon-fly, I should be at no loss for an answer, even if I thought fit to envelope it in the fine periphrasis which I once heard spoken by a witness before a Select Committee of the House of Commons. A question was addressed to him to which any common mortal might have replied "I don't know"; but this witness, being a Civil Servant, thought it incumbent upon him to use phraseology appropriate to the dignity of his department. "The honourable member," said he, "is interrogating me upon a subject, cognisance of which on my part is a matter of impossibility."

—Sir Herbert Maxwell, *Memories of the Months,* 1919

Of all the birds the ostrich is the greatest, and the American humming-bird the least. In these the gradations of nature are strongly marked, for the ostrich in some respects approaches the nature of that class of animals immediately above him, namely quadrupeds, being covered with hair, and incapable of flying; while the humming-bird, on the other hand, approaches that of insects.

—Oliver Goldsmith, *Preface and Familiar Introduction*
to the Study of Natural History, 1763

Why have not these monsters of the sky been appropriated to the use of man? How comes it that he who has subdued the ocean and cultivated the earth; who has harnessed elephants, and even lions, to

his chariot wheels, should never have availed himself of the wings of
the eagle, the vulture, or the frigate pelican? That, having conquered
the difficulty of ascending into the atmosphere, and ascertained the
possibility of traveling at the rate of eighty miles an hour through
its void regions, he should yet allow himself to be the mere sport of
the whirlwind, and not tame to his use, and harness to his car, the
winged strength of some of these aerial racers, and thus stamp with
reality some of the boldest fictions of the heathen poets? The hint
has, indeed, long been thrown out; and the perfection to which the
art of falconry was carried in former times sufficiently secures it
against the charge of absurdity or extravagance.

—John Mason Good, *The Book of Nature*, 1839

Every part of their mechanism . . . seems adapted for the im-
provement of their flight; their bones are extremely light and thin
and their muscles feeble, except the large pectoral muscle, by means
of which they move their wings with such ease and rapidity. This
very strong muscle fills up all that space on each side of the breastbone, which, though small in quadrupeds is in these large, broad,
and externally of a very great surface; by means of this a bird can
move its wings with a degree of strength, which, when compared to
the animal's size, is almost incredible. No machines that human art
can contrive are capable of giving such force to so light an apparatus;
and for this reason alone the art of flying must remain one of those
perfections which man may desire but can never attain.

—Oliver Goldsmith, *Preface and Familiar Introduction
to the Study of Natural History*, 1763

How should one describe the wing of a bird, as one sees it in
flight?

The Dictionary, obscure and inaccurate as Dictionaries usually
are, defines a wing as "the organ of a bird, or other animal, or insect,
by which it flies—any side-piece." Might not the impression one
gathers of a wing, during flight, be defined as of a lateral extension of
the body, presenting a relatively large surface, but having no appreciable thickness? That surface, examined in a dead bird, is seen to be

formed, for the most part, of a series of parallel tapering, elastic rods, fringed with an innumerable series of smaller, similar, but much shorter rods, closely packed, and linked together by some invisible means to form an elastic web. These we call the "quill," or "flight-feathers." The rest of the wing, and the body itself, is clothed with precisely similar structures, differing only in their smaller size. We call them "feathers" commonly, without realizing that they are the "Hall-mark" of the bird, for no other creature has ever been similarly clothed.

—W. P. Pycraft, *Birds in Flight*, 1922

Flight, the chief and characteristic mode of locomotion in birds, results principally from the construction and form of the anterior extremities. The form of the body has reference thereto, the trunk being an oval with the large end forward: being also short and inflexible, the muscles act with advantage, and the centre of gravity is more easily changed from above the feet as in the stationary position, to between the wings as during flight. The long and flexible neck compensates for the rigidity of the trunk, and alters the poise according to the required mode of progression, by simply projecting the head forward, or drawing it back. The head of the bird is generally small, and the beak pointed, which is a commodious form for dividing the air.

—Richard Owen, *On the Anatomy of Vertebrates, Volume 2, Birds and Mammals*, 1866

A year or two ago a man wrote to me enquiring as you now do about the vent feathers (under tail covers if you like it better) of the Blackcock. I could only tell him that I knew nothing beyond the fact that they are sometimes marked with black and sometimes not. Never having lived in Blackcock country my opportunities of observation have been nil, and I could not find out that anybody, here or on the continent, had explained or attempted to account for the variation; but I remember noticing the fact when a boy, in some Blackcock sent to my father from Perthshire.

By way of starting a theory, to be kicked over if need be, I should surmise that the young birds have the bigger marks, the "T" or anchor shape, which gradually lessens to the arrow-head, that to an "ermine" spot and finally disappears. This is just the reverse of the "return marking" on the Waxwing's pinons, for they, I am pretty sure, are only seen in old birds, and they seem to increase with age.

—Alfred Newton, in a letter of November 17, 1900

Birds form the best characterised, most distinct, and natural class in the whole animal kingdom, perhaps even in organic nature. Birds float by the specific levity of their body, arising from the extension of the air-cells and the lightness of the plumage; but to swim requires an expanse of sole, either by marginal membranes of the toes (Water-rails, Coots), or by the extension of webs between and uniting the toes. In such true swimmers the under side of the trunk is boat-shaped, the down is thick and covered by closely imbricated well-oiled feathers, the bulk of the bird being enlarged and its specific gravity diminished by the air intercepted in the plumage. Much of the body is thus sustained above the water by hydrostatic pressure, and muscular action is needed solely for the horizontal movements. The broad oars, acting at the end of a long lever, strike the water backward with great force, the webs being fully expanded; but they collapse, the toes coming together, in the forward movement, and in some of the best swimmers the metatarsal is compressed to further diminish the resistance in preparing for the next effective stroke.

—Richard Owen, *On the Anatomy of Vertebrates, Volume 2, Birds and Mammals*, 1866

Even the little sparrow, which flits about by the roadside, can laugh at us with his impudent little chirp, as he flies up out of reach to the topmost branch of a tree. And yet a glance at his skeleton will show us that he has the same framework as a reptile, only it is altered to suit his mode of life.

True, his breastbone is deep and thin instead of flat, and those joints of his backbone which lie between his neck and tail are sol-dered firmly together, more like those of the tortoise, and he stands only upon two feet. Yet this last difference is merely apparent, for if you look at the bones of his wings you will find that they are, bone for bone, the same as those in the front legs of a lizard, only they have been drawn backwards and upwards so as to work in the air.

—Arabella B. Buckley, *The Winners in Life's Race*, 1898

The muscles and delicate plumage of their wings, give them not merely the power of flight, but, under different modifications, a nearly equal command over earth, air, and water: for such a provision enables the rail, destitute as he is of a webbed foot, to rival, in swimming and diving, the guillmot; the ostrich, as we have observed, to outstrip in running the speed of a race-horse; and even the diminutive swallow, and various other migratory birds, to double, when on the wing, the pace of the fleetest ostrich; and to dart, twice a year, across the Atlantic or Mediterranean, often at the rate of a mile a minute for several minutes in succession; and perhaps generally, and with perfect ease, at the rate of a mile every two minutes, or upwards of seven hundred miles every twenty-four hours, till it reaches the precincts of its summer or winter residence.

—John Mason Good, *The Book of Nature*, 1839

But where have the feathers come from—those wonderful beautiful appendages, without which he could not fly? They are growths of the bird's skin, of the same nature as the scales of reptiles, or those on the bird's own feet and legs; and on some low birds such as the penguins they are so stiff and scale-like that it is often difficult to say where the scales end and the feathers begin. All feathers, even the most delicate, are made of horny matter, though it splits up into so many shreds as it grows that they look like the finest hair, and Dr. Gadow has reckoned that there must be fifty-four million branches and threads upon one good-sized eagle feather.

When these feathers first begin to grow they are like little grooved pimples upon the flesh, then soon these pimples sink in till a kind of cup is formed all round them, and into this cup the soft layer just under the outer skin sends out fibres, which afterwards form the pith. Round these fibres rings of horny matter form, and then within these rings, in the grooves of the soft pimple, the true feather is fashioned. First the tips of the feathery barbs, then the shaft, and then the quill appear, as the feather grows from below, fed by an artery running up into the pimple; till at last, when the whole is full-grown, the quill is drawn in at the base, and rests in its socket, complete.

—Arabella B. Buckley, *The Winners in Life's Race*, 1898

Birds may be distinguished, like quadrupeds, into two kinds or classes, granivorous and carnivorous; like quadrupeds too, there are some that hold a middle nature, and partake of both. Granivorous birds are furnished with larger intestines, and proportionally longer than those of the carnivorous kinds. Their food, which consists of grain of various kinds, is conveyed whole and entire into the first stomach or craw, where it undergoes a partial dilution by a liquor secreted from glands spread over its surface; it is then received into another species of stomach, where it is further diluted; after which it is transmitted in to the gizzard, or a true stomach, consisting of two very strong musles covered externally with a tendinous substance, and lined with a thick membrane of prodigious power and strength; in this place the food is completely triturated, and rendered fit for the operation of the gastric juices.

—Thomas Bewick, *The History of English Birds*, 1797

In carnivorous birds, whose stomachs are membranous alone, and, consequently, whose food is chymified by the sole action of the gastric juice, without any collateral assistance or previous mastication, this fluid is secreted in much larger abundance; as it is also in those who labour under that morbid state of the stomach which is called canine appetite; or when, on recovery from fevers, or in consequence of long abstinence, the system is reduced to a state of great exhaustion, and a keen sense of hunger induces a desire to devour food voraciously and almost perpetually.

—John Mason Good, *The Book of Nature*, 1839

Grosbeak

The bill in this genus is strong, convex above and below, and very thick at the base.
Nostrils small and round.
Tongue as if cut off at the end.
Toes placed three before and one behind.

—John Latham, *A General Synopsis of Birds*, 1781

The Great Auk is (or, rather, was) in every particular except the wing a Razorbill on a very much larger scale. It is as if the Razorbill's wings had been fitted on to a bird nearly twice as long, and many times as heavy as the bird for which they were intended. The Auk's wing was merely a flipper. Ages ago, doubtless, the Great Auk could fly, but through long disuse the wing gradually degenerated. Flight was sacrificed for increased proficiency in swimming under water.

Under these circumstances the bird fell an easy prey to fishermen, who used to salt down the bodies for food; and so indiscriminate was the slaughter that by the beginning of the nineteenth century the Great Auk had already become a rarity, while in 1844 the last specimens were obtained off Iceland . . . many have hoped the Great Auk will yet be found in some remote northern island home, and many have sought for it carefully and long, but with every passing year the probability merges more and more into the certainty that the only memorials of this kind are some 79 skins or mounted specimens in various museums and about 74 eggs.

—A. J. R. Roberts, *The Bird Book*, 1903

Raptors

Hawks are beautiful objects when on the wing I have often stood to view a hawk in the sky trembling its wings & then hanging quite still for a moment as if it was as light as a shadow & could find like the clouds a resting place upon the still blue air.

—John Clare, journal, 1820s

Rapacious birds, or those which subsist chiefly on flesh, are much less numerous than ravenous quadrupeds; and it seems wisely provided by nature, that their powers should be equally confined and limited as their numbers; for if, to the rapid flight and penetrating eye of the Eagle, were joined the strength and voracious appetite of the Lion, the Tiger, or the Glutton, no artifice would evade the one, and no speed could escape the other.

—Thomas Bewick, *The History of English Birds*, 1797

The Peregrine's powers on the wing are remarkable, and a friend of mine at Lundy saw a striking exhibition of them. The Falcon was flying leisurely seawards, followed by some half-dozen clamouring Crows, of whom he took not the slightest notice. They were, however, persistent in their efforts to move him, and one, bolder than the rest, flew at him. The Peregrine rose in the air, made one swift swoop, and the Crow fell headlong into the sea. The lesson was repeated, whereon the Crows thought that discretion was, after all, the better part of valour, and returned hurriedly to the island.

—A. J. R. Roberts, *The Bird Book*, 1903

If ever a bird deserved the title of feathered freebooter the sparrow-hawk does.

—Jordan Denham, *From Spring to Fall*, 1894

Falco communis. A pair appeared in September, 1875, and worked great havoc among the night herons. I have seen one fly into a flock of young, and kill three without picking up any.

—Theodore Roosevelt, *Notes on Some of the Birds of Oyster Bay, Long Island*, 1879

In all birds of the eagle, or rapacious kind, which live upon flesh, the beak, talons, and stomach are peculiarly formed . . . The talons are large and extremely tenacious, the muscles which contract the claw being infinitely stronger than those which expand it. Thus furnished for war, all of this kind spread terror wherever they approach. The variety of music which but a moment before enlivened the grove, at their appearance instantly ceases. All is silent, every order of lesser birds seek for safety either in flight or obscurity, and some are even found to seek protection from man, in order to avoid their less merciful pursuers.

—Oliver Goldsmith, *Preface and Familiar Introduction to the Study of Natural History*, 1763

Duck Hawk

I never have seen this Hawk in life, but others tell me that several have been observed in this County in the Autumn.

—Wilbur Webster Judd, *The Birds of Albany County*, 1907

I never saw but one bald eagle in America: he was beating for his prey over the mountain of Montreal; his snow-white head and tail being discernible at a great distance. They are more numerous on the sea coast, near the haunts of the fish-hawk (osprey). When this latter bird has taken a fish, the bald eagle who has been watching his movements from a neighbouring height, will commence a most furious attack upon him, will force him to drop his prey, and frequently seize it before it can disappear under water.

—Godfrey T. Vigne, *Six Months in America*, 1832

One wonders how the man who named this bird the "Screech" Owl, would feel about a real screech, and how he would describe it. For the bird's characteristic cry is a singularly mournful and plaintive little wail, with never the slightest suggestion of a screech about it. Any term which would have denoted lament, apprehension, and incidentally a severe chill, would have been appropriate; in fact the name, "Shivering" Owl, by which the bird is commonly known in the South, has the advantage of being double significant, since the shivering note gives superstitious folk the "shivers" also.

—T. Gilbert Pearson, *Birds of America*, 1917

If by any chance an Owl leaves its dark retreat in the day-time, it is surrounded by innumerable small birds, who pursue it with cries and menace, just as they do if they perceive a fox or any other beast of prey.

—Charlotte Smith, *A Natural History of Birds intended Chiefly
for Young Persons*, 1819

Little Owl

This bird has undoubtedly occured on many occasions as a straggler in this country, but its claim as a British Bird now rests on introductions which have been made in Kent, Northampton, Bedford, Yorkshire, and other places where it has more or less established itself as a breeding species, and is slowly extending its range from at least one of these centres. It is a small species, living chiefly on insects and mice, and is generally found in well-wooded country, where it may be often seen sitting on a dead tree or post, sunning itself, for it is largely diurnal in its habits.

The plumage above is a warm brown spotted with white; under parts white striped with brown. The female is rather larger than the male. Length about 9 in.; wing 6 in.

In this species the feathers on the legs and toes are quite short, being little more than bristles on the latter, a point by which it may be easily distinguished from the Tengmalm's Owl.

—J. Lewis Bonhote, *Birds of Britain and Their Eggs*, 1907

Bloxworth
September 20, 1877

Concerning Owls: both last year and this I have been exercised in regard to an Owl that comes and hoots in trees near this house. On more than one occasion last year my brother Edward and myself saw a Barn Owl fly from a tree whence such hooting had been heard but a few minutes before, and no Brown Owl could be found in or flushed from the said tree. It is possible that after all the Barn Owl may hoot after a fashion; for I sought to say that this note is not the regular "Tu-whit, Tu-whoo," but a wavering "whoo-yoo-o-yoo-yoo," preceded and followed by horrid and unholy shrieks.

—Alfred Newton, in A. F. R. Wollaston's *Life of Alfred Newton*

The Great Horned Owl is found over almost the whole of North America. In strength and ferocity it has no equal among our rapacious birds. Of all the owls which we have, it is the only one distinctly harmful. During the day it keeps very closely hidden, more to escape persecution from crows and other birds that delight to torment it than because the light of day is painful to it. As a matter of fact, there is scarcely a keener-visioned creature in the woods than this owl, in spite of the general impression that it cannot see well when the sun shines.

—Clarence M. Weed and Ned Dearborn, *Birds in Their Relations to Man*, 1903

In the twilight of an evergreen thicket sits a great horned owl like a hermit in his cell in pious contemplation of his own holiness and the world's wickedness. But this recluse hates not sin, only daylight and mankind.

—Rowland E. Robinson, *In New England Fields and Woods*, 1896

I have thrice been so fortunate as to see a snowy owl in the Ipswich dunes. On the first occasion I had nearly walked by the bird, as it sat in its characteristic attitude, bent at an angle of forty-five degrees, when I discovered that the gray stump about seventy yards away was a snowy owl. His eyes were narrow slits more than twice as long as broad, but he kept one of them on me, and he occasionally turned his head so that one eye relieved the other. After watching his in return for fifteen minutes I relaxed my "frozen" posture, and dropping to the ground, endeavored to stalk him. Notwithstanding all my care, he took alarm at once, and, spreading his great wings and throwing his feathered feet out behind, he flew off with broad wing sweeps.

—Charles Wendell Townsend, *Sand Dunes and Salt Marshes*, 1913

Burrowing Owl

Having spent the last four seasons collecting on the Pacific coast, I have had abundant opportunity to observe the habits of the Burrowing owl during the breeding season. In parts of California, where I have spent considerable time, these interesting little owls are very numerous, and a ride of a few miles over the uncultivated plains usually shows them by the dozens, sitting, either singly or in pairs, at the entrance to their underground homes. At such times they are very tame and stare wonderingly until you are within a few feet of them, when they either drop into the burrow or fly a few rods away. After these short flights they almost invariably alight on the mound in front of another burrow, when they turn about so as to face you, and at short intervals make a sharp, un-owl-like note, at the same time comically bowing themselves almost to the ground. It is quite amusing to those who see them for the first time.

—F. T. Pember, *The Ornithologists' and Oologists' Semi-Annual*, 1889

May 25th

Early this morning there was great agitation in the tree-tops waving near us. For an hour or more there was high tragedy hovering over the pines and maples. The birds, of course, are in the midst of their spring joys, and family cares, and they are more numerous than usual this year. The large pine overshadowing our cottage roof at the northward has several nests, and appears a favorite resort of the robins. Early in the morning a great hawk came sailing over the river, from the eastern hills, wheeling in airy circles above the pine. Indescribable agitation fell upon the robins; their anxious, hurried flight about their nests, coming and going, wheeling and watching, was painful to see; their cries of horror, of wrath, of indignation, as the tyrannical hawk drew nearer and nearer, and, at last, alighted on the pine, were truly distressing. Oh for a gun! Oh for a sportsman's hand, and a sportsman's eye to aim straight at this Gessler of the woods! But, alas, the female garrison could do nothing beyond playing the part of the sympathizing chorus in Greek tragedy, while Niobe was mourning over her slaughtered children. In a moment perhaps fifty robins and other small birds had gathered about the pine, utterly fearless for themselves, but full of sympathy for the afflicted households of their brethren, and mad with powerless rage against the hawk. Oh for a valiant king-bird to put the monster to flight by boldly dashing at his eyes, as king-birds often do! But alas! there was neither man nor king-bird near enough to avert the catastrophe. With the utmost coolness the hawk perched himself near a nest, and after helping himself to a young robin, utterly regardless of the turmoil and agony around him, sailed proudly away. Perhaps some fifteen minutes passed, and again the wicked wretch came sailing over the meadows, towards the pine. The same agitation or rather increasing agony among the robins followed—they appeared absolutely frantic with anxiety for their little ones, and wrath against the invader. But of course it was fruitless. The arrogance and impudence of the hawk were intolerable to behold. He picked out another nestling from the young brood, and again sailed away. Four or five times in the course of an hour he repeated the same performance, sailing grandly over the river, alighting on the pine, picking out a bird first from one nest and then from another, and on each occasion flying away with the utmost composure, though a score of light skirmishers were fluttering in impotent rage about him. Alas for the bereaved mother birds, and their mates! Their sharp cries of grief were heard throughout the day; the agitation among the feathered tribe in our neighborhood continued more or less until evening.

—Susan Fenimore Cooper, *Rural Hours*, 1850

The sparrow-hawk (Accipter nisus) is a splendid sprinter, dashing with lightning speed into a flock of small birds, or swooping round the corner of a building upon a brood of young chickens. It meets with scant mercy from gamekeepers, by whom it is commonly known as the blue hawk, from the prevailing slaty hue of the plumage on its upper parts, whereby it may easily be distinguished on the wing from the harmless, mouse-hunting kestrel (Falco tinnunculus), whose attire is mainly of rich russet. Both birds, of course, go by the name of hawk, though the kestrel is a true falcon, distinguished as such by its long pointed wings, the notch on the upper part of the beak, and the dark-brown iris, while the sparrow-hawk displays the insignia of its clan, namely, shorter rounded wings, a notchless beak, and a yellow iris.

—Sir Herbert Maxwell, *Memories of the Months*, 1919

Eagles are destructive but not cruel birds, for although they deprive many birds and beasts of their lives, they effect this purpose with a single blow, sweeping down upon the doomed creature and striking it so fiercely with the death-dealing talons that the victim is instantaneously killed with the shock. The Eagle never uses its beak for the purpose of killing its prey. Instances have been known when the Eagle has seized and attacked human beings. A few years ago one attacked a traveler on a lonely mountain road in Germany, but he seized the bird by the neck and strangled it, not before it had done considerable damage to his clothes, legs and arms. Prof. Wilson tells a touching story of a Golden Eagle descending and carrying off an infant, whose mother had laid it beside a haycock while she was working in the harvest field close by. The eagle was traced to its eyrie in the precipice, some distance off, and the poor mother, blind to all danger in her efforts to recover her babe, safely scaled the precipice, high up in which the nest was placed; though no man, however skillful a cragsman, had ever dared attempt the ascent. Here the mother found her child alive and unhurt, and clasping it to her arms, she descended again—a more perilous feat still; reached the ground in safety and then swooned away.

—Walter Raine, *The Ornithologists' and Oologists' Semi-Annual*, 1889

Sharp-Shinned Hawk

The flight of this hawk is so peculiar that it can be easily recognized in the distance. It is swift, vigorous, and somewhat varied and irregular. When in quest of prey, it moves moderately high at first, but gradually descends to a lower level, moving athwart the ground with surprising swiftness, and pouncing upon its quarry with such suddenness, that escape is out of the question. We have often observed it in pursuit of birds which would exert themselves to the utmost to escape their swift and powerful enemy, and, which, as a *dernier ressort*, would innocently seek shelter in a clump of briers, apparently congratulating themselves on their supposed security, when the object of their alarm, nothing daunted, would dash through the thicket with impetuosity, and transfix its victim before the latter had time to recover its self-possession.

—Thomas G. Gentry, *Life-Histories of the Birds of Eastern Pennsylvania*, 1877

When the peregrine appears speeding through the air in a straight line at a great height, the feathered world, as far as one is able to see, is thrown into the greatest commotion, all birds, from the smallest up to species large as duck, ibis, and curlew, rushing about in the air as if distracted. When the falcon has disappeared in the sky, and the wave of terror attending its progress subsides behind it, the birds still continue wild and excited for some time, showing how deeply they have been moved; for, as a rule, fear is exceedingly transitory in its effects on animals.

—W. H. Hudson, *The Naturalist in La Plata*, 1895

The Golden Eagle is fond of fish. One in Scotland was found drowned, attached to a large pike; it had pounced upon the fish and being unable to extricate itself was drawn under and drowned.

—Walter Raine, *The Ornithologists' and Oologists' Semi-Annual*, 1889

Osprey or Fish Hawk

This bird receives its name from his food which is generally fish; it skims over the lakes and rivers, and sometimes seems to lie extended on the water, as he hovers so close to it, and having by some attractive power drawn the fish within its reach, darts suddenly upon him.

The charm it makes use of is supposed to be an oil contained in a small bag in the body, and which nature has by some means or other supplied him with the power of using for this purpose; it is however very certain that any bait touched with a drop of the oil collected from this bird is an inresistible lure for all sorts of fish, and insures the angler great success.

—Anonymous, *Travels Through the Interior Parts of North America*, 1766

First I shall name the eagle, of which there are three species: the great grey eagle is the largest, of great strength and high flight; he chiefly preys on fawns and other young quadrupeds.

The bald eagle is likewise a large, strong, and very active bird, but an execrable tyrant: he supports this assumed dignity and grandeur by rapine and violence, extorting unreasonable tribute and subsidy from all the feathered nations.

The last of this race I shall mention is the falco piscatorius or fishing-hawk: this is a large bird, of high and rapid flight; his wings are very long and pointed, and he spreads a vast sail, in proportion to the volume of his body. This princely bird subsists entirely on fish, which he takes himself, scorning to live and grow fat on the dear earned labours of another; he also contributes liberally to the support of the bald eagle.

—William Bartram, *Travels*, 1791

Often as we stood in the breakers fishing for surf bass, we looked up and saw the two eagles high above us like airplanes against the blue. Once, while I watched them thus, one eagle—I think the male—climbed in wide spirals without a discernible movement of his wings until he was far above his circling mate; then, tipping suddenly forward, he came down headforemost, diving straight for her, a mighty spearhead plunging from the sky, his body rocking violently from side to side. Just over her, his broad pinions widened and flattened, his white tail opened like a fan—and when in another fraction of a second he would have crashed into her, he shot upward in a long curve, having passed so close to her that she must have felt the wind of his rushing wings.

There was one day when I saw eagle matched against eagle not in battle but in a contest only less stirring than the actual battle would have been. Far away across the marshlands I saw an eagle hurrying toward the sea. He was flying at high speed, his dark wings powerfully beating the air; and, in a few moments, I saw behind him another eagle also rushing at utmost speed toward the ocean. I looked seaward in the direction in which the two great white-headed birds were flying, but I could distinguish nothing there; yet I judged from the manner and the velocity of their flight that their keen eyes saw what I did not or could not see.

The leading eagle, which was some hundreds of yards ahead of the other, crossed the narrow strip of beach between the marshes and the ocean, heading straight out over the Atlantic; then, suddenly, I saw in front of him, well out over the water, an osprey circling and spiraling upward. At that distance I could not discern the fish in the osprey's claws, but I knew that it was there—that this was the prize which had brought the two monarchs hurrying across the marsh-lands from their lookout stations perhaps a mile or several miles away.

I knew what would happen, for I had seen it often before; but this time the sequel was a surprise. The osprey, a large and strong-winged hawk, often fights hard to keep his fish, circling upward, dodging and twisting, refusing to surrender until his last chance of escape has gone. This osprey, however, gave up quickly. At the first swoop of the eagle the sea hawk dropped his fish, and the larger bird, shooting downward with half-closed wings, seized it in his talons before it struck the surface of the water.

He did not keep it long. The other eagle, arriving at this moment upon the scene, drove at him with furious speed, and for a few minutes I saw a thrilling contest in the air above the ocean—the two great birds swooping and swerving, dodging and twisting this way and that, the one trying to escape, the other and apparently more powerful bird cutting it off at every turn. If these eagles were mates, perhaps the male had taken the fish from the osprey only to give it to his consort: in that case, this chase above the ocean was only a game—a phase, perhaps, of the eagles' autumnal love-making. But to my eyes it had all the appearance of deadly earnestness, and, in any case, it was, while it lasted, perhaps the finest display of the sort that I have witnessed. It was too furious to last long. Presently the first eagle released the fish, and the other, with a magnificent downward gliding swoop, caught it in her talons and bore it off through the air.

—H. R. Sass, *On The Wings of a Bird*, 1928

Mississippi Kite

This new species I first observed in the Mississippi Territory, a few miles below Natchez, on the plantation of William Dunbar, Esq. . . . This excellent man, whose life has been devoted to science, though at that time confined to bed by a severe and dangerous indisposition, and personally unacquainted with me, no sooner heard of my arrival at the town of Natchez, than he sent a servant and horses, with an invitation and request to come and make his house my home and head-quarters, while engaged in exploring that part of the country. The few happy days I spent there I shall never forget.

In my perambulations I frequently remarked this Hawk sailing about in easy circles, and at a considerable height in the air, generally in company with the Turkey Buzzards, whose manner of flight it so exactly imitates as to seem the same species, only in miniature, or seen at a more immense height. Why these two birds, whose food and manners, in other respects, are so different, should so frequently associate together in air, I am at a loss to comprehend. We cannot for a moment suppose them mutually deceived by the similarity of each other's flight: the keeness of their vision forbids all suspicion of this kind. They may perhaps be engaged, at such times, in mere amusement, as they are observed to soar to great heights previous to a storm, or what is more probable, they may both be in pursuit of their respective food;—one, that he may reconnoitre a vast extent of surface below, and trace the tainted atmosphere to his favorite carrion; the other in search of those large beetles, or coleopterous insects, that are known often to wing the higher regions of the air.

—Alexander Wilson, *American Ornithology*, 1826

Sometimes in the midst of a troop of Vultures may be recognized the white head and white tail of the Bald Eagle, the rest of his plumage being similar to that of his less dignified companions, but from whom he may be readily distinguished by the greater ease of his motions, as well as his more majestic appearance. While the Turkey Buzzard sails in contracted circles, or swims off in a wide curve, the Eagle, as if conscious of his superiority, floats upon his unmoving wing as though he would compass in one vast sweep the broad expanse of heaven; or sometimes, when at his greatest altitude, hardly appearing as more that a black speck in the dim distance, he will fold his wings and descend with the velocity of thought toward the earth, when suddenly unfurling his broad pinions, he checks his downward course, and glides off like an arrow to a distant quarter. . . .

The Golden Eagle is a large and powerful bird, noble and majestic in appearance. Its food consists principally of lambs, fawns, rabbits, turkeys, ducks and other large birds. In capturing its prey it does not manifest the same agility as the Bald Eagle in pursuing and seizing it upon the wing, but it is obliged to descend from a considerable height upon it to insure success. The keenness of its vision, however, enables it to discern at a great distance the objects of its desire, upon which it generally falls with the swiftness of a meteor, and with an unerring and deadly aim. The feathers of this Eagle are much sought after by the Indians of North America, as an ornament of their dress; and so highly are they prized, that it is said a warrior will often exchange a valuable horse for the tail feathers of a single bird.

—William L. Baily, *Our Own Birds*, 1869

Sometimes when I have been riding over marshy ground, one of the hawks has placed himself directly over my head, within fifteen or twenty yards of me; and it has perhaps acquired the habit of following a horseman in this way in order to strike at any birds driven up. On one occasion my horse almost trod on a couple of snipe squatting terrified in the short grass. The instant they rose the hawk struck at one, the end of his wing violently smiting my cheek as he swooped, and striking at the snipe on a level with the knees of my horse. The snipe escaped by diving under the bridle, and immediately dropped down on the other side of me, and the hawk, rising up, flew away.

—W. H. Hudson, *The Naturalist in La Plata*, 1895

Having a good spirited horse under me, I generally kept a-head of my companions, which I often chose to do, as circumstances offered or invited, for the sake of retirement and observation.

The high road being here open and spacious, at a good distance before me, I observed a large hawk on the ground, in the middle of the road; he seemed to be in distress, endeavouring to rise; when, coming up near him, I found him closely bound up by a very long coach-whip snake, that had wreathed himself several times round the hawks body, who had but one of his wings at liberty; beholding their struggles a while, I alighted off my horse with the intention of parting them; when, on coming up, they mutually agreed to separate themselves, each one seeking his own safety, probably considering me as their common enemy. The bird rose aloft and fled away as soon as he recovered his liberty, and the snake as eagerly made off, I soon overtook him but could not perceive that he was wounded.

I suppose the hawk had been the aggressor, and fell upon the snake with an intention of making a prey of him, and that the snake dexterously and luckily threw himself in coils round his body, and girded him so close as to save himself from destruction.

—William Bartram, *Travels*, 1791

Birdsong

Books! 'tis a dull and endless strife;
Come, hear the woodland linnet,
How sweet his music! on my life,
There's more of wisdom in it—

—William Wordsworth

It is hard to tell just how much of the attraction in any bird-note lies in the music itself and how much in the associations. This is what makes it so useless to try to compare the bird songs of one country with those of another. A man who is worth anything can no more be entirely impartial in speaking of the bird songs with which from his earliest childhood he has been familiar than he can be entirely impartial in speaking of his own family.

—Theodore Roosevelt, *Theodore Roosevelt: An Autobiography*, 1920

April 19, 1832

Heard the Nightingale for the first time this season—in Hilly wood
Same morning Frederic heard the cuckoo sing in Royce Wood
—John Clare, journal

I was asked to imitate the Wild Turkey call, and I did, to the surprise of all the circle. Hooted like a Barred owl, and cooed like the doves. I am glad, really, that I was not desired to bray! "Why?" Why! Because an ass is an ass and it would have been rude even in an ass to bray in such company.

—John James Audubon, journal, 1826

The flight song of the horned lark I have heard in Labrador. The bird springs up from the ground and mounts silently into the air, rising in irregular circles or almost vertically until it appears but a little speck in the sky, or perchance is lost to sight in the scudding fog. Then it soars and pours forth in great ectasy a song that begins with one or two notes followed by a series of squeaks, high notes and fine trills, suggestive at times of distant sleigh bells and again of unoiled gates. The song finished, the bird flaps its wings a few times, closes them and then sails again, and again repeats its song. One bird I timed remained in the air three minutes, during which it repeated its song thirty-two times. When the bird has finished singing it silently and very rapidly plunges back to earth. The performance is well worth hearing and, although not highly musical, is very pleasing and decidedly spectacular.

—Rowland E. Robinson, *In New England Fields and Woods*, 1896

The catbirds have such an attractive song that it is extremely irritating that at any moment they may interrupt it to mew and squeal.

—Theodore Roosevelt, *Theodore Roosevelt: An Autobiography*, 1920

Judged from its structure, the rook family is supposed to come next in intelligence to man himself. Judging from the intelligence displayed by certain human families with whom I have come in contact, I can quite believe it. That rooks talk I am positive. No one can spend half-an-hour watching a rookery without being convinced of this. Whether the talk be always wise and witty, I am not prepared to maintain; but that there is a good deal of it is certain. A young French gentleman of my acquaintance, who visited England to study the language, told me that the impression made upon him by his first social evening in London was that of a parrot-house. Later on, when he came to comprehend, he, of course, recognized the brilliancy and depth of the average London drawing-room talk; but that is how, not comprehending, it impressed him at first. Listening to the riot of a rookery is much the same experience. The conversation to us sounds meaningless; the rooks themselves would probably describe it as sparkling.

—Jerome K. Jerome, *Second Thoughts of an Idle Fellow*, 1890

Once I heard a blue jay sing as sweetly as the mocking-bird when trilling in a tender minor key. I could hardly believe my own sight and hearing as the beautiful, tricky creature sat before me with drooping crest and half-raised wings, swaying his body lightly up and down and uttering a low, almost bewildering flute medley full of the cadences of dreams.

—Maurice Thompson, *Young Folks' Cyclopedia of Natural History*, 1895

The timidity of many a songbird is your own fault. Treat them with kindness and they will treat you to melody.

—Charles C. Abbott, *Young Folks' Cyclopedia of Natural History*, 1895

Many birds utter the same notes over and over again; others sit on a branch and sing the same song, as the thrush; but the starling has a whole syllabary of his own, every note of which evidently has its meaning, and can be varied and accented at pleasure.

His whistle ranges from a shrill, piercing treble to a low, hollow bass; he runs a complete gamut, with "shakes," trills, tremulous vibrations, every possible variation. He intersperses a peculiar clucking sound, which seems to come from the depths of his breast, fluttering his wings all the while against his sides as he stands bolt upright on the edge of the chimney. Other birds seem to sing for the pure pleasure of singing, shedding their notes broadcast, or at most they are meant for a mate hidden in the brush. The starling addresses himself direct to his fellows: I think I may say he never sings when alone, without a companion in sight.

—Richard Jeffries, *Wild Life in a Southern County*, 1881

The song of the Bachman Sparrow is a thing of surprising beauty. In delivering it the bird chooses a prominent station at the top of weed-stalk, fencepost, or sapling, or stands well out on a bare limb of a tree. Here he throws his head back and draws, as it appears, a full breath in a note of ravishing sweetness; then sends it forth again in a tinkling rill of uniform or varied notes. Nothing can excel the fine poetic rapture of the inspirited note. It sets the veins a-tingle and makes one wish to put his shoes from off his feet. The characteristic opening note is given with constantly varying pitch and intensity. Sometimes it sounds like a dream voice floating gently from the summer land of youth, and again it vibrates with startling distinctness like a present call to duty. Occasionally a dainty trill is substituted for this inspired and inspiring opening, while the remainder of the song may consist of a half-dozen notes precisely alike, or of a succession of groups three or four in number. There is a soulful quality, an ethereal purity, and a caressing sweetness about the whole performance which makes one sure the door is opened into the third heaven of bird music.

Once as I sat entranced before this new-found Orpheus a Lark Sparrow broke into song at half the distance. In pained astonishment and wrath I turned upon him—him even! "Oh, please not now! Mon enfant! Please not now!"

—W. Leon Dawson, *Birds of Ohio*, 1902

What, then, is the Passion Song? It is an outburst of melody of such richness and fullness, such thrilling ecstasy, that the singer is lifted into the air on quivering wings to pour out his melody without a pause until the inspiration has passed. The call song is the product of a deliberate purpose, but the passion song wants no purpose.

—Unattributed, Warbler Songs, 1900

Worcester, Massachusetts

Early last summer while standing on my back steps, I heard a cheerful voice say, "You're a pretty bird. Where are you?" I supposed it to be the voice of a Parrot, but wondered how any Parrot could talk loud enough to be heard at that distance, for the houses on the street back of us are quite a way off.

Almost before I had done laughing, the voice came again, clear, musical, and strong—"You're a pretty bird. Where are you?"

For several days I endured the suspense of waiting for time to investigate. Then I chased him up. There he was in the top of a walnut tree, his gorgeous attire telling me immediately that he was a Rose-breasted Grosbeak.

At the end of a week he varied his compliment to, "Pretty, pretty bird, where are you? Where are you?" With a kind of impatient jerk on the last "You." He and his mate stayed near us all last summer and though I heard him talk a hundred times, yet he always brought a feeling of gladness and a laugh.

Our friend has come back again this spring. About May 1, I heard from him the same endearing compliment as before.

Several friends whom I have told about him have asked, "Does he really say the words plainly? Do you mean that he really talks?" My reply is, "He says them just as plainly as a bird ever says anything, so plainly, that even now I laugh whenever I hear him."

He is not very easily frightened and sometimes talks quite a while when I am standing under the tree where he is.

—Emily B. Pellet, Bird-Lore, 1901

When ten or twelve larks are singing at once, all within a narrow radius—a thing that may be often witnessed from these downs in the spring—the charm of their vivacious notes is greater than when one solitary bird alone discourses sweet music which is lost in the blue dome overhead.

—Richard Jeffries, *Wild Life in a Southern County*, 1881

The Pine-woods Sparrow (*peucaea aestivalis*) is a common summer resident at Eubanks, Ky. It frequents the sedge fields and meadows. It begins to sing on its arrival in the spring, (March 20). It sings at all hours of the day, but is at its best in the evening from sunset until it is quite dark. On several occasions these sparrows have been heard singing quite late at night after a thunder shower. As they have never been heard singing at night except after a storm, it is supposed to be caused by the rain having awakened them.

They sing from the top of a fence, a tree or any other convenient perch. The song is not very powerful, but sweet, clear and far-reaching. It is always uttered slowly and deliberately, and carries with it a sense of calm, peace and contentment which places it among the sweetest of our native song-birds.

—John B. Lewis, *The Ornithologists' and Oologists' Semi-Annual*, 1889

The birds are turkeys, turkey-buzzards, prairie-fowls, quails, pigeons, doves, wild-geese, wild-ducks, wood-cocks, snipes, black-birds, moching-birds, red-birds, yellow-birds, humming-birds, wip-perwills, blue-jays, paroquets, larks, wood-peckers, black-martins, and a few other small birds. But birds are not so numerous as in En-gland; some of them have very beautiful plumage, but not many of them are birds of song.

—John Woods, *Two Years' Residence in the Settlement
on the English Prairie in the Illinois Country*, *United States*, 1822

Wood-thrush

He is truly a royal minstrel, and considering his liberal distribu-tion throughout our Atlantic seaboard, perhaps contributes more than any other bird to our sylvan melody. One may object that he spends a little too much time in tuning his instrument, yet his careless and uncertain touches reveal its rare compass and power.

He is the only songster of my acquaintance, excepting the canary, that displays different degrees of proficiency in the exercise of his musical gifts. Not long since, while walking one Sunday in the edge of an orchard adjoining a wood, I heard one that so obviously and unmistakably surpassed all his rivals, that my companion, though slow to notice such things, remarked it wonderingly; and with one accord we paused to listen to so rare a performer. It was not different in quality so much as in quantity. Such a flood of it! Such copiousness! Such long, trilling, accelerating preludes! Such sudden, ecstatic overtures would have intoxicated the dullest ear. He was really without a compeer—a master-artist. Twice afterward I was conscious of having heard the same bird.

—John Burroughs, *Wake Robin*, 1893

Crested Flycatcher

This Bird, by its ungrateful brawling Noise, seems at Varience and displeased with all others.

—Mark Catesby, *The Natural History of Carolina, Florida, and the Bahama Islands*, 1818

Birds are in general social and benevolent creatures; intelligent, ingenious, volatile, active beings; and this order of animal creation consists of various nations, bands or tribes, as may be observed from their different structure, manners and languages or voice, as each nation, though subdivided into many different tribes, retain their general form or structure, a similarity of customs, and a sort of dialect or language, particular to that nation or genus from which they seem to have descended or separated: what I mean by a language in birds, is the common notes or speech, that they use when employed in feeding themselves and their young, calling on one another, as well as their menaces against their enemy; for their songs seem to be musical compositions, performed only by the males, about the time of incubation, in part to divert and amuse the female, entertaining her with melody, &c. This harmony, with the tender solicitude of the male, alleviates the toils, cares and distresses of the female, consoles her in solitary retirement whilst setting, and animates her with affection and attachment to himself in preference to any other. The volatility of their species, and operation of their passions and affections, are particularly conspicuous in the different tribes of the thrush, famous for song; on a sweet May morning we see the red thrushes (turdus rufus) perched on an elevated sprig of the snowy Hawthorn, sweet flowering Crab, or other hedge shrubs, exerting their accomplishments in song, striving by varying and elevating their voices to excel each other, we observe a very agreeable variation, not only in tone but in modulation; the voice of one is shrill, another lively and elevated, others sonorous and quivering. The mock-bird (turdus polyglottos) who excels, distinguishes himself in variety of action as well as air; from a turret he bounds aloft with the celerity of an arrow, as it were to recover or recall his very soul, expired in the last elevated strain. The high forests are filled with the symphony of the song of wood-thrush (turdus minor).

—William Bartram, *Travels*, 1791

I do not think his best friend will claim that the common house sparrow has the soul of music in him; certainly not if he has ever been wakened in a glorious dawn by the indescribable jangle of harsh sounds which constitutes this bird's only morning hymn, at the hour when every bird in the woods, from the noble singers of the thrush family down to the least chipping sparrow, is greeting the new day in his most musical fashion.

The matin song of the house sparrow, in which he indulges unsparingly, being of similar quality, harmonizes perfectly with the jarring sounds of man's contriving; the clatter of shod wheels over city pavements, the war-whoop of the ferocious milkman, the unearthly cries of the venders, and above all the junkman's pandemonium of "bells jangled, out of tune." The harshest cries of our native birds, if not always musical in themselves, seem at least to accord in some way with sounds of nature. The house sparrow alone is entirely discordant,—the one bird without a pleasing note, whose very love-song is an unmusical squeak. Nor is his appearance more interesting than his voice, and on looking into his manners and customs we discover most unlovely characteristics.

—Olive Thorne Miller, *Bird-Ways*, 1885

I noticed this summer that the little thrush that commenced singing in april sung till the middle of july & that he had got many variations from the nightingale in the last month which he did not commence with in april—indeed his song was so like that of the nightingale that it might be mistaken for it by careless observers.

—John Clare, journal, 1820s

Mockingbird

Hernandez justly calls it the Queen of all singing Birds. The *Indians*, by way of eminence or admiration call it *Cencontlatolly*, or *four hundred tongues;* and we call it (tho' not so elevated a name, yet very properly) the *Mock-bird*, from its wonderful mocking and imitating the notes of all Birds, from the Humming Bird to the Eagle. From *March* till *August* it sings incessantly day and Night with the greatest variety of Notes; and, to compleat his compositions, borrows from the whole Choir, and repeats to them their own Tunes with such artful Melody, that it is equally pleasing and surprising. They may be said not only to sing but dance, by gradually raising themselves from the place where they stand, with their Wings extended, and falling with their Head down to the same place; then turning round, with their Wings continuing spread, have many pretty antic Gesticulations with their Melody.

—Mark Catesby, *The Natural History of Carolina,*
Florida, and the Bahama Islands, 1818

Our birds are like our men of genius. As in the literary world there is a description of talent that must be discovered and pointed out by an observing few, before the great mass can understand it or even know its existence,—so the sweetest songsters of the wood are unknown to the mass of the community, while many very ordinary performers whose talents are conspicuous, are universally known and admired.

—T. W. Higginson, *The Birds of the Pasture and Forest*, 1858

On Redwings

For weeks past the laurels and holly-bushes of our gardens have sheltered small flocks of these little northern thrushes—for the birds are gregarious, though never going in very great numbers. Even though unseen, the approach of the birds may be easily detected by the soft piping sounds which they utter in coming to roost at evening.

—Anonymous, *Winter Birds*, 1889

I can scarcely believe the account which you mention at the end of your letter respecting the mans "puzzling himself with doubts about the Nightingales singing by day & about the expression of his notes whether they are grave or gay"—you may well exclaim "what solemn trifling" it betrays such ignorance that I can scarcely believe it—if the man does but go into any village solitude a few miles from London next may their varied music will soon put away his doubts of its singing by day—nay he may get rid of them now by asking any country clown the question for its such a common fact that all know of it—& as to the "expression of its notes" if he has any knowledge of nature let him ask himself whether Nature is in the habit of making such happy seming songs for sorrow as that of the nightingales—the poets indulgd in fancys but they did not wish that those matter of fact men the Naturalists shoud take them for facts upon their credit—What absurditys for a world that is said to get wiser and wiser every day—yours &c

—John Clare, letter, 1820s

Veery

He sings neither in the orchard, nor the garden, nor in the sub-urbs of the city. He shuns the exhibitions of art, and reserves his wild notes for those who frequent the inner sanctuary of the groves. All who have once become familiar with his song await his arrival with impatience, and take note of his silence in midsummer with regret. Until this little bird has arrived, I always feel as an audience do at a concert, before the chief singer has made her appearance, while the other performers are vainly endeavoring to soothe them by their inferior attempts.

—T. W. Higginson, *Birds of the Garden and Orchard*, 1858

And what is a bird without its song? Do we nor wait for the stranger to speak? It seems to me that I do not know a bird till I have heard its voice; then I come nearer it at once, and it possesses a human interest to me. I have met the gray-cheeked thrush in the woods, and held him in my hand, still I do not know him. The silence of the cedar bird throws a mystery about him which neither his good looks nor his petty larcenies in cherry time can dispel. A bird's song contains a clue to its life, and establishes a sympathy, an understanding, between itself and the listener.

—John Burroughs, *Wake Robin*, 1893

I spread my skins and blanket by my chearful fire, under the pro-tecting shade of the hospitable Live-oak, and reclined my head on my hard but healthy couch. I listened, undisturbed, to the divine hymns of the feathered songsters of the groves, whilst the softly whispering breezes faintly died away.

The sun now below the western horizon, the moon majestically rising in the east; again the tuneful birds become inspired; how melo-dious is the social mock-bird! The groves resound the unceasing cries of the whip-poor-will; the moon about an hour above the hori-zon; lo! a dark eclipse of her glorious brightness comes slowly on; at length, a silver thread alone encircles her temples: at this boding change, an universal silence prevails.

—William Bartram, *Travels*, 1791

The common sounds which birds make can be divided into two or three classes. They are generally called call notes, alarm notes, and recognition notes. The cock gives a call note when he has found something to eat; when the hens hear it, they run to the spot. Alarm notes are given by the hen when she wishes her chickens to hide under her wing, or by any bird when he is suddenly startled.

Recognition notes are used very largely by birds who travel in companies, and are given and answered constantly, so that the different members of the band may keep together.

—J. H. Stickney, *Bird World*, 1898

Birds with the flocking-instinct sometimes sing in concert. The prettiest instance known to me of this habit among our birds is that of the goldfinches, which in spring have their musical reunions—a sort of *sangerfest* which often continues for days, and during which the matches appear to be made. But with most of our birds the song is a sort of battle-flag of the males, and when they unfurl it, if it is not a challenge, it certainly indicates that they have the "fighting edge." It is a notice to other males that "this grove, or this corner of the field is *my* territory, and I will tolerate no trespassers."

—John Burroughs, *Wake Robin*, 1893

The morning-song is the most cherished of the bird-lover's day.

—Olive Thorne Miller, *With the Birds in Maine*, 1904

How harmonious the shrill tuneful songs of the wood thrush, and the soothing love lays of the amorous cuckoo! seated in the cool leafy branches of the stately magnolias and shadowy Elms, Maples and Liquid-amber, together with gigantic Fagus sylvatica, which shade and perfume these sequestered groves. How unexpected and enchanting the enjoyment, after traversing a burning sandy desert!

—William Bartram, *Travels*, 1791

On the Dabchick

We have another pleasure in hearing this bird's long bubbling or trilling love-call, like a peep of laugher, or a sound between a bird's prolonged cry and the musical laugh of a child.

—W. H. Hudson, *London Birds*, 1899

After dashing off the concluding words of our Essay, ("the most glorious age of British Poetry,") our thoughts began to wander away, by some fine associations, into the woods of our childhood, "Bards of Scotland! Birds of Scotland!" and at that very moment, we heard the loud, clear, mellow, bold song of the Blackbird. There he flits along upon a strong wing, with his yellow bill visible in distance, and disappears in the silent wood, no longer silent. It is a spring day in our imagination,—his clay-wall nest holds his mate at the foot of the silver-fir, and he is now perched on its pinnacle. That thrilling hymn will go vibrating down the stem till it reaches her brooding breast. The whole vernal air is filled with the murmur and the glitter of insects,—but the blackbird's song is over all other symptoms of love and life, and seems to call upon the leaves to unfold into beauty.

—Christopher North, *Birds*, 1826

There is no singing-bird in New England that enjoys the notoriety of the Bobolink (Icterus agripennis). He is like a rare wit in our social or political circles. Everybody is talking about him and quoting his remarks, and all are delighted with his company. He is not without great merits as a songster; but he is well known and admired, because he is showy, noisy, and flippant, and sings only in the open field, and frequently while poised on the wing, so that everybody who hears him can see him, and know who is the author of the strains that afford him so much delight. He sings also at broad noonday, when everybody is out, and is seldom heard before sun-rise, while other birds are pouring forth their souls in a united con-cert of praise. He waits until the sun is up, and when most of the early performers have become silent, as if determined to secure a good audience before exhibiting his powers. . . .

There is not a plaintive strain in his whole performance. Every sound is as merry as the laugh of a young child; and one cannot listen to him without fancying that he is indulging in some jocose raillery of his companions. If we suppose him to be making love, we cannot look upon him as very deeply enamored, but rather as highly delighted with his spouse, and overflowing with rapturous admira-tion. The object of his love is a neatly formed bird, with a mild expression of countenance, a modest and amiable deportment, and arrayed in the plainest apparel. It is evident that she does not pride herself on the splendor of her costume, but rather on its neatness, and on her own feminine graces. She must be entirely without vanity, unless we suppose that it is gratified by observing the pomp and display which are made by her partner, and by listening to his delightful eloquence of song; for if we regard him as an orator, it must be allowed that he is unsurpassed in fluency and rapidity of utterance; and if we regard him only as a musician, he is unrivalled in brilliancy of execution.

—T. W. Higginson, *Birds of the Garden and Orchard*, 1858

That's the wise Thrush; he sings his song twice over,
Lest you would think he never could recapture
The first fine careless rapture!

—Robert Browning, "Home-Thoughts, from Abroad,"
in *Dramatic Lyrics*, 1842

Birds of Sea and Shore

I know of no more interesting shore bird to watch than the stately black-bellied plover, as it runs hither and thither on the sand, dabbing here and there with its short bill, or standing pensively, slowly folding its great wings after alighting. In the spring one may study all phases of plumage in a single flock, from those in winter dress with pure white breasts and bellies, through the slightly and profusely spotted ones, to those with splendid jet black breasts that contrast well with their white sides and necks. Thus on May 21, 1905, a flock of sixty-six of these birds ran by me as I lay concealed on the beach within a hundred yards, and I made the following census: nineteen were full black bellies; twenty seven were in various stages of incompleteness; twenty were pale bellies.

Their whistle is somewhat like that of the piping plover, but is deeper and longer and differs in accent. As a flock flies over, their voices come down as a shower of sweet yet mournful sounds.

—Charles Wendell Townsend, *Sand Dunes and Salt Marshes*, 1913

A fresh surprise and pleasure awaited me when I explored the coast east of the village; it was bold and precipitous in places, and from the summit of the cliff, a very fine view of the coast-line cliff itself was the breeding place of some hundreds of herring-gulls. The eggs at the period of my visit were not yet hatched, but highly incubated, and at that stage both parents are almost constantly at home, as if in a state of anxious suspense . . .

I spent hours of rare happiness at this spot in watching the birds. I could not have seen and heard them to such advantage if their breeding place had been shared with other species. Here the herring-gulls had the rock to themselves, and looked their best in their foam-white and pearly-grey plumage and yellow legs and beaks. While I watched them, they watched me; not gathered in groups, but singly or in pairs, scattered up and down all over the face of the precipice above me, perched on ledges and on jutting points of rock. Standing motionless thus, beautiful in form and colour, they looked like sculptured figures of gulls, set up on the projections against the rough dark wall of rock, just as in niches on a cathedral front. At first they appeared quite indifferent to my prescence, although in some instances near enough for their yellow irides to be visible. While unalarmed they were very silent, standing in that clear sunshine that gave their whiteness something of a crystalline appearance; or flying to and fro along the face of the cliff, purely for the delight of bathing in the warm lucent air. Gradually a change came over them. One by one those that were on the wing dropped on to some projection, until they had all settled down, and, letting my eyes range up and down over the huge wall of rock, it was plain to see that all the birds were watching me. They had made the discovery that I was a stranger. In my rough old travel-stained clothes and tweed hat I might have passed for a Branscombe villager, but I did no hoeing and digging in one of the cultivated patches; and when I deliberately sat down on a rock to watch them, they noticed it and became suspicious; and as time went on and I still remained immovable, with my eyes fixed on them, the suspicion and anxiety increased and turned to fear; and those that were sitting on their nests got up and came close to the edge of the rock, to gaze with the others and join in the loud chorus of alarm. It was a wonderful sound, not like the tempest of noise that may be heard at the breeding season at Lundy Island, and at many other stations where birds of several species mix their various voices—the yammeris and the yowlis and skrykking, screeking, skrymming scowlis, and meickle noyes and shoutes, of old Dunbar's wonderful onomatopoetic lines. Here there was only one species, with a clear resonant cry, and as every bird uttered that one cry, and no other, a totally different effect was produced. The herring-gull and lesser black-backed gull resemble each other in language as they do in general appearance; both have very powerful and clear voices unlike the guttural black-headed and common gull. But the herring-gull has a shriller, more piercing voice and resembles the black-backed species just as, in human voices, a boy's clear treble resembles a baritone. Both birds have a variety of notes; and both, when the nest is threatened with danger, utter one powerful importunate cry, which is repeated incessantly until the danger is over. And as the birds breed in communities, often very populous, and all clamour together, the effect of so many powerful and unisant voices is very grand; but it differs in the two species, owing to the quality of their voices being different; the storm of sound produced by the black-backs is deep and solemn, while that of the herring-gulls has a ringing sharpness that is almost metallic.

It is probable that in the case I am describing the effect of sharpness and resonance was heightened by the position of the birds, perched motionless, scattered about on the face of the rock, all with their beaks turned in my direction, raining their cries upon me. It was not a monotonous storm of cries, but rose and fell; for after two or three minutes the excitement would abate somewhat and the cries grow fewer and fewer; then the infection would spread again, bird after bird joining the outcry; and after a while there would be another lull, and so on, wave following wave of sound. I could have spent hours, and the hours would have seemed like minutes, listening to that strange chorus of running chiming cries, so novel was its effect, and unlike that of any other tempest of sound produced by birds which I had ever heard.

—W. H. Hudson, *Branscombe and Its Birds*, 1898

In swimming under water the black guillemot uses its wings only—the rose-red legs trail behind it, a fading fire as it goes down. The body becomes one great glaucous-green bubble, which has, still more, a luminous appearance. The effect may almost be called beautiful, but it is still more odd and bottle-imp-like. Most diving sea-birds exhibit this appearance under water, but not all in the same degree. . . .

A pair of these birds are now feeding their young. The nest is in a hole in the earth, on a ridge of the precipitous grass-slope of the cliff, just above where it breaks into rocks, and drops sheer to the sea. Both parents feed the chick—for their family is no larger—but one more often than the other. They bring, each time, a single fish—a sand-eel, often of a fair size—and disappear with it into the hole, reappearing shortly afterwards. Once both are in the hole together, having entered in succession, each with a fish, but generally when the two meet at the entrance one only brings a fish and goes in, and the other, having nothing, stays outside. When the parent bird has fed its young and come out again, it will often sit for a little on the steep slope, above or below the hole, before flying away. It looks solicitously at the hole, and from time to time utters a little thin note that just reaches me where I am. Once both the birds sat like this, one above and one below the hole. What I particularly noticed was that when the bird that had taken a fish in had come out again, the other, even though it had nothing, would always go in too, as though to pay the chick a little visit.

—Edmund Selous, *The Bird Watcher in the Shetlands*, 1905

Far from the loud sea beaches,
  Where he goes fishing and crying,
Here in the inland garden,
  Why is the sea-gull flying?

Here are no fish to dive for;
  Here is the corn and lea;
Here are the green trees rustling;
  Hie away home to the sea!

Fresh is the river water,
    And quiet among the rushes;
This is no home for the sea-gull,
    But for the rooks and thrushes.

Pity the bird that has wandered!
    Pity the sailor ashore!
Hurry him home to the ocean,
    Let him come here no more!

High on the sea-cliff ledges,
    The white gulls are trooping and crying;
Here among rooks and roses,
    Why is the sea-gull flying?

—Robert Louis Stevenson, "A Visit from the Sea,"
in *Underwoods*, 1887

Young kittewakes—as no doubt the old ones, too, though I have not yet noticed them doing so—bathe, or rather play about in the sea, very prettily. They flap their wings in an excited way, or hold them spread on the water whilst turning round, or half round in it, then, with their wings still spread, they make a little spring upwards, and flop down on it again, like a kite falling flat, and repeat the performance any number of times. . . .

I can, I think, see . . . why the bathing of aquatic birds has passed, as I believe it has in several instances, into an antic or something partaking of that character. They bathe in their own element—water— in which they are thoroughly at home, whilst the wide expanse of it around them allows of free and extended movement. But when a land-bird washes itself it does so under very different conditions, and a more or less lively tubbing is the utmost one would expect it to evolve out of the situation.

—Edmund Selous, *Bird Watching*, 1901

Although gulls often alight and leave their tracks in the dunes, the footprints of sea birds are best studied on the damp beach, and a chapter might be written on this subject alone. The most character-istic of these tracks are those of the shore birds, and one can easily distinguish the records of plover from the records of sandpipers, both by the footprints and by the bill-marks. Flocks of plover spread out irregularly on the sand, and leave tracks running in various directions and constantly crossing, while the sandpipers have more team play, and run along the beach, up and down before the ad-vancing and retreating waves, but always together. The sandpiper, with head down nearly all the time, drills the sand with his long bill, and leaves behind him an almost uninterrupted series of holes close together for the space of a foot or more, then a blank space where only his footprints show as he hurries along, swallowing his prey, then another series of holes, and so on. Not so the plover; he strides along with head up, but every few seconds he strikes the sand a blow with his short bill for a minute crustacean or worm below the sur-face. These dabbings of the semi-palmated or ring-neck plover are small, while those of the black-bellied plover are large and are usu-ally two or three feet apart and generally double, which means that the eager bird struck the sand with bill partly open. The footprints show three toes wide apart.

—Charles Wendell Townsend, *Sand Dunes and Salt Marshes*, 1913

Now for Sea-fowl—and here I must plead guilty to the charge (if it be a charge) of being open to a little bit of sentiment. At the pres-ent time I believe there is no class of animals so cruelly persecuted as the sea-fowl which throng to certain portions of our coast in the breeding season. At other times of the year they can take good care of themselves, as every gunner on the coast knows; but in the breeding season, in fulfilment of the high command to "increase and multiply" they cast off their suspicions and wary habits and come to our shores. No one that I have ever heard of has complained of them as injurious in any way. Some few, as the "Scoulton Peewits," settle far inland, and their usefulness as they follow the plough is every-where recognised. But of the rest—I have never heard the Willocks or Kittiwakes of the Yorkshire coast accused of raising the price of herrings, sprats, and oysters! I think we may fairly assume that they are innocuous in every respect. But how do we treat them? Excursion trains run to convey the so-called "sportsmen" of London and Lancashire to the Isle of Wight and Flamborough Head, where one of the amusements held out is the shooting of these harmless birds. But it is not merely the bird that is shot that perishes—difficult as it is to say where cruelty begins or ends—that alone would not be cruelty in my opinion. The bird that is shot is a parent—it has its young at home waiting for the food it is bringing far away from the Dogger Bank or the Chops of the Channel—we take advantage of its most sacred instincts to waylay it, and in depriving the parent of life, we doom the helpless offspring to the most miserable of deaths, that by hunger. If this is not cruelty, what is? Can we blaze away hour after hour at these wretched inoffensive birds and call it "Sport" without being morally the worse for it?

—Alfred Newton, *The Zoological Aspect of Game Laws*, 1868

May 27, 1826

I must now change for a moment my theme and speak of birds awhile. Mother Carey's Chickens (*Procellaria*) came about us, and I longed to have one in my possession. I had watched their evolutions, their gentle patting of the sea when on the wing with their legs hanging and webbs expanded. I had seen them take large and long ranges in search of food, and return repeatedly for the bits of fat thrown overboard and for them intended . . .

During many weeks following this date I discovered that many flew mated side by side, and, occasionally, particularly in calm and pleasant weather, caressed each other as Ducks are known to do. . . .

When full one hundred leagues at sea, a female Rice Bunting came aboard and remained with us over-night and part of next day. A Warbler also came but remained only a few minutes and made for the land we had left. It moved, whilst on board, with great activity and sprightliness; the Bunting to the contrary was exhausted, panted, and, I have no doubt, died of inanition. Many Sooty Terns were in sight during several days. I saw one Frigate Pelican high in the air, and could only judge it to be such through the help of the telescope. Flocks of unknown birds were also about the ship during the whole day. They swam well and preferred the water to the air. They resembled large Phalaropes, but could not be certain . . . In Latitude 24. 27' a Green Heron came on board and remained until frightened by me, then flew toward the brig "Gleaner." It did not appear in the least fatigued.

June 26, 1826

We have been becalmed many days, and I should be dull indeed were it not for the fishes and birds, and my pen and pencil. I have been much interested in the Dusky Petrel; the mate killed four at one shot, so plentiful were they about our vessel, and I have made several drawings from these, which were brought on board for that purpose. They skim over the sea in search of what is here called Gulf Wood, of which there are large patches, perhaps half an acre in extent. They flap the wings six or seven times, then soar for three or four seconds, the tail spread, the wings extended. Four or five of these birds, indeed sometimes as many as fifteen or twenty, will alight on this weed, dive, flutter, and swim with all the gaiety of ducks on a pond, which they have reached after a weary journey. I heard no note from any of them. No sooner have the Petrels eaten or dispersed the fish than they rise and extend their wings for flight, in search of more. At times, probably to rest themselves, they alighted, swam lightly, dipping their bills frequently in the water as mergansers and fishy Ducks do when trying, by tasting, if the water contains much fish.

—John James Audubon, journal

A tern that either eludes or is not molested by a skua at sea, flies home with its fish, to feed its young. But here it has often to run the gauntlet of other skuas, who wait and watch for it upon the land, sitting amidst the short stunted heather, with the brown of which their plumage, as a rule, harmonises. There are, therefore, land-robbers

and sea-robbers—pirates, and highwaymen—among these aristo-
cratic birds, and it would be interesting to know whether the two
roles are performed by different individuals, or indifferently by the
same one. To ascertain this satisfactorily I have found a difficult
matter, but I believe that here as elsewhere—in everything, as soon
as one begins to watch it—a process of differentiation is going on.

Where there are terns to be robbed, the skuas—I am speaking
always of the smaller and, as I have found it, the more interesting
species—seem to prefer them to any other quarry, so that the gulls,
generally, benefit by their presence; otherwise all are victimised,
except, as I think, the great black-backed gull. The latter will, himself, attack the skua, who flies before him, so that, taking this and his
size into consideration, it does not seem very likely that the parts
should ever be reversed between them, nor can I recall any clear
instance in which they were. Of all the birds attacked, the common
gull—which, like common sense, seems to be anything but common—
makes, in my experience, the stoutest resistance; for it will turn to
bay and show fight, both in the air and on the water, when it has been
driven down upon it . . .

The skuas love brigandage so much that, amongst themselves,
they play at it; swooping, fleeing, and pursuing, each feigns, in turn,
to be spoiler or spoiled. So, at least, I understand it, for nothing ever
comes of these mock skirmishings, no real fight or flight, or anything
approaching to one. It is fun, frolic, with a sense of humour, maybe,
as though two pirates were playfully to hoist the black at each other. I
love the humour of it. I love the birds. Above all, I love that wild cry
of theirs that rings out so beautifully "to the wild sky," to the mists
and scudding clouds. By its general grace and beauty, by its sportings
and piracies, its speed of flight and the rushing sweeps of its attack,
this bird must ever live in the memories of those who have known it:
but, most of all, it will live there by the inspiring music of its cry.

—Edmund Selous, *The Bird Watcher in the Shetlands*, 1905

Among the family of Gulls, none are more interesting than the
Skuas or Jaegers. They are the pirates of the sea-coast, being very

bold and insolent, and in many cases do not take the trouble to fish for themselves; but, watching the fishing operations of the Gull, seize their opportunity of assailing a successful fisher and compelling him to disgorge his prey which they take to themselves. They not only pitilessly persecute the Kittiwake and other Gulls in order to obtain their own food second-hand; but also destroy and devour the eggs of other birds.

—Walter Raine, *The Ornithologists' and Oologists' Semi-Annual*, 1889

> He thought he saw an Albatross
> That fluttered round the lamp:
> He looked again, and found it was
> A penny-postage stamp.
> "You'd best be getting home," he said,
> "The nights are very damp."

—Lewis Carroll, *Sylvie and Bruno*, 1889

The spotted sandpiper, aside from the charm of his voice, is one of the most winsome of birds, and graceful in every movement. His use of the wings is particularly expressive. They never seem to be mere means of flitting, like wings in general; they are far more, they almost take the place of speech. By their movements he expresses his emotions, his sentiments, till, in watching him one realizes how much may be said without words, and longs for ability to interpret. On alighting, he holds them far above the head for a moment before carefully folding them down in proper position. Sometimes when singing he keeps them vibrating rapidly, adding wonderfully to the effect upon the listener. Again, he will glide down through the air, holding them almost straight up, forming a sharp-pointed V. To drive away intruders or to meet an enemy he spreads the wings while ruffling up the plumage and making himself as formidable as possible; and in courtship he drags them on the ground. I have once or twice seen one of these birds express some emotion—alas, I could only guess what—by holding one wing up while looking with clear, calm eyes, full in my face, "scanning me with a fearless eye."

The "tipping," which everywhere gives a sandpiper his local name of "tip-up," is not graceful. It reminds one of the rocking of a light canoe near the shore as the waves rush by.

There was never a prettier sight than a little flock of sandpipers flying over the edge of the water in zigzag fashion, moving as one bird, as if animated by one will. . . .

Sandpipers have a curious habit, when they alight on the shore in a flock, of standing a few seconds perfectly still as if turned to stone, then suddenly with one accord beginning to run around for food. Once I caught a young family out with their mother foraging for their supper. They were about half the size of the mother, and she stood perfectly still while the little flock ran about in the liveliest way, catching, or at any rate chasing, insects, with jerky motions like a grasshopper, and never intermitting for a moment the "teter." When the mother wished to go she called, and the obedient little ones at once followed her away.

—Olive Thorne Miller, *With the Birds in Maine*, 1904

On the Song of the "Peep," or the Least Sandpiper

In the spring one is sometimes treated to their flight song, a musical quavering trill, which the bird pours out continuously as it rises on quivering wings. The song ends with a few sweet notes that suggest some of those of the goldfinch, and, after the excited bird has fallen to the ground, it emits a few low clucks. The whole performance is altogether delightful and unexpected.

—Charles Wendell Townsend, *Sand Dunes and Salt Marshes*, 1913

From the edge of the turf something runs on to the sand, to the edge of the pure water, and some small grey dots with it. It is a hen sandpiper. As the birds run they look like grey stones moving about, when they are reflected in the water; so closely do they fall in with their surroundings that even with a glass, at very short range, we are barely able to follow them.

—Jordan Denham, *From Spring to Fall*, 1894

Like most burrowing birds the Puffin occasionally annexes the hole of some other creature, that of a rabbit, especially, but in the great majority of instances it is its own architect. This bird burrows into . . . sea-cliffs, as well as into that level ground, whilst in other cases it finds a convenient shelter in old and ruined masonry. The formidable beak—shaped somewhat like a coulter of a plough—and the excessively sharp claws are both used in the excavation of the burrow. Like the Burrowing owl, the Puffin casts out the loose earth and stones behind it with its legs and feet, and I have often stood below the cliffs and watched the almost continual shower of debris as the active little birds have worked away hundreds of feet above me. . . . Some of these colonies of Puffins, notably those at St. Kilda and the Farne Islands, are intensely interesting places to visit, as the number of birds is past all belief. One of these colonies at St. Kilda, situated in a sandy bank on the shores of Village Bay, close to the store, is almost exactly like a colony of Sand Martins, the great height of the cliff—and the consequent distance at which the holes are viewed—assisting to make the comparison complete.

—Charles Dixon, *Birds' Nests*, 1902

The laughing gull nests abundantly on the Louisiana islands and after the breeding season visits the Alabama coast in numbers to feed. The species is common in Mississippi Sound and in the bays along the coast both in summer and winter, but it does not at present nest within the borders of the State. A small flock was seen on Petit Bois Island, February 12, 1912, and about 20 on Dauphin Island, March 22, 1912. In the latter flock there was one black-headed adult. About 20 or 30 birds were seen on Dauphin Island, July 5, 1913, and by the end of the month they were common there. Small numbers also were seen there June 1–5, 1914. Two immature birds were seen near Mobile, May 9, 1911, and 50 or more, both young and adults, in scattered flocks, on July 14, 1913. The latter were flying toward the city early in the morning, evidently intending to feed in the river. On Grand Bay, November 16, 1915, several laughing gulls flew over my duck blind, and near Point-aux-Pines, November 26, 1915, I saw a flock of about 6 birds.

—Arthur H. Howell, *Birds of Alabama*, 1924

All is flesh that a Gull can find to eat as long as it is not vegetable.

—John Hall Sage and Louis Bennett Bishop, *The Birds of Connecticut*, 1913

A curious habit of herring gulls leads to peculiar tracks. I refer to the fact that they not infrequently drag dead fish in tortuous courses from the upper beach down to the water. A dead hake eighteen inches long I found had been dragged one hundred and thirty-four paces to the water, and, from the tracks, it was evident that the gull had laboriously walked backwards all the way, pausing from time to time and relinquishing its beak-hold on the fish. The fish was certainly gamey enough to need a salt water souse, but the gull's object was possibly to soften it. This action on the part of the gull seems to me to deserve credit for something more than mere instinct. I cannot help thinking that the lower animals, in unusual actions of this sort, display an intelligence akin to our own, and that the sharp line between instinct for them and reasoning power for us should not be drawn. The Lord only knows how much of our own boasted intelligence is merely instinctive; I have known dogs that have shown more reasoning power than I have seen displayed by some stupid people. I have a parrot that shows its intelligence in the same manner as the gull by taking hard bits of cracker to its water jar and soaking them before it eats them.

—Charles Wendell Townsend, *Sand Dunes and Salt Marshes*, 1913

It is a bright, frosty morning early in January. The sky is almost cloudless, though a haze hangs thickly on the horizon, obscuring the distant hills and cliffs. It is almost low water, and a wide belt of sand, left uncovered, rises gently till about a quarter of a mile from the sea it ends in a barrier of sand-dunes, at once crowned and held together by rushes, effectually enforcing its command on the waves, "thus far and no further!"

The tide is, however, rising, and the waves struggle shorewards against a stiff easterly wind, which catches the crests of the breakers, causing the manes of the miniature "white horses" to trail yards behind them.

A few Herring Gulls sail swiftly along just above the waves. Theirs is the very poetry of motion; no effort, only an occasional adjustment of the angle at which the wing is held. Another slight change, almost imperceptible to the eye, and the bird rises with a graceful curve into the air, wheels and swoops down, gathering the necessary impetus for the return journey. Very difficult is the laboured flapping of the Cormorant as he passes us flying just above the waves with his long neck outstretched.

In front of us is a Ringed Plover, running nimbly out after a receding wave, stooping daintily to pick up some morsel, then re-treating to escape a wetting, as the next comes in. He is a pretty little bird, light brown above and white below, except for a broad black collar across the foreneck. The crown of the head is pale brown, separated from the white frontal band by a broad band of black. His short bill is orange, tipped with black; legs and feet are the same colour. Such is his portrait, but it is hard to convey in words the impression of sprightliness and grace he leaves upon our minds.

As we approach the estuary bird-life become more plentiful. A spit of sand running out into the sea is occupied by a flock of Gulls, which apparently have fed well, for they stand complacently preening their feathers. Even at this distance a pair of Great Black-backed Gulls are conspicuous among their fellows owing to their size, and we are able to recognize the immature Herring Gulls by their mottled brown plumage.

Near by is a flock of Dunlins, a little silvery line on the sand. The Gulls look giants beside them. Now they rise as one bird and fly with amazing swiftness, their white underparts flashing in the sunlight at one moment; the next, their brown backs are towards us, and the birds are hardly visible till they wheel again.

—A. J. R. Roberts, *The Bird Book*, 1903

One March day I notice a gull rise from the water and fly with all speed directly at a golden-eye duck who was peacefully swimming not far off. The duck dove to avoid the blow that seemed imminent, and the gull took its place on the surface of the water. In a few seconds he was off to repeat the game on another duck, and so it went on. The victim always dove in time, the gull never picked up any food or appeared to be looking for anything the duck might have dropped, and the other ducks swam close to the marauding gull without any show of fear on their part or of malice on the part of the gull. I believe that the whole performance was in the nature of play between the different species living in a familiar and friendly manner in the same region.

—Charles Wendell Townsend, *Sand Dunes and Salt Marshes*, 1913

Gull-fights are sometimes very fierce and determined, and when this is the case they often cause great excitement among a number of others. As on the human plane, fights between birds make impressions upon one according to the greater or lesser amount of intensity manifested, becoming sometimes quite tragic in their interest. Not only is this the case with oneself, but birds that are not fighting seem affected in the same way. I have noticed this with partridges somewhat—but more in the gullery. An ordinary scuffle between two birds attracts little if any notice from the others, but when it is sustained and bitter, supported with great courage on either side, there may be quite a crowd of excited on-lookers. I have seen a very desperate combat which I at first thought was a general scrimmage. It was not so, however. Two alone were engaged, but a cloud of gulls swept over and hovered about them, often hiding them from view.

—Edmund Selous, *The Bird Watcher in the Shetlands*, 1905

I treasure in my memory a stormy July day, when the wind was sweeping down cold and wet on to the shore, when a fog-bank lay to the east and great dark cumuli to the north of a gray sea studded with white-caps, when patches of fleecy scud drove overhead, revealing here and there spots of blue sky, and when the surf moaned on the bar. Herring gulls were everywhere, for the sea had cast up for them a bountiful feast. The sand flats were splashed with great patches of young herring, here shining like silver, there looking dark and colorless, while windrows of hake and pollack and schools of dog-fish dotted the shore. The sand was covered with the gulls' footprints, and marked with great white splashes, while feathers were blowing about as from an open feather-bed. As I stood on the edge of the beach, bracing myself against the wind, I noticed that a bar on one side was so thickly covered with the great birds that no sand was to be seen, while on the other that the broad flat beach for at least a mile was thronged with them, a great army of gray and white. Overhead they were continually passing and repassing, drifting along before the wind or sailing straight into the teeth of it.

—Charles Wendell Townsend, *Sand Dunes and Salt Marshes*, 1913

But with the gulls here—and still more with the terns—there is more than mere indifference. It is a disagreeable reflection that all these many birds—these beings everywhere about one—resent one's presence and wish one away, that every one of all the discordant notes uttered as one walks about under this screaming cloud of witnesses has a distinct and very unflattering reference to oneself, upbraids one, almost calls one a name. To be hated by thousands—and rightly hated too!

—Edmund Selous, *The Bird Watcher in the Shetlands*, 1905

Birds in Winter

GOLDEN-CRESTED WRENS.

Outside, here in the north, the lands are deeply covered with snow, and the usual supplies of food are cut off. The bright winter's berries of the hedgerows have vanished, and the thrushes are more destitute than other birds. The evergreens of the gardens are full of them. In their aimless flying to and fro they shake a feathery rain from the snow-plumed branches, and many are so emaciated that they cower with drooping wings beneath the thicker shrubs. There the blackbird darts out, as though to show how cleanly cut is his trim figure against the snow. He is more hardy than some of his congeners, and is self-assertive and bold wherever food is to be had. Few winter notes are so characteristic as his metallic "chink! chink!" coming through the thin frosty air at sundown.

—Anonymous, *Winter Birds*, 1889

November 8, 1853

Birds generally wear the russet dress of nature this season. They have their fall no less than the plants; the bright tints depart from their foliage or feathers, and they flit past like withered leaves in rustling flocks. The sparrow is a withered leaf.

—Henry David Thoreau, journal

In walking through the Park on the 28th [of December], a rather sizable bird flew over my head and lighted in a distant tree. If robins had been plentiful I should have thought this to be one, as it was about as large, and yet with something unusual in its appearance that made me curious to follow it up. It showed little timidity, but still kept a sharp eye on me as I reconnoitered close enough to see that its plumage was dingy white beneath and ashy above; not a robin certainly, possibly a shrike. At that instant it flew out of sight, but following its direction I soon found it perching in a low bush, furtively looking about and jerking its tail like a cat-bird. I mentally requested him to hold his head still for examination, for the characteristic markings of a bird radiate from the seat of intelligence. A shrike's bill is stout, and curved at the the end, and a black stripe passes through the eye; this one's bill was straight and slender, and the side of the face of uniform color; while in flying off again it disclosed pure white outer tail-feathers, with much white on the remainder,—no shrike, but the mocking-bird!—the genius of the thrush family,—the cat-bird, before the latter fell from grace. But what brought him to New York the last of December? It is a thoroughly Southern species, and it is quite the thing to explain its occasional appearance in the Northern States, and especially in winter, by calling it an escaped caged specimen; an inference that seems somehow to detract not a little from the credit of finding it. But I am convinced that in the present instance such a supposition is an injustice both to the bird and to myself. Without any doubt, this particular specimen wandered up from the

South entirely of its own volition, and lingered about the Park for my special benefit—a sort of Christmas present, a little belated in the delivery.

—Howard E. Parkhurst, *The Birds' Calendar*, 1894

A November gale sweeps over the marshes from the north-east, causing the alder and willow branches to crack and snap. The green plovers are all huddled up with their heads to the wind. The lap of the tide on the saltings, the shriek of the curlew, and the twitter of the dunlins tell you plainly birds will keep close to cover if they can get it. A dunlin shoots over the wall, then another, at last a whole flock. What is driving them? See, there comes a short-eared owl. A little to leeward a shore shooter is making his way towards the saltings; a snipe springs from a clump of rushes in front of him. He fires and wounds the snipe; only the tip of its wing is injured, so it does not drop at once, but wavers in its flight, crying, "Scape, scape." The owl sees this and takes in the situation at once; with a dash he catches it and is off, elated with his success.

—J. A. Owen, *Within an Hour of London Town:*
Among Wild Birds and Their Haunts, 1892

I draw a great fund of pleasure from the quails which inhabit my farm; they abundantly repay me, by their various notes and peculiar tameness, for the inviolable hospitality I constantly show them in the winter. Instead of perfidious taking advantage of their great and affecting distress, when nature offers nothing but a barren universal bed of snow, when irresistible necessity forces them to my barn doors, I permit them to feed unmolested; and it is not the least agreeable spectacle which that dreary season presents, when I see those beautiful birds, tamed by hunger, intermingling with all my cattle and sheep, seeking in security for the poor scanty grain which but for them would be useless and lost. Often in the angles of the fences where the motion of the wind prevents the snow from settling, I carry them both chaff and grain; the one to feed them, the other to prevent their tender feet from freezing fast to the earth as I have frequently observed them to do. I do not know an instance in which the singular

barbarity of man is so strongly delineated, as in the catching and mur-
thering those harmless birds, at that cruel season of the year. Mr.__,
one of the most famous and extraordinary farmers that has ever done
honour to the province of Connecticut, by his timely and humane
assistance in a hard winter, saved this species from being entirely
destroyed. They perished all over the country, none of their delightful
whistlings were heard the next spring, but upon this gentleman's farm;
and to his humanity we owe the continuation of their music.

—Crèvecoeur, *Letters from an American Farmer*, 1782

There are few of our land-birds that flock together in summer,
and few that are solitary in winter,—none that I recollect, except
birds of prey. And not only do birds of the same kind associate, but
certain species are almost always found together. Thus, the chickadee, the golden-crested wren, the white-breasted nuthatch, and, less
constantly, the brown creeper and the downy woodpecker, form a
little winter clique, of which you do not often see one of the members without one or more of the others. No sound in nature is more
cheery and refreshing than the alternating calls of a little troop of this
kind echoing through the glades of the woods on a still, sunny day in
winter: the vivacious chatter of the chickadee, the slender, contented
pipe of the goldcrest, and the emphatic, business-like hank of the
nuthatch, as they drift leisurely along from tree to tree.

—T. W. Higginson, *Our Birds, and Their Ways*, 1857

How winter emphasizes the movements of wild life! The snow
and the cold are the white paper upon which the print is revealed. A
track of a mouse, a bird, a squirrel, or a fox shows us at a glance how
the warm pulse of life defies the embargo of winter. From cracks and
rents in the frigid zone which creep down upon us at this season there
issue tiny jets of warm life which play about here and there as if in the
heyday of summer. The woods snap and explode with the frost, the
ground is choked with snow, no sign of food is there for bird or beast,
and yet here are these tiny bundles of cheer and contentment in
feathers—the chickadees, the nuthatches, and their fellows.

—John Burroughs, *Birds and Bees*, 1919

For hours from my look-out have I been seeking with my glass the snow-plumed pines in search of a flock of interesting birds that do not appear. But in such weather as this the crossbills always arrive. In severe winters I have never looked in vain for them in the pinewood. There they'are!—now on the upper, now on the lower branches, so tame that we may approach unheeded, the birds give out a constant twitter, and ever repeat their not unmusical call-notes. Never still, they are constantly changing position, fluttering from branch to branch, constantly sending down showers of cones and scales, and themselves hanging in every conceivable position. Nimbly they go, parrot-like, along the undersides of the boughs, climbing and holding with bill and feet. What a babble of self-satisfied chatter comes from the feeding flock!

—Anonymous, *Winter Birds*, 1889

The truth is, that birds are remarkably well guarded against cold by their quick circulation, their dense covering of down and feathers, and the ease with which they can protect their extremities. The chickadee is never so lively as in clear, cold weather;—not that he is absolutely insensible to cold; for on those days, rare in this neighborhood, when the mercury falls to fifteen degrees or more below zero, the chickadee shows by his behavior that he, too, feels it to be an exceptional state of things. Of such a morning I have seen a small flock of them collected on the sunny side of a thick hemlock, rather silent and quiet, with ruffled plumage, like balls of gray fur, waiting, with an occasional chirp, for the sun's rays to begin to warm them up, and meanwhile not depressed, but only a little sobered in their deportment, and ready, if the cold continued, to get used to that too.

—T. W. Higginson, *Our Birds, and Their Ways*, 1857

Extinction

Lovers of birds alive and free have reason to rejoice that our most interesting birds are not gaudy in coloring. The indiscriminate and terrible slaughter of some of these beautiful creatures, to appear in some horrible, unnatural position on ladies' hats, is surely enough to make the most long-suffering lover of nature cry out in grief and pain. To me—let me say it frankly—they look not like an adornment of feathers, but like the dead bodies of birds, foully murdered to minister to a passing fashion.

—Olive Thorne Miller, *With the Birds in Maine*, 1904

Carolina Parrots

They seem entirely unsuspicious of danger, and after being fired at, only huddle closer together, as if to obtain protection from each other, and as their companions are falling about them, they curve down their necks, and look at them fluttering upon the ground, as though perfectly at a loss to account for so unusual an occurrence. It is a most inglorious sort of shooting; down right, cold-blooded murder.

—John Kirk Townsend, journal, 1834

I made a very attractive camp among the giant sycamores, sweet-gums, and cotton-woods. The warm sunshine penetrated into this sheltered spot, while the wind had fallen to a gentle zephyr, and came in refreshing puffs through the lofty trees. Here birds were numerous, and briskly hopped about my fire while I made an omelet and boiled some wheaten grits.

In this retired haunt of the birds I remained through the whole of that sunny Sunday, cooking my three meals, and reading my Bible, as became a civilized man. While enjoying this immunity from the disturbing elements of the great public thoroughfare, the river, curious cries were borne upon the wind above the tree-tops like the chattering calls of parrots, to which my ear had become accustomed in the tropical forests of Cuba. As the noise grew louder with the approach of a feathered flock of visitors, and the screams of the birds became more discordant, I peered through the branches of the forest to catch a glimpse of what I had searched for through many hundred miles of wilderness since my boyhood, but what had so far eluded my eager eyes. I felt certain these strange cries must come from the Carolina Parrot, or Parakeet (*Conurus Carolinensis*), which, though once numerous in all the country west of the Alleghanies as far north as the Great Lakes, has so rapidly diminished in number since 1825, that we find it only as an occasional inhabitant of the middle states south of the Ohio River. In fact, this species is now chiefly confined to Florida, western Louisiana, Texas, Arkansas, and the Indian Territory. . . .

The birds soon reached the locality of my camp, and circling through the clear, warm atmosphere above the tree-tops, they gradually settled lower and lower, suspiciously scanning my fire, screaming as though their little throats would burst, while the sunlight seemed to fill the air with the reflections of the green, gold, and carmine of their brilliant plumage. They dropped into the foliage of the grove, and for a moment were as quiet as though life had departed from them, while I kept close to my hiding-place behind an immense fallen tree, from beneath which I could watch my feathery guests. . . .

This interesting parakeet may, during the next century, pass out of existence, and be known to our descendents as the Great Auk (Alca impennis) is now known to us, as a very rare specimen in the museums of natural history.

—Nathaniel H. Bishop, *Four Months in a Sneak-Box*, 1879

Of the hundred and sixty-eight kinds of Parrots enumerated by European writers as inhabiting the various regions of the globe, this is the only species found native within the territory of the United States. The vast and luxuriant tracts lying within the torrid zone seem to be the favorite residence of these noisy, numerous, and richly-plumaged tribes. . . .

In descending the River Ohio, by myself, in the month of February, I met with the first flock of Paroquets at the mouth of the Little Scioto. I had been informed, by an old and respectable inhabitant of Marietta, that they were sometimes, though rarely, seen there. I observed flocks of them, afterwards, at the mouth of the Great and Little Miami, and in the neighborhood of numerous creeks that discharge themselves into the Ohio. At Big Bone Lick, thirty miles above the mouth of the Kentucky River, I saw them in great numbers. They came screaming through the woods in the morning, about an hour after sunrise, to drink the salt water, of which they, as well as the Pigeons, are remarkably fond. When they alighted on the ground, it appeared at a distance as if covered with a carpet of the richest green, orange, and yellow; they afterwards settled, in one body, on a neighboring tree, which stood detached from any other, covering almost every twig of it, and the sun, shining strongly on their gay and glossy plumage, produced a very beautiful and splendid appearance.

—Alexander Wilson, *American Ornithology*, 1826

On Dodos

These singular birds, which for distinction we shall henceforth designate by the technical name Didinae, furnish the first clearly attested instances of the extinction of organic species through human agency. It has been proved, however, that other examples of the kind had occurred both before and since; and many species of animals and plants are now undergoing this inevitable process of destruction before the ever-advancing tide of human population. We cannot see without regret the extinction of the last individual of any race of organic beings, whose progenitors colonized the pre-adamite Earth; but our consolation must be found in the reflection, that Man is destined by his Creator to "be fruitful and multiply and replenish the Earth and subdue it." The progress of Man in civilization, no less than his numerical increase, continually extends the geographical domain of Art by trenching on the territories of Nature, and hence the Zoologist or Botanist of future ages will have a much narrower field for his researches than that which we enjoy at present.

—H. E. Strickland and A. G. Melville, *The Dodo and Its Kindred*, 1848

I hope that the efforts of the Audubon societies and kindred organizations will gradually make themselves felt until it becomes a point of honor not only with the American man, but with the American small boy, to shield and protect all forms of harmless wild life.

—Theodore Roosevelt, *Theodore Roosevelt: An Autobiography*, 1920

The yellow plover frequents the prairies in the spring in immense flocks, and a nice little bird it is, graceful to shoot at, and very delicious to swallow.

—James Hall, *The West*, 1848

Birds are of value to the State as (1) destroyers of noxious insects, their eggs and larvae, and also of small mammals, especially when such injurious animals appear in excessive numbers; (2) destroyers of weed seed; (3) replanters of forests; (4) food; (5) sport; (6) scavengers; (7) guides to fishermen; (8) means of mental enjoyment. . . . To provide mental enjoyment may not seem at first sight a part of the function of the State, but there is a large and steadily increasing body of people, valuable citizens, who derive great enjoyment from listening to the songs and studying the habits of birds, who will go where birds are and keep away where birds are not. Surely it is more to the advantage of the state to protect birds and encourage these people to live with us than it is to allow our smaller birds to be shot for the morsel of meat their bodies may afford. From this standpoint alone, the protection of birds is certainly a good investment for the state.

—John Hall Sage and Louis Bennett Bishop, *The Birds of Connecticut*, 1913

There is scarcely a hotel in New Orleans where small birds do not form an item on the bill of fare. At certain seasons the robin, wood-thrush, thrasher, olive-backed thrush, hermit-thrush, che-wink, flicker, and many of our beautiful sparrows form the bulk of the victims; but catbirds, cardinals, and almost all small birds, even swallows, can be found in the markets.

—Professor Henry Nehrling, *Our Native Birds of Song and Beauty*, 1893

A still more striking example of wholesale egg-collecting, and probably the most important one in the United States, from a financial stand-point, is that of the Farallones. These islands, or rather rocks, situated on the coast of California, thirty miles west of the Golden Gate, are the breeding-grounds of myriads of sea-birds, chiefly western gulls (Larus occidentalis) and murres, or California guillemots (Urea troile Californica). For nearly fifty years murre eggs were collected here and shipped to San Franciscan market, where they found a ready sale at from twelve to twenty cents a dozen, a price only a little less than that of hens' eggs. During the season, which lasted about two months, beginning near the middle of May, the eggs were shipped regularly once or twice a week. The main crop was gathered on South Farralone, the principal island, and mainly from the "great rookery" at the west end. The birds lay only one egg, which is deposited on the bare rock. When the season opened the men went over the ground and broke all the eggs in sight, so as to avoid taking any that were not perfectly fresh. The ground was then gone over every day, and the eggs were systematically picked up and shipped to market. . . . It is said that in 1854 more than five hundred thousand eggs were sold in less than two months, and that between 1850 and 1856 three or four millions were taken to San Francisco.

—Dr. T. S. Palmer, in Clarence M. Weed and Ned Dearborn's
Birds in Their Relation to Man, 1903

Half a century ago the penguin (great auk) was very plenty. It is a handsome bird about the size of a goose, with a coal-black head and back, a white belly, and a milk-white spot under the right eye. They cannot fly well—their wings are more like fans.

—Anonymous, *Newfoundland and Its Missionaries*, 1860s

In Japan it is said that when travelling artisans see an eagle, they take out their sketching tablets and record its beautiful shape and attitudes. The barbarians of this part of the world try to shoot it, a fate they have often meted out to every large or unusual bird they came across, even if it were of no value to them, and they left it to rot where it fell. Fortunately times are changing and the people are gradually awakening to the idea that money value in food and plumage, or even in work done for man, is not the only thing for which birds should be protected. We are also beginning to realize that the interest which finds pleasure in the sport of bird destruction is a very limited and a very selfish one, and that the claims of the sportsman are not paramount to those of the nature student or even of the lover of natural beauty.

—Charles Wendell Townsend, *Sand Dunes and Salt Marshes*, 1913

The ducks, too, still resort to our rivermouth, in spite of the railroads and the tall chimneys by which their old feeding-grounds are surrounded. As long as the channel is open, you may see the goldeneyes, or "whistlers," in extended lines, visible only as a row of bright specks as their white breasts rise and fall on the waves; and farther than you can see them, you may hear the whistle of their wings as they rise. Spring and fall the "black ducks" still come to find the brackish waters which they like, and to fill their crops with the seeds of the eel-grass and the mixed food of the flats. In the late twilight you may sometimes catch sight of a flock speeding in, silent and swift, over the Mill-dam, or hear their sonorous quacking from their feeding-ground.

At least, these things were,—and not long since,—though I cannot answer for a year or two back. The birds long retain the tradition of the old places, and strive to keep their hold upon them; but we are building them out year by year. The memory is still fresh of flocks of teal by the "Green Stores" on the Neck; but the teal and the "Stores" are gone, and perhaps the last black duck has quacked on the river, and the last whistler taken his final flight. Some of us, who are not yet old men, have killed "brown-backs" and "yellow-legs" on the marshes that lie along to the west and south of the city, now cut up by the railroads; and you may yet see from the cars an occasional long-booted individual whose hopes still live on the tales of the past, stalking through the sedge with "superfluous gun," or patiently watching his troop of one-legged wooden decoys.

—T. W. Higginson, *Our Birds, and Their Ways*, 1857

Not even genuine piety can make the robin-killer quite respectable. Saturday is the great slaughter day in the bay region. Then the city pot-hunters, with a ragtag of boys, go forth to kill, kept in countenance by a sprinkling of regular sportsmen arranged in self-conscious majesty and leggins, leading dogs and carrying hammerless, breech-loading guns of famous makers. Over the fine landscapes the killing goes forward with shameful enthusiasm. After escaping countless dangers, thousands fall, big bagfuls are gathered, many are left wounded to die slowly, no Red Cross Society to help them. Next day, Sunday, the blood and leggins vanish from the most devout of the bird butchers, who go to church, carrying gold-headed canes instead of guns. After hymns, prayers, and sermon they go home to feast, to put God's songbirds to use, put them in their dinners instead of in their hearts, eat them, and suck the pitiful little drumsticks. It is only race living on race, to be sure, but Christians singing Divine Love need not be driven to such straits while wheat and apples grow and the shops are full of dead cattle. Songbirds for food! Compared with this, making kindlings of pianos and violins would be pious economy.

—John Muir, *Among the Birds of the Yosemite*, 1898

"Who killed Cock Robin?"
"I," said the Sparrow,
"With my bow and arrow,
I killed Cock Robin."
All the birds of the air fell a-sighing and a-sobbing
When they heard of the death of poor Cock Robin.

—Anonymous, *Tom Thumb's Pretty Song Book*, circa 1744

The Passenger Pigeon is quite abundant in almost all parts of the Union,—roaming in wild and uncontrollable masses from one place to another, now appearing in one section of the country, and then quitting it for an absence of years. Its plumage, though plain, is beautifully varied on the neck and shoulders with glossy feathers, reflecting in different lights the resplendent colors of the rainbow.

—William L. Baily, *Our Own Birds*, 1869

Happening to go ashore, one charming afternoon, to purchase some milk at a house that stood near the river, and while talking with the people within doors, I was suddenly struck with astonishment at a loud rushing roar, succeeded by instant darkness, which, on the first moment, I took for a tornado, about to overwhelm the house and every thing in destruction. The people, observing my surprise, coolly said, "It is only the Pigeons;" and, on running out, I beheld a flock, thirty or forty yards in width, sweeping along very low, between the house and the mountain, or height, that formed the second bank of the river. These continued passing for more than a quarter of an hour, and at length varied their bearing so as to pass over the mountain behind which they disappeared before the rear came up.

—Alexander Wilson, *American Ornithology*, 1826

Jackson, Minnesota

Sunday, April 7 [1901], while walking through a small scrubby oak grove, I flushed seven large pigeons. It being Sunday I carried no gun, and consequently cannot prove the identity of the birds. They flushed rapidly and were soon out of sight. I am certain they were not Mourning Doves, and am satisfied that they were Passenger Pigeons. This is the first record I have here for many years.

—J. C. Knox, letter to the editor in *American Ornithology for the Home and School*, Volume 1, 1905

To my mind, many "professionals" shoot a score of birds where they ought to shoot but one. The long record of slaughtered birds is sickening . . . Even our most scientific journals print many of these bloody annals. It is true, a reasonable number of specimens must be collected for scientific purposes, but surely no adequate excuse can be given for shooting hundreds of individuals of the same species merely to have the honor of saying that an astounding number of specimens were "taken." If the cause of natural history cannot be promoted without destroying the humane instincts of the naturalist himself, the price is too great; it were better left unpaid. A bird in the bush is worth forty in the hand, especially if the forty are dead; worth more, too, I venture to add, to the cause of science itself.

—Leander S. Keyser, *In Bird Land*, 1897

The Wild Turkey, once so abundant in that part of the country lying between the Alleghenies and the Mississippi river, appears now to have become quite a scarce, shy, and in some places an obsolete bird. Like the poor Red Man who once roamed unrestrained through the same trackless woods, the march of civilization has encroached upon its freedom. And as the Indian has folded his blanket and gradually retired before the irresistible step of the avaricious white man, to the plains of the Far West, so this noblest game of the forest has taken its flight from haunts where once the murderous gun was seldom heard to echo, to nestle among the secluded wilds west of the

Mississippi. Straggling companies, however, still remain in the yet unsettled parts of Pennsylvania, New York, and several of the Western States, though only relics of what was formerly a numerous and powerful tribe.

—William L. Baily, *Our Own Birds*, 1869

Women will then be no longer able to wear hats, to adorn which the most beautiful of earth's creatures have been ruthlessly slaughtered, and, therefore, faith in them will begin once more to revive. Faith in woman, we know, is a very important thing.

—Edmund Selous, *Bird Watching*, 1901

We, the Song birds of Massachusetts and their Playfellows, make this our humble petition.

We know more about you than you think we do. We know how good you are. We have hopped about the roofs and looked in at the windows of the houses you have built for poor and sick and hungry people and little lame and deaf and blind children. We have built our nests in the trees and sung many a song as we flew about the gardens and parks you have made so beautiful for your own children, especially your poor children, to play in.

Every year we fly a great way over the country, keeping all the time where the sun is bright and warm; and we know that whenever you do anything, other people all over the great land between the seas and the great lakes find it out, and pretty soon will try to do the same thing. We know; we know. We are Americans just as you are. Some of us, like some of you, came from across the great sea, but most of the birds like us have lived here a long while; and birds like us welcomed your fathers when they came here many years ago. Our fathers and mothers have always done their best to please your fathers and mothers.

Now we have a sad story to tell you. Thoughtless or bad people are trying to destroy us. They will kill us because our feathers are beautiful. Even pretty and sweet girls, who we should think would be our best friends, kill our brothers and children so they may wear their plumage on their hats. Sometimes people kill us from mere wantonness. Cruel boys destroy our nests and steal our eggs and our young ones. People with guns and snares lie in wait to kill us, as if the place for a bird were not in the sky, alive, but in a shop window, or under a glass case. If this goes on much longer, all your song birds will be gone. Already, we are told, in some other countries that used to be full of birds, they are almost gone. Even the nightingales are being all killed in Italy.

Now we humbly pray that you will stop all this, and will save us from this sad fate. You have already made a law that no one shall kill a harmless song bird or destroy our nests or our eggs. Will you please to make another that no one shall wear our feathers, so that no one will kill us to get them? We want them all ourselves. Your pretty girls are pretty enough without them. We are told that it is as easy for you to do it as for Blackbird to whistle.

—Hon. George F. Hoar, manuscript, early 1900s

Boston, Massachusetts

As far as I can see, the continued agitation against the wearing of birds as ornaments, has had little effect here in Boston. Nearly half the hats seen on the street have on them various parts of what once were beautiful, happy birds. On some, heads; some, tails; some, wings; and on some the entire bird. Can you imagine anything more ridiculous than a young woman sporting an entire Herring Gull on her head? I have seen one such, and scores with smaller gulls and terns. It seems a pity that women would cling to this barbarous fashion until actually forced to put it aside to escape prosecution. Perhaps they do not realize what they do.

—"Effie," letter to the editor, in *American Ornithology for the Home and School*, Volume 2, 1905

Birds are but a part of the life on this our earth, and the hatred of destruction, once kindled by them will, like the ripples made by a stone flung into the water, extend outwards through the whole animal and vegetable kingdom till it include, at last, man himself.

—Edmund Selous, *Bird Watching*, 1901

Prairie Birds

THE PRAIRIE HEN.

Council Bluffs, Missouri Territory
May 8th, 1843

We have seen extensive Prairie (low & flat) that have been so innundated as to have at present deposits of mud to the depth of 6 inches to 20 through which no grass can force its way this year! — Glorious times this for the Geese Ducks and Gulls which are breeding all over these great plains now of mud and water puddles, instead of the lovely flowers that usually at this season adorn them.

—John James Audubon, journal

On Burrowing Owls and Their Harmonious Relations
with Prairie Dogs and Rattlesnakes

According to the dense bathos of such nursery tales, in this underground Elysium the snakes give their rattles to the puppies to

play with, the old dogs cuddle the owlets, and farm out their own lit-
ters to the grave and careful birds; when an owl and dog come home
paw-in-wing, they are often mistaken by their respective progeny,
the little dogs nosing the owls in search of the maternal font, and the
old dogs left to wonder why the baby owls will not nurse. It is a pity
to spoil a good story for the sake of a few facts.

—Elliott Coues, *Field Ornithology*, 1874

Birds of song but seldom enliven the gloomy monotony of the
forest. Few, if any, of these, are carnivorous, and it is not until
the labor of the farmer has covered the soil with fields of grain, that
the cheerful notes of the songster are heard. We have now a great
variety of singing birds, which have rapidly followed the population
from the other side of the mountains.

Of birds, that which is most peculiar to this country, as well as
most numerous, is the prairie fowl, or grouse. It is nearly as large as
the common hen. The flesh is delicate and finely flavored. The
female resembles the quail in shape and color, and the male, who
erects his plumage and struts like the turkey and peacock, is chiefly
distinguished by a tuft of feathers on the head, and a tail longer and
more ornamented than that of his mate. Their only note is a low,
strong, melancholy sound, resembling the cooing of the dove, which
may be heard at a considerable distance and the traveler in passing
over the prairie at sunrise, hears this singular noise in every direction, and if unacquainted with its source, is at a loss whether to
attribute it to a numerous colony of doves, of owls, or of tremendous
bull frogs, for it partakes of the tone of each of these animals.

—James Hall, *The West*, 1848

Thursday, June 7th 1849

In the afternoon Capt S Liet W & I took a ride over the
prairie   it was a magnificent sight to me not having seen anything
before   i saw nothing new to me in the Bird line   here I find numbers of the Hirundo fulva [cliff swallow] very abundant and the

praries are roling containing many handsome plants partages
abound also the black throated Bunting & Meadow Lark I rode on
an Indian pony Capt & Liet in a buggy the pony when I would
touch him with the spr would return it with a Kick as though a fly
had bit him We returned at 10 p.m.

Tuesday November 6th, 1849

Cloudy until nine a.m. it then commenced clearing and we had
a fine day. rose at day light but the teams did not get started until
7 a.m. just as they started it commenced raining but did not last
long and one hour after we left. after going about 3 miles we left the
Military road & took the Whiskey road as they said it was the best
and avoided the mountains we rode several miles before we over
took the wagons two of which broke which detained us about an
hour. when we took our lunch. we saw great numbers of wild
pigeons all day in some places the trees were almost breaking down
with them. Grouse also in great flocks in one of which I counted 72
and some flocks there were greater numbers . . . we continued our
march until 4 ½ p.m. when we came to a halt on the edge of the
Prarie which place we concluded bivouacs . . . The trees in this
timber was filled with Grouse.

Friday August 23rd, 1850

Indian sign plenty going west but few buffalo 3 were killed
today. two of them however too far from camp to bring in the
meat. The other was killed late this evening and will be sent after
in the morning. wolves continue numerous. . . . Plovers (Tringa
Bartramii) are very numerous they are in immense flocks.

—S. W. Woodhouse, journals

Wild geese frequent the Prairies in a wet season; they much
resemble some I saw at the Earl of Egremont's, at Petworth, in
Sussex. Wild ducks also, in a wet season, larger than English wild-
ducks. There are woodcocks and snipes on the creeks.

Blackbirds,—often seen in large flocks, much like starlings. Mocking-birds;—all I know of them is, they mock the notes of others. Red-bird,—a most beautiful scarlet bird, the size of a black-bird. Yellow-bird,—a handsome yellow bird with dark wings. Humming-birds are scarce; I mentioned one on our journey. Wipper-will, or whip-poor-will, or wippervill,—a brown bird that is named from the cry it makes, of "whip-poor-will;" it is generally heard of an evening in spring and summer.

Paroquets are the same as are seen in cages in England,—a mischievous bird. Blue-jays are a very noisy busy bird. The larks are much larger than those of England; but the most common birds are wood-peckers, of many sorts.

The Americans frequently fix boxes on poles, or on the cabin, in which the black-martins build. I have seen them begin their nests in a few minutes after the boxes were fixt up.

> —John Woods, *Two Years' Residence in the Settlement on the English Prairie in the Illinois Country, United States,* 1822

Prairie Marsh Wren. *Telmatodytes palustris iliacus.*

This is the Mississippi Valley form of the common long-billed marsh wren. It is a dweller in wet marshes along the borders of rivers and lakes, where its globular nests are fastened to the upright stalks of cattail flags over the water. In migration it is sometimes found in strange situations, as in the case of one which I caught in the railroad station at Blytheville about 11 p.m., May 5, or of another which I saw in a dry broom sedge field at McGehee, May 17. . . . The species breeds locally in the State, having been observed in summer on the St. Francis River at Lake City and Bertig.

> —Arthur H. Howell, *Birds of Arkansas,* 1911

Upland Birds

Blue or Dusky Grouse

I have seen young broods running beneath the firs in June at a height of eight thousand feet above the sea. On the approach of danger, the mother with a peculiar cry warns the helpless midgets to scatter and hide beneath leaves and twigs, and even in plain open places it is almost impossible to discover them. In the meantime the mother feigns lameness, throws herself at your feet, kicks and gasps and flutters, to draw your attention from the chicks. The young are generally able to fly about the middle of July; but even after they can fly well they are usually advised to run and hide and lie still, no matter how closely approached, while the mother goes on with her loving, lying acting, apparently as desperately concerned for their safety as when they were featherless infants. Sometimes, however, after carefully studying the circumstances, she tells them to take wing; and up and away in a blurry birr and whirr they scatter to all points of the compass, as if blown up with gunpowder, dropping cunningly out of sight three or four hundred yards off, and keeping quiet until called, after the danger is supposed to be past. If you walk on a little way without manifesting any inclination to hunt them, you may sit down at the foot of a tree near enough to see and hear the happy reunion. One touch of nature makes the whole world kin; and it is truly wonderful how love-telling the small voices of these birds are, and how far they reach through the woods into one another's hearts and into ours. The tones are so perfectly human and so full of anxious affection, few mountaineers can fail to be touched by them.

—John Muir, *Among the Birds of the Yosemite*, 1898

Ruffed Grouse or Partridge

One of his favorite covers is in a quiet spot where I go to gather ferns—a grove that "fronts the rising sun" and is full of dappled maple saplings interspersed with the white birches that gleam in the morning light and keep birchbark scrolls rolled up along their sides ready for the birds to carry away for their nests. At the foot of the trees, and close to the moss-covered drumming-log, ferns stand in pretty groups in all growths from the tiny green sprays and the soft uncurling downy balls to the full grown arching fronds whose backs are dotted with brown fruit; while, as a protecting hedge along the front of the grove, great masses of the tender green mountain fern give their delicate fragrance to the air. But pass by this hiding place, and a sudden whirr through the bushes, first from one startled bird and then another, tells you they have flown before you. Approach the drumming-log when the air has been resounding with exultant blows—the noise stops, not a bird is to be seen.

—Florence Merriam, *Birds Through an Opera Glass*, 1889

In some parts of California the mountain quail is much wilder than in others. But throughout the great mountains of the south they are generally the most guileless little things imaginable. The valley quail, even where never disturbed, is often very wild; but the mountain quail, even when wild, has a wildness of an entirely different kind. He seems to elude you in a manner quite accidental. In his actions there is no trace of stupidity. All is innocent faith and trusting curiosity. . . .

For the tourist who goes to the mountains to enjoy deep shades, cold brooks, and quiet retreat from the dust and bustle of the lowland towns, this quail has a charm scarcely second to that of the trout or the deer. When, in the heat of the day, one comes to some little portrero where pine-clad hills inclose a soft green meadow, where a clear, cold stream gurgles through grassy banks, and ferns wave darkly green even in the noon of summer, then this bird makes a strange, sweet feeling in the wanderer's heart, whether his mellow call ring from the bristling heights above or the delicate ch-ch-ch-ch-cheeah, cheeah come from the ferns beside one as he steals softly away. As a companion in the impressive solitude that broods over these high places, so far from the haunts of men, no other bird can take his place. His friendly coyness, the soft sparkle in the little black eye that so plainly says he would like to be your friend if only it were safe; his lingering look, as if he would like to meet you, but is too well-bred to force his acquaintance upon you; the tenderness of his notes, and the artlessness of his motions, all seeming to deprecate the necessity of keeping at a judicious distance—all these will quickly disarm your intentions, and you will love him too much in life to care to see him in death.

—Theodore S. Van Dyke, *Southern California: Its Valleys, Hills, and Streams; Its Animals, Birds, and Fishes; Its Gardens, Farms and Climate*, 1886

Mountain Quail or Plumed Partridge

I think he is the very handsomest of all the American partridges, larger and handsomer than the famous Bob White, or even the fine California valley quail or the Massena partridge of Arizona and Mexico. That he is not so regarded, is because as a lonely mountaineer he is not half known.

His plumage is delicately shaded, brown above, white and rich chestnut below and on the sides, with many dainty markings of black and white and gray here and there, while his beautiful head plume, three or four inches long, nearly straight, composed of two feathers closely folded so as to appear as one, is worn jauntily slanted backward like a single feather in a boy's cap, giving him a very marked appearance . . .

Once when I was seated at the foot of a tree on the head-waters of the Merced, sketching, I heard a flock up the valley behind me, and by their voices gradually sounding nearer I knew that they were feeding toward me. I kept still, hoping to see them. Soon one came within three or four feet of me, without noticing me any more than if I were a stump or a bulging part of the trunk against which I was leaning, my clothing being brown, nearly like the bark. Presently along came another and another, and it was delightful to get so near a view of these handsome chickens perfectly undisturbed, observe their manners, and hear their low peaceful notes. At last one of them caught my eye, gazed in silent wonder for a moment, then uttered a peculiar cry, which was followed by a lot of hurried muttered notes that sounded like speech. The others, of course, saw me as soon as the alarm was sounded, and joined the wonder talk, gazing and chattering, astonished but not frightened. Then all with one accord ran back with the news to the rest of the flock. "What is it? what is it? Oh you never saw the like," they seemed to be saying. "Not a deer, or a wolf, or a bear; come see, come see." "Where? where?" "Down there by that tree." Then they approached cautiously, past the tree, stretching their necks, and looking up in turn as if knowing from the story told them just where I was. For fifteen or twenty minutes they kept coming and going, venturing within a few feet of me, and discussing the wonder in charming chatter. Their curiosity at last satisfied, they began to scatter and feed again, going back in the direction they had come from; while I, loath to part with them, followed noiselessly, crawling beneath the bushes, keeping them in sight for an hour or two, learning their habits, and finding out what seeds and berries they liked best.

—John Muir, *Among the Birds of the Yosemite*, 1898

In that blue shadow at the bottom of that winding furrow are the dainty footprints of a grouse, and you wonder why he, so strong of wing, should choose to wade laboriously the clogging snow even in his briefest trip, rather than make his easy way through the unresisting air, and the snow-written record of his wayward wanderings tells not why. Suddenly, as if a mine had been strung where your next footstep should fall and with almost as startling, though harmless effect, another of his wild tribe bursts upward through the unmarked white floor and goes shirring and clattering away, scattering in powdery ruin the maze of delicate tracery the snowfall wrought; and vanishes, leaving only an aerial pathway of naked twigs to mark his impetuous passage.

—Rowland E. Robinson, *In New England Fields and Woods*, 1896

That handsome bird the red-legged partridge is supposed to have been introduced into this country by that royal bird-fancier Charles II. This tradition can be received for what it is worth.

—Jordan Denham, *From Spring to Fall*, 1894

The popular name "Fool Hen" is applied to the Franklin's Grouse and various other species of northern Grouse, and to other species of gallinaceous game birds, who fail to act promptly on the well-known fact that the average man will murder them on sight.

—Edward Howe Forbush, *Birds of America*, 1917

No pheasant, partridge, or quail, is strictly speaking found in North America. The partridge, so called in the States, is the quail of the Canadas: but although on account of its size and general appearance it might easily be mistaken for the latter bird, it is in fact a species of the new genus, "ortyx." The difference between the real quail and the ortyx of America, like that between the long and short-winged hawks, consists in the structure of the wing: in the one, the second feather is longest; in the other, the fourth, which evidently unfits it for taking a long flight. . . . The pheasant of the States is the partridge of the Canadas, and is in fact a very handsome species of grouse, feathered down to the toes, and having in a great measure the habits of the capercaily, living entirely in the woods, and treeing readily when put up by a small dog. I have before noticed the grouse, or barren, or prairie hen. In the Canadas there is also a darker coloured species, called, the spruce partridge. A large grouse, nearly allied to the capercaily in size and colour, is found near the Rocky Mountains; and although five or six different kinds of grouse are to be found in North America—including, I believe, the ptarmigan—yet the black and red game of Scotland are not among them. A smaller species of red grouse is plentiful in Newfoundland.

—Godfrey T. Vigne, *Six Months in America*, 1832

A bevy of quails is the term corresponding with a covey of partridges.

—Jordan Denham, *From Spring to Fall*, 1894

Capercaillie

Although originally an inhabitant of Great Britain, this species became extinct over a hundred years ago from causes which are by no means clear. In 1837 it was introduced into Perthshire and a few other districts in Scotland, where it has increased largely, and is at the present time gradually spreading southwards through the pine, oak, and birch forests.

It is essentially a forest-haunting species, rarely, if ever, wandering far from the woods, where its call of "peller, peller, peller," may be continually heard during the spring months, and sometimes again in autumn.

Like most game birds, it is polygamous, and an old cock is very jealous of his hens, savagely attacking other males that come near him. When courting he performs various evolutions, drooping his wings and erecting his tail, and calling out vigorously at the same time. Their food consists chiefly of various seeds and berries, and in their season the tender shoots of the Scotch fir.

—J. Lewis Bonhote, *Birds of Britain and Their Eggs*, 1907

On Quail in New Jersey

These birds are numerous . . . On going but a little way you meet with great coveys of them. However, they keep at a great distance from town, being either extirpated or frightened there by frequent shooting. They are always in lesser or greater coveys, do not fly very much, but run in the fields and keep under the bushes and near the enclosures where they seek their food. When they sleep at night they come together in a heap. They scratch in the bushes and upon the fields like common chickens. In spring they make their nests, either under a bush or in the maize fields, or on the hills in the open air; they scratch some hay together, into which they lay about thirteen white eggs.

—Peter Kalm, *Travels in North America*, 1757

There are pheasants in some parts of this country, but they are seldom seen.

—James Hall, *The West*, 1848

One of the most prominent and most frequent of the sounds which strike a stranger here, and one which cannot fail to awaken the curiosity and excite the inquiries of even the most unobservant, is the call of the Quail (*Ortyx Virginian*). All day long, from morning till night, we hear the words "Bob White," whistled with invincible pertinacity in every direction. The sound is exactly what may be produced by a person attempting to whistle these words, making the second syllable seven or eight notes higher than the first. It is loud and clear, and may be heard a long way off. The position of the bird, when uttering his call, may be the top of an out-house, or a pile of logs; but his favorite place is the topmost rail of the fence; for it is to the plantations he chiefly resorts, being rarely seen in the forest.

—Philip Henry Gosse, *Letters from Alabama Chiefly Relating to Natural History*, 1859

As you saunter on your devious way you may hear a rustle of quick feet in the dry leaves and a sharp, insistent cry, a succession of short, high-pitched clucks running into and again out of querelous "ker-r-r-r," all expressing warning as much as alarm. Your ears guide your eyes to the exact point from which the sounds apparently come, but if these are not keen and well trained they fail to detach any animate form from the inanimate dun and gray of dead leaves and underbrush.

With startling suddenness out of the monotony of lifeless color in an eddying flurry of dead leaves, fanned to erratic flight by his wing-beats, the ruffed grouse bursts into view, in full flight with the first strokes of his thundering pinions, and you have a brief vision of untamed nature as it was in the old days.

—Rowland E. Robinson, *In New England Fields and Woods*, 1896

On Pheasants

The colour schemes of the male birds of this order are as varied as they are daring and fantastic. Hardly could one devise more startling contrast with the sombre austerity of the aforesaid Mikado than is presented in the lavish splendour of the golden pheasant, which, by the by, is only a pheasant by courtesy, modern ornithologists having placed him in a separate genus under the name of Thaumalea picta— the Painted Wonder-bird. But that does not concern us here; if he is not a true pheasant, he is next door to it, although no amount of compulsory education will train him to be a decent rocketer. It used to be thought that golden pheasant required the protection of an aviary in our climate; but in fact, they may be naturalized in British woodland as easily as the common ring-necked and Colchic species. Most delightful objects they are in a landscape, especially about the garden, the cock bird having but one fault—inveterate self-consciousness. He seems to be as painfully aware of being over-dressed as one might feel if overtaken by daylight in walking back from a fancy-dress ball. His one impulse seems to be to run away and get hidden out of sight. Except in spring. Then you may study him to your heart's content, as I did one evening lately, strutting about on a sunlit lawn, surrounded by his dusky harem in mute admiration of his glittering raiment.

—Sir Herbert Maxwell, *Memories of the Months*, 1919

From John Clare's Bird List of 1825–26

Bittern—
the bittern called here the butter bump from the odd loud noise resembling that word haunts Whittlesea Mere lays in the reed shaws—
about the size of the heron flyes up right into the sky morning &
evening & hides all day

Little Bittern—

Little brown Bittern—

Glossy Ibis—

Curlew—
very common here in winter coming down with the floods they
haunt Marshe & boggy heathes in summer & makes their nests
like the pewit on the bare ground among rushes &c laying from 3 to
5 eggs of a dirty white color

Whimbrel—
not known by this name here

Woodcock—
I have seen odd ones here till the beginning of may & I often
thought that such never went away but bred here

Snipe—
Snipes are often seen with us in summer & their nests have been
found but I cannot say further
I saw one yesterday (12th of may) it sat so close that I likend to set
my foot on it i examined the place & I fancied it was preparing a nest
in the midst of a large tuft of fog or dead grass common on the
heaths

Judcock or Jack Snipe—
not known here

Water Birds

The Canvass-Back Duck arrives in the United States from the north about the middle of October; a few descend to the Hudson and Delaware, but the great body of these birds resort to the numerous rivers belonging to and in the neighborhood of the Chesapeake Bay, particularly the Susquehannah, the Patapsco, Potomac, and James Rivers, which appear to be their general winter rendezvous. Beyond this, to the south, I can find no certain accounts of them. At the Susquehannah, they are called Canvass-Backs; on the Potomac, White-Backs; and on James River, Sheldrakes. They are seldom found at a great distance up any of these rivers, or even in the salt-water bay; but in that particular part of tide water where a certain grass-like plant grows, on the roots of which they feed. This plant, which is said to be a species of *valisineria,* grows on fresh-water shoals of from seven to nine feet, (but never where these are occasionally dry,) in long, narrow, grass-like blades, of four or five feet in length; the root is white and has some resemblances to celery. The grass is in many places so thick that a boat can with difficulty be rowed through it, it so impeded the oars. The shores are lined with large quantities of it, torn up by the Ducks, and drifted up by the winds, lying, like hay, in windrows. Wherever this plant grows in abundance, the Canvass-Backs may be expected either to pay occasional visits, or to make it their regular residence during the winter. It occurs in some parts of the Hudson; in the Delaware, near Gloucester, a few miles south of Philadelphia; and in most of the rivers that fall into the Chesapeake, to each of which particular places these Ducks resort; while, in waters unprovided with this nutritive plant, they are altogether unknown.

On the first arrival of these birds in the Susquehannah, near Havre-de-Grace, they are generally lean; but such is the abundance of their favorite food that, towards the beginning of November, they are in pretty good order. They are excellent divers, and swim with great speed and agility. They sometimes assemble in such multitudes as to cover several acres of the river, and, when they rise suddenly, produce a noise resembling thunder. They float about these shoals, diving, and tearing up the grass by the roots, which is the only part they eat. They are extremely shy, and can rarely be approached, unless by stratagem. . . .

In the severe winter of 1779–80, the grass, on the roots of which these birds feed, was almost wholly destroyed in James River. In the month of January, the wind continued to blow from W.N.W. for twenty-one days, which caused such low tides in the river, that the grass froze to the ice everywhere; and, a thaw coming on suddenly, the whole was raised by the roots, and carried off by the fresh. The next winter, a few of these Ducks were seen, but they soon went away again; and, for many years after, they continued to be scarce; and, even to the present day, in the opinion of my informant, have never been so plenty as before.

—Alexander Wilson, *American Ornithology*, 1826

The duck was all jewels combined, showing different lustres as it turned on the unrippled element in various lights, now brilliant glossy green, now dusky violet, now a rich bronze, now the reflections that sleep in the ruby's grain.

—Henry David Thoreau, journal

Among the water-fowl, the wood-duck, and blue-winged teal of the Mississippi Valley, and the black duck of the Atlantic coast are absent; but their places are supplied by birds extremely rare, if not entirely unknown, on the Atlantic shores. There is a blue-winged teal here, but different from the Western blue-wing. In place of the latter is the cinnamon teal, very common in all the little inland ponds and streams. His whole body, from the blue tail feathers to the bill, is robed in rich, glossy cinnamon, beamy as the bronze of a wild turkey. The wings are a gamy gray with sky-blue bands upon the top which flash brightly in the sun as the bird springs from the water. The black brant (Bernicula nigricans, and not the common brant, sometimes called "black brant" by way of distinction from "white brant") is found only in the Bay of San Diego, and False Bay, three miles above, skipping all the wild-fowl resorts and bays from there to Tomales Bay, above San Francisco. It is almost black in front, with a white collar around the jet-black neck, and almost pure white behind. It is very rapid in flight, being almost equal to a mallard duck in activity, and is the gamiest by far of all American water-fowl. It never goes inland, and does not even fly over a narrow point of land if it can be easily avoided.

—Theodore S. Van Dyke, *Southern California: Its Valleys, Hills, and Streams; Its Animals, Birds, and Fishes; Its Gardens, Farms, and Climate*, 1886

Bearded Reedling

Extremely scarce and local in our islands, being confined to not more than half-a-dozen localities, this charming little bird, more than any others perhaps of our rarer species, is worth a journey to see. Inhabiting large and extensive reed-beds, it used formerly to be abundant in the fens of Huntingdon, Cambridge, and other eastern counties, but with the reclaiming and draining of the land it has slowly died out, only holding its own in those few places where nature still reigns supreme. Its exact systematic position is doubtful, as it shows no close affinity with any other known species; one point, however, is absolutely certain, namely that its popular name of "Tit" is quite a misnomer, as it has no connection in appearance or habits with those delightful birds. The naturalist, therefore, who goes to visit him at home must not search for him on trees or look for his nest in holes. As the boat glides quietly past some reed-bed his first acquaintance of this bird will be the clear and unmistakable "ping-ping," a note answered almost immediately by another close by. Soon, if he remains quiet, he will see a small light-brown bird with long tail rise from the reeds and, progressing with undulating flight, settle again a short distance on. Although very tame and un-suspicious, the bearded Reedling is very hard to watch, owing to the thickness of the reeds in which he lives, but if we wait about patiently we can see a good deal of him as he searches the mud at the base of the reeds for minute molluscs, of which he is extremely fond. These he swallows whole, and having exhausted the treasures of one spot he will run up two reeds, resting one foot on each alternately, with surprising rapidity and then fly off with a merry "ping-ping" to renew his search in some other spot, and possibly, if the place be more open, we may see him scratch up the soft ooze with a peculiar backward motion of both feet and then eagerly scan the spot to see if his labours have met their reward. Early in April he pairs, and a nest of leaves and rushes, deeply cup-shaped and lined with the feathery tops of the reeds, is built. Materials are collected by both sexes, but especially by the cock, while the building itself is entirely carried on by the hen. A clutch of six eggs is laid; they are very round in shape and dead white, freckled with minute black markings. Two broods are reared in the season, the young being fed chiefly on insects. It is essentially a resident species and spends the whole year wandering over the reed-beds in family parties, feeding on insects, molluscs, or seeds, the party keeping together by a continual use of the call-note. At nightfall they all gather close together on some broken reed, where they sleep securely till dawn awakens them to another day of restless work and energy.

—J. Lewis Bonhote, *Birds of Britain and Their Eggs*, 1907

The heron and its allies are all aquatic birds, living on the banks of rivers, lakes, and in the marshy tracts that have a certain amount of free water in them; but this broad statement must not be taken as equally applicable to all the race. Some of these birds find health and happiness in localities that are more damp than wet, and find abundance of food where others would starve. None of them are beautiful on close inspection, but most are graceful in their movements when walking, and many exceedingly so when on the wing. It is eminently true of them that "distance lends enchantment to the view," and the less said about the merits of their singing the better. But if they do not sing, they can make themselves heard, and the united voices of a hundred night-herons, migrating after the gloaming, and high overhead, is, to say the least, not an inspiriting sound to the lonely wayfarer who has gone astray in the wilderness.

—Charles C. Abbott, *A Naturalist's Rambles About Home*, 1885

Swans
Monday Dec. 3rd, 1804

The land on either hand continues to improve in quality; there appears to be in general a superficial stratum of good earth of a dark brown color, upon which vegetation is sufficiently luxuriant; hills frequently arose out of the level country, full of rocks & stones, generally of an extremely hard flinty kind ... of this kind was a promontory which came in from the right hand, a little before we arrived at the Chutes: this promontory presented some appearance at a distance, of the ancient ruined fortifications & Castles so frequent in Europe, the effect was greatly heightened by a flock of swans which had taken their stations under the Walls which rose out of the Water; as we approached the Birds floated about magestically upon the glassy surface, and in tremulous melancholy accents seemed to consult each other on measures of safety, the ensemble produced a truly sublime picture.

—William Dunbar, journal

As we paced along the lochside, the still air was filled suddenly with strange clamour, and, looking up, we beheld a flight of great birds. Swans—wild swans—would they alight on our lake? Or would they tantalise us by continuing their flight to the bay, distant but a mile, or to one of the many other lochs and tarns of the neighbourhood? Scarcely, methought, would they venture down, for we had no time to attempt concealment; yet, as luck would have it, these fair creatures heeded not the presence of three human beings and a black terrier. They swung round in wide circles, trumpeting loudly, and lit upon the glass-calm surface of the loch about three hundred yards from where we stood. They were whoopers, nineteen of them, all, except three dusky cygnets, in spotless white. Of course I had left my field-glasses behind; whenever I do so something of special interest is sure to present itself.

—Sir Herbert Maxwell, *Memories of the Months*, 1919

Snowy Egret

Like the other white herons, this exquisite little egret, although once abundant, has been practically exterminated by persistent hunting for its plumes. It formerly nested in the Mississippi Valley State as far north as southern Illinois, but in recent years has been driven out from all but the more inaccessible parts of Louisiana. In 1886 it was reported as arriving at Osceola April 3, and in 1889 a few were seen at Clinton July 4. In June and July, 1902, Oberholser saw a few along Red River north of Texarkana.

—Arthur H. Howell, *Birds of Arkansas*, 1911

The beautiful legs and feet of the heron, when in the water, resemble the stems of aquatic plants, and the faintest ripple or flow heightens the illusion.

—Jordan Denham, *From Spring to Fall*, 1894

Whooping-Cranes

Great numbers of them are seen early in the Spring, about the Mouths of Rivers, near St. Augustine in Florida, and . . . they retire to the Mountains in Summer. Our late Discovery of this Bird in Hudson's Bay during the Summer, is, I think, a sufficient Proof that these are Birds of Pasage, and change their Situation just as the Stork doth in Europe; going Northward to breed in the Summer, and returning to the South at the Approach of Winter.

—George Edwards, *A Natural History of Birds*, 1750

Whooping Crane

This is the tallest and most stately species of all the feathered tribes of the United States, the watchful inhabitant of extensive salt marshes, desolate swamps, and open morasses in the neighborhood of the sea. Its migrations are regular, and of the most extensive kind, reaching from the shores and inundated tracts of South America to the arctic circle. In these immense periodical journeys, they pass at such a prodigious height in the air as to be seldom observed. They have, however, their resting-stages on the route to and from their usual breeding places, the regions of the north. A few sometimes make their appearances in the marshes of Cape May, in December, particularly on and near Egg Island, where they are known by the name of Storks. The younger birds are easily distinguished from the rest by the brownness of their plumage. Some linger in these marshes the whole winter, setting out north about the time the ice breaks up. During their stay, they wander along the marsh and muddy flats of the sea-shore in search of marine worms, sailing occasionally from place to place, with a low and heavy flight, a little above the surface; and have at such times a very formidable appearance. At times, they utter a loud, clear, and piercing cry, which may be heard at the distance of two miles. They have also various modulations of this singular note, from the peculiarity of which they derive their name. When wounded, they attack the gunner, or his dog, with great resolution; and have been known to drive their sharp and formidable bill, at one stroke through a man's hand.

—Alexander Wilson, *American Ornithology*, 1826

Saw a crane of the largest size flying over the lake, a mile or two to the northward of our boat. A pair of them have been about the lake all summer; they are said to be the large brown crane. We found one of their young this afternoon lying dead upon the bank of a brook, to which we gave the name of Crane Brook on this occasion. It was a good-sized bird, and seemed to have been killed in a fight with some winged enemy, for it had not been shot. As for the boldness of calling the brook after it, the pretty little stream had no name before; why not give it one now?

—Susan Fenimore Cooper, *Rural Hours*, 1850

We observed a kind of muscle in the sand; the shell of an oval form, having horns or protuberences near half an inch in length and as thick as a crow-quill, which I suppose serve the purpose of grapnels to hold their ground against the violence of the current. Here were great numbers of wild fowl, wading in the shore water that covers the sandy points, to a vast distance from the shores; they were geese, brant, gannet, and the great and beautiful whooping crane. Embarked again, doubled the point of the island and arrived at Point Coupe in the evening

—William Bartram, *Travels*, 1791

On Whooping Cranes

The social customs of these birds are most entertaining to the observer who may lie hidden in the grass and watch them through a glass. Their tall, angular figures, made up of so much wing, leg, neck, and bill, counterpoised by so little body, incline the spectator to look upon them as ornithological caricatures. After balancing himself upon one foot for an hour, with the other drawn up close to his scanty robe of feathers, and his head poised in a most contemplative attitude, one of these queer birds will suddenly turn a somersault, and, returning to his previous posture, continue his cogitations as though nothing had interrupted his reflections. With wings spread, they slowly winnow the air, rising or hopping from the ground a few feet at a time, then whirling in circles upon their toes, as though going through the mazes of a dance. Their most popular diversion seems to be the game of leap-frog, and their long legs being specially adapted to this sport, they achieve a wonderful success. One of the birds quietly assumes a squatting position upon the ground, when his sportive companions hop in turn over his expectant head. They then pirouette, turn somersaults, and go through various exercises with the skill of gymnasts. Their sportive proclivities seem to have no bounds; and being true humorists, they preserve through their gambols a ridiculously sedate appearance. Popular accounts of the nidification of these birds are frequently untrue. We are told that they build their cone-shaped nests of mud, sticks, and grass in shallow water, in colonies, and that their nests, *being placed on rafts* of buoyant material, float about in the bayous, and are propelled and guided at the will of the sitting bird by the use of her long legs and feet as oars. The position of the bird upon the nest is also ludicrously depicted. It is described as sitting astride the nest, with the toes touching the ground; and to add still more comicality to the picture, it is asserted that the limbs are often thrust out horizontally behind the bird. The results of close observations prove that these accounts are in keeping with many others related by parlor naturalists. The cranes sit upon their nests like other birds, with their feet drawn up close to the body. The mound-shaped nests are built of sticks, grass, and mud, and usually placed in a shallow pond or partially submerged swamp, while at times a grassy hassock furnishes the foundation of the structure. In the saucer-shaped top of the nest two eggs are deposited, upon which the bird sits most assiduously, having no time at this season for aquatic amusements, such as paddling about with her nest.

—Nathaniel H. Bishop, *Four Months in a Sneak-Box*, 1879

Paul Smiths August 7th/71

Father, Uncle Hill and we three boys went off on an excursion (with our lunch). Of course we went in boats. We passed through the lower St. Regis (on which Paul Smiths is located), through Spitfire into upper St. Regis. Here we got off the boats upset them (first taking out the lunch) and swam around them. We finally got the boats right-side up again and rowed to an island where we had some revolver practice. While in the boats some wild ducks (Anas boschas?) started out just before the bows of our boats. After this we went to a spring of cold water where we took our lunch. We boys and our guide then rowed home, stopping on the way to pick some blueberries. In passing through Spitfire lake we saw several loons (Colymbus torquatus). In the afternoon we flyfished for trout and caught—two minnows.

—Theodore Roosevelt, aged 13

The grebes and divers are moderately well known. Few country boys who have lived near a creek or a millpond but have seen the little brown "devil-divers," as they are so frequently called, although why it is not quite readily explained. What of deviltry there is about them no one has yet made plain.

The grebes proper are found in most parts of the globe, and being migratory the same species is often found at vast distances from its proper home, if its nesting-place is to be so considered They are divers, and in this word we describe the prominent feature of their lives. On land they are hopeless, awkward, and ill at ease; upon the water nothing can exceed their gracefulness of motion.

—Charles C. Abbott, *Young Folks' Cyclopedia of Natural History*, 1895

Horned Grebe

If one can get close enough to this Grebe to observe its strange head, identification will be easy, for there is no other bird at all like it.

—Wilbur Webster Judd, *The Birds of Albany County*, 1907

Common Grebe. Dipper Duck.

Above, dark brownish, the feathers with paler edges; beneath, silky-white. Length 13 inches.

Not uncommon in Adam's and Hadley ponds and the Connecticut River. Very possibly breeds.

Loon. Great Northern Diver.

Above, black marked with white on the back; beneath, white. Length, 32–35 inches. A irregular and rare visitant during the migrations.

Dovekie.

Above, blue-black; beneath, pure white. Length, 8–9 inches.
Belchertown ponds, winter of 1872; many were blown inland by a severe storm. Entirely accidental.

—Hubert Lyman Clark, *The Birds of Amherst and Vicinity*, 1906

Hukweem the loon must go through the world crying for what he never gets, and searching for one whom he never finds, for he is the hunting-dog of Clote Scarpe. So said Simmo to me one night in explaining why the loon's cry is so wild and sad.

—William J. Long, *Wilderness Ways*, 1903

Pelicans are large flat-footed Water-Fowls, almost as big as Geese, and their Feathers in Colour like them: they have short Legs, long Necks, and their Bills are about two Inches broad, and seventeen or eighteen Inches long: The Fore-Part of their Neck or Breast is bare of Feathers, but covered with a soft, smooth, yet loose Skin, like that about the Necks of Turkies. This Skin is of the Colour of their Feathers, mixed with a dark and light Grey, so exactly interwoven that it appears very beautiful. They are very heavy Birds, and seldom fly far, or very high from the Water: They commonly sit on Rocks at some Distance from the Shore, where they may look about them: They seem to be very melancholy Fowls, by their perching all alone: They sit as if they were sleeping, holding their Heads upright, and resting the Ends of their Bills on their Breasts.

—George Edwards, *A Natural History of Birds*, 1750

We come now to consider the well-known pelicans, which have, wherever found, attracted a great deal of attention. Primarily, it may be said, that they are utterly devoid of beauty, have an ungraceful, wrinkled bag the whole length of their under jaw or bill, and grunt as unattractively as many birds sing sweetly. There are about ten species, of which two are found, in summer, in high latitudes; the others in the tropics and warm temperate regions. In North America there are two, the white and brown. In Indian times the native white pelican was not uncommon to the rivers and coast of the Middle states, now it is unknown there, except as the rarest of rare stragglers. In the Mississippi Valley they are not uncommon.

—Charles C. Abbott, *Young Folks' Cyclopedia of Natural History*, 1895

On the Teal

A winged rolling pin

—Henry David Thoreau, journal

Tuesday, March 7

Milder; thawing. Walking near the river saw three large waterfowl moving northward; we believed them to be loons; they were in sight only for a moment, owing to the trees above us, but we heard a loud howling cry as they flew past, like that of those birds. It is early for loons, however, and we may have been deceived. They usually appear about the first of April, remaining with us through the summer and autumn until late in December, when they go to the seashore; many winter about Long Island, many more in the Chesapeake. Not long since we saw one of these birds of unusual size, weighing nineteen pounds; it had been caught in Seneca Lake on the hook of what fishermen call a set-line, dropped the depth of ninety-five feet, the bird having dived that distance to reach the bait. . . . It may be doubted if any other feathered thing goes so far beneath the water.

—Susan Fenimore Cooper, *Rural Hours*, 1850

The loon is a very remarkable bird, from the formation of its feet: but having no anatomical knowledge, I cannot describe it technically. They are so made, that it can scarcely walk; it is therefore seldom seen on land. In calm weather it rises from the water with great difficulty, and flies as impelled by the wind, on which it seems to depend . . . In Chippeway language it is called a maunk, which agrees with the French word manquer, to fail; it being, from its shyness, very difficult to kill.

—John Long, *J. Long's Voyages and Travels*, 1791

Chenomorphae

By this harsh term the birds known as screamers, geese, ducks, and flamingoes are referred to.

There are nine American species of geese and about twice as many more in the whole world. In the habits of those that visit temperate regions in winter and nest in the arctic region, there is no marked difference. Very largely what is true of one is true of all of them.

—Charles C. Abbott, *Young Folks' Cyclopedia of Natural History*, 1895

One day I startled a moorhen in a shallow pond; instantly the bird dived, and I watched to see where it would come up, knowing that the moorhen cannot stay long under water. . . . After waiting some time, and wondering what had become of the bird, I fancied I saw some duckweed slightly agitated. Looking more carefully, it seemed as if there was something very small moving now and then just there—the spot was not more than fifteen yards distant. It was as if the beak of a bird, the body and most of the head quite hidden and under water, were picking or feeding among the duckweed. This continued for some few minutes. . . . As the pond was very shallow the bird must have stood on the bottom, and so resumed its feeding with the beak just above the surface.

—Richard Jeffries, *Wild Life in a Southern County*, 1881

These ibises are said to be all dull, stupid birds, quite harmless, and not timid. They live in flocks, but pair for life.

—Susan Fenimore Cooper, *Rural Hours*, 1850

I have records of some thirty . . . different kinds of ducks of this region, but it is possible to speak of only a few and that but briefly. Of these there are three species that go by the name of "coots," and their pursuit is called "cooting," although the name coot belongs properly to that species of rail which is commonly called a mud hen. With such confusion of popular epithets it is no wonder that scientific names are preferred by those who wish to be exact. These "coots" that I speak of are really ducks, and they are known as the American scoter or butter-bill, the surf scoter or skunk-head and the white-winged scoter.

—Charles Wendell Townsend, *Sand Dunes and Salt Marshes*, 1913

Four ducks on a pond,
A grass bank beyond,
A blue sky of spring,
White clouds on the wing:
What a little thing
To remember for years—
To remember with tears!

—William Allingham, *A Memory*, 1850

The little green heron: It is common enough in the marshes, especially on the muddy edges of the creeks at low tide, where the hunting is good. As it stands or walks it may draw in its head until it appears to have no neck, or it may extend it as long as its body. If one has ever blown a blade of grass stretched tightly between the thumbs side by side, one will recognize the voice of this bird, which mimic exactly the music of the grass blade.

—Charles Wendell Townsend, *Sand Dunes and Salt Marshes*, 1913

Another interesting trait possessed by the bittern is its power of concealment. This is due partly to the streaked brown and pale buff plumage which matches admirably the dead tufts of grass, but chiefly to the motionless and un-bird-like posture, with upward pointing bill, assumed by the bird. It is sometimes almost impossible to point out a bird in this position that one has been fortunate enough to see, to another who has not seen it, so perfect is the protection afforded by the colors and the posture. I once started a bittern from the black-grass region of the marsh on a June day, and soon after realized that four objects that I had supposed were the stakes of a dilapidated gunner's blind were, in reality, the outstretched necks of four young bitterns. When closely approached they abandoned this method of deception, snapped their bills loudly in anger, erected the feathers of their necks, spread their feeble pin-feathered wings and, emitting faint hissing snarls, sprang defiantly at me.

—Charles Wendell Townsend, *Sand Dunes and Salt Marshes*, 1913

April 13, 1820

[This] morning we were awakened by the loud cries of the sand-hill crane, performing evolutions in the air, high over their feeding grounds. This stately bird is known . . . [as] *grus canadensis* [and] . . . is very distinct from the grus Americanus of authors, or hooping crane, although many persons have supposed it to be no other than the young of that gigantic species. The sandhill crane, in the spring of the year, removes the surface of the soil by scratching with its feet, in search of the radical tubers of the pea vine, which seem to afford them a very palatable food.

This crane is a social bird, sometimes assembling together in considerable flocks. They were now in great numbers, soaring aloft in the air, flying with an irregular kind of gyratory motion, each individual describing a large circle in the air independently of his associates, and uttering loud, dissonant, and repeated cries. They sometimes continue thus to wing their flight upwards, gradually receding from the earth, until they become mere specks upon the sight, and finally altogether disappear, leaving only the discordant music of their concert to fall faintly upon the ear.

—Thomas Say, journal

Here in this river and in the waters all over Florida, a very curious and handsome bird, the people call them Snake Birds, I think I have seen paintings of them on the Chinese screens and other India pictures: they seem to be a species of cormorant or loon (Colymbus cauda elongata) but far more beautiful and delicately formed than any other species that I have ever seen. The head and neck of this bird are extremely small and slender, the latter very long indeed, almost out of all proportion, the bill long, strait and slender, tapering from its base to a sharp point, all the upper side, the abdomen and thighs, are as black and glossy as a raven's covered with feathers so firm and elastic, that they in some degree resemble fish-scales, the breast and upper part of the belly are covered with feathers of a cream colour, the tail is very long, of a deep black, and tipped with a silvery white, and when spread, represents an unfurled fan. They delight to sit in little peaceable communities, on the dry limbs of trees, hanging over the still waters, with their wings and tails expanded, I suppose to cool and air themselves, when at the same time they behold their images in the watery mirror: at such times, when we approach them, they drop off the limbs into the water as if dead, and for a minute or two are not to be seen; when on a sudden at a vast distance, their long slender head and neck only appear, and have very much the appearance of a snake, and no other part of them is to be seen when swimming in the water, except sometimes the tip end of their tail. In the heat of the day they are seen in great numbers, sailing very high in the air, over lakes and rivers.

I doubt not but if this bird had been an inhabitant of the Tiber in Ovid's days, it would have furnished him with a subject, for some beautiful and entertaining metamorphoses.

—William Bartram, *Travels*, 1791

Ducks are not famous as songsters, but there is a somewhat musical duck that appears in these waters, namely the old squaw, old-wife, or long-tailed duck. This handsome bird comes with the winter in a livery of snow white and jet black, and he bears a long and slender tail which he jauntily cocks up at an angle. In Labrador these ducks were spoken of as "hounds" by Cartwright over a hundred years ago, and they still bear this name there, and it is an appropriate one, for the voice of a flock is like the music of a pack of hounds in full cry. According to Preble the Cree Indians along the Athacasca call this bird ca-ca-wee, the Chipewayans of the Mackenzie River refer to it as a-ha-lik; while the Eskimos give it the name a-ha-lin. All of these names are very fair attempts to repeat some of the notes used by these birds.

—Charles Wendell Townsend, *Sand Dunes and Salt Marshes*, 1913

Wood Duck or Summer Duck

[They] make their Nests in the Holes of tall Trees (made by Wood-peckers) growing in Water, particularly Cypress Trees. While they are young and unable to fly, the Old ones carry them on their Backs from their Nests into the Water; and at the Approach of Danger, they fix with their Bills on the Backs of the Old ones, which fly away with them.

—Mark Catesby, *The Natural History of Carolina,
Florida, and the Bahama Islands*, 1818

From John Clare's Bird List of 1825–26

Shore Sand Piper—
unknown to me

Green Sand piper—
unknown

Gamblet—
unknown to me

Ash colored Sandpiper—
unknown here

Common Sandpiper—
has been seen here

Greenwich Sandpiper—
unknown

Black sand piper—
unknown to me

Spotted Sand piper—

Red legged Sandpiper—
said to be common here

Lincolnshire Sandpiper—
unknown to me

Dunlin—
unknown to me

Flight

Who needs to be told that birds fly?

—W. P. Pycraft, *Birds in Flight*, 1922

The impression left after watching the motions of birds is that of extreme mobility— a life of perpetual impulse checked only by fear.

—Richard Jeffries, *Wild Life in a Southern County*, 1881

FIG. 20. — Chimney Swift.

The Woodcock is properly a nocturnal bird, feeding chiefly at night, and seldom stirring about till after sunset. At such times, as well as in the early part of the morning, particularly in spring, he rises, by a kind of spiral course, to a considerable height in the air, uttering at times a sudden *quack*, till, having gained his utmost height, he hovers around in a wild, irregular manner, making a sort of murmuring sound; then descends with rapidity as he rose.

—Alexander Wilson, *American Ornithology*, 1826

Not so very long ago a great controversy was waged as to what birds did with their legs during flight. Many of the older artists invariably depicted them drawn up under the breast. But as a matter of fact, this method seems to be confined to the Passerine birds—the "perching birds," such as crows and finches and their kin. It has yet to be settled what obtains among what are known as the "Picarian" birds, such as kingfishers, bee-eaters, woodpeckers, and so on. The legs and feet of these birds are so small, and their flight is so rapid, that the matter is by no means an easy one to settle. But all other birds carry the legs and toes bent backwards, under the tail. In the gulls, this can easily be seen, and easier still in the case of the common heron, where they are, as it were, trailed out behind— owing to the shortness of the tail and the great length of the leg. The puffin carries them "splayed" out on each side of his tail, and so also do his kinsmen, the razor-bills, and guillemots.

—W. P. Pycraft, *Birds in Flight*, 1922

Velocity of flight depends upon the rapidity with which the wing-strokes succeed each other; and the raon of the resistance of the air is not as the velocity simply, but as the square of the velocity. A downward stroke would only tend to raise the bird in the air; to carry it forward the wings require to be moved in an oblique plane, so as to strike backward as well as downward. The turning in flight to the right or to the left is principally effected by an inequality in the vibrations of the wings. To wheel to the right the left wing must be plied with greater frequency or force, and vice versa.

The outspread tail contributes to sustain the posterior part of the body; and, its plane being horizontal, serves chiefly by its movements to lift or lower the head.

—Richard Owen, *On the Anatomy of Vertebrates, Volume 2,
Birds and Mammals*, 1866

Now in a bird's wing the feathers are so arranged that they lap one under the other from the outside of the wing to the body, so that when the bird strikes downwards they are firmly pressed together, and the whole wing, which is hollow like the bowl of a spoon, encloses a wingful of air, and as this is forced out behind, where the tips of the feathers are yielding and elastic, he is driven upwards and forward. When, however, he lifts his wing again, the feathers turn edgeways and are separated, so that the air passes through them, and he still rises while preparing for the next stroke. All this goes on so rapidly that even the heron makes 300 strokes in a minute, and the wild duck 500, while in most birds they are so rapid that it is impossible to count them; yet all the while the little creature can direct his flight where he will, can pause and direct his wings to the breeze so as to soar, can swoop or hover, wheel or strike, guiding himself by the outspread tail and a thousand delicate turns of the wing.

—Arabella B. Buckley, *The Winners in Life's Race*, 1898

Presently a small swift shadow passes across—it is that of a hawk flying low over the hill. He skirts it for some distance, and then shoots out into the air, comes back half-way, and hangs over the fallow below, where there is a small rick. His wings vibrate, striking the air downwards, and only slightly backwards, the tail depressed counteracting the inclination to glide forwards for awhile. In a few moments he slips, as it were, from his balance, but brings himself up again in a few yards, turning a curve so as to still hover above the rick. If he espies a tempting morsel he drops like a stone, and alights on a spot almost exactly below him—a power which few birds seem to possess. Most of them approach the ground gradually, the plane of their flight sloping slowly to the earth, and the angle decreasing every moment till it becomes parallel, when they have only to drop their legs, shut their wings, and, as it were, stand upright in the air to find themselves safe on the sward. By that time their original impetus has diminished, and they feel no shock from the cessation of motion. The hawk, on the contrary, seems to descend nearly in a perpendicular line. The lark does the same, and often from a still greater height, descending so swiftly that by comparison with other birds it looks as if she must be dashed to pieces; but when within a few yards of the ground, the wings are outstretched, and she glides along some distance before alighting. This latter motion makes it difficult to tell where a lark actually does alight. So, too, with snipe: they appear to drop in a corner of the brook, and you feel positive that a certain bunch of rushes is the precise place; but before you get there the snipe is up again under your feet, ten or fifteen yards closer than you supposed, having shot along hidden by the banks, just above the water, out of sight.

Sometimes, after soaring to an unusual elevation the lark comes down, as it were, in one or two stages: after dropping say fifty feet, the wings are employed, and she shoots forward horizontally some way, which checks the velocity. Repeating this twice or more, she reaches the ground safely. In rising up to sing she often traces a sweeping spiral in the air at first, going round once or twice; after which, seeming to settle on the line she means to ascend, she goes up almost perpendicularly in a series of leaps, as it were—pausing a moment to gather impetus, and then shooting upwards till a mere speck in the sky.

—Richard Jeffries, *Wild Life in a Southern County*, 1881

My companion passengers lay strewn about the deck and on the cotton bales, basking like crocodiles during all the intervals granted to the sun to peep at them through the smoky haziness that accompanied us. Yet the breeze was strong, the waves moved majestically, and thousands of Large Petrels displayed their elegant aerial movements to me. How much I envied their power of flight to enable me to be here, there, and all over the globe, comparatively speaking, in a moment, throwing themselves edgeways against the breeze as if a well sharpened arrow, shot with the strength and grace of one sprung from the bow of an Apollo.

—John James Audubon, journal, 1826

Though, really, their plumage is all of gleaming, purply blues, at a little distance, and when they fly, ravens look a dead ugly black, which is also the case with rooks, who are almost equally handsome when seen closely. Their flight is peculiar, and though it strikes the imagination, yet it cannot be called at all grand or majestic in the ordinary sense of those words. The wings, which are broad, short, and rounded—or at any rate present that appearance to the eye— move with regular, quick little beats, or, when not flapped, are held out very straightly and rigidly. When thus extended, they are on a level with or, perhaps, a little below the line of the back, and from this, in beating, they only deviate downwards, and do not rise above it, or very triflingly so, giving them a very flat appearance. A curious curve is to be remarked in the anterior part of the spread wing, at first backwards towards the tail, and then again forwards towards the head. All the primary quills seem to partake of this shape and they are also very noticeably disjoined one from another, so that the interspace, even whilst the wing is beaten, looks almost as wide as the quill—by which I mean the whole feather—itself. I tried to imagine the effect of a number of these sombre, quickly-beating pinions with the short eager croak, having something of a bellowing tone in it over the wide-extended carnage of an ancient battlefield, and I thought I could do it pretty well—in spite of the difficulty, in the present day, of conjuring up such scenes.

But, though the ordinary flight of ravens be as I have described, it does not at all follow that they may not sometimes soar or sail for long distances through the air, or descend through it at great speed, and with all sorts of whirring and whizzing evolutions. For all these things do the rooks, and yet their ordinary flight is of a heavy and plodding character. One very peculiar antic, or "tirk i' the air," the raven certainly has. Whilst flapping steadily along with regular, though quick beat of the wings, it closes these all at once, quite tightly, as though it were on the ground, and immediately rolls over to one side or the other. Either the roll is complete, so that the bird comes right round again into its former position, or else, having got only so far as to be back downwards, it rolls back the reverse way. This has a most extraordinary appearance. The bird is stretched horizontally in the position in which it has just been flying, and in rolling over makes one think of a barrel or a man rolling on the ground. Being in the air, however, it may, by dropping a little as it rolls, make less, or possibly, no progress in a latitudinal direction, though whether this is the case or not I am not sure.

To watch this curious action through the glasses is most interesting. Each time there is a perceptible second or two during which the bird remains completely reversed, back to earth and breast to sky. The appearance presented is equally extraordinary, whether it makes the half roll and returns, or goes completely round. I have sometimes seen rooks make a turn over in the air, but his was more a disorderly tumble, recalling that of the peewit, and, though striking enough, was not nearly so extraordinary as this orderly and methodical, almost sedate, turning upside down. The feat is generally performed four or five times in succession, at intervals of some seconds, during which the steady flight is continued. Most often it is done in silence, but sometimes, at each roll over, the raven cries "pyar," a penetrating and striking note.

—Edmund Selous, *Bird Watching*, 1901

The Wagtails are the smallest birds that walk, the Thrushes the largest that hop. Their flight, too, is peculiar, for the birds proceed by a series of undulations, rising with a few rapid beats of the wing, and almost closing them as they sink, accompanying each dip with the utterance of their call-note, which is well rendered by the words "chiz-zit." This method of flight is shared by the Green Woodpecker, but I am unable to give any reason for the peculiarity.

—A. J. R. Roberts, *The Bird Book*, 1903

The upward sweep from near the ground—sometimes from nearly touching it—with its attendant sweep back again, is one of the greatest beauties of the peewit's flight—a flight that is full of beauties. He does it often, but not always in quite the same way; it is a varying perfection, for each time it is perfect, and sometimes it semes to vie with almost any aerial master-stroke. The bird's wings, as it shoots aloft, are spread half open, and remain thus without being moved at all. The body is turned sideways, sometimes more, sometimes less—and the light glancing on the pure soft white of the under part, makes it look like the crest of foam on an invisible and swiftly moving wave. As the uprush attains its zenith, there is a lovely, soft, effortless curling over of the body, and the foam sinks again with the wave. Such motions are not flight, they are passive abandonings and giving-up-to, drifting on unseen currents, bird-swirls and feathered eddies in the thin ocean of the air.

—Edmund Selous, *Bird Watching*, 1901

From Gilbert White's Journals, 1780

Mar. 6. Sky-larks mount and sing.

Mar. 8. Mrs. Snooke dyed, aged 86.

Mar. 12. No turnips to be seen on the road.

Mar. 14. Chaffinches sing but in a shorter way than in Hants.

Mar. 15. Mrs. Snooke was buried.

Mar. 17. Brought away Mrs. Snooke's old tortoise, Timothy, which she valued very much, & had treated kindly for near 40 years. When dug out of it's hybernaculum, it resented the Insult by hissing.

Mar. 18. No turnips to be seen on the road. Green plovers [lapwings] on the common. The uncreasted wren, the smallest species, called in this place the Chif-chaf, is very loud in the Lythe. This is the earliest summer bird of passage, & the harbinger of spring. It has only two piercing notes.

Eggs

I think, that, if required, on pain of death, to name instantly the most perfect thing in the universe, I should risk my fate on a bird's egg.

—T. W. Higginson, *The Life of Birds*, 1862

Last year a pair of goldfinches built in a plum tree by the side of a carriage drive, so low that on tiptoe I could reach into the nest to count over the eggs from day to day. And what dainty light blue shells they had. Just as if bits of blue sky had fallen into the nest!

—Florence Merriam, *Birds Through an Opera Glass*, 1889

I think I have now a new fact—at least new to me—to prove design in the formation of birds' eggs. It was casually mentioned to me by Mr. Edon, curator of my Fish Museum, South Kensington. He has remarked a very striking difference in the shape and form of the eggs of birds, which build in nests or holes, as contrasted with the shape of the eggs of those birds which build on flat surfaces. The kingfisher will place her eggs at a considerable depth in the earth in rats' holes, sand martin's holes, etc. Her eggs are nearly round. The owl builds in holes in trees, etc., and her eggs are perfectly round. The long-tailed tit builds in a very deep nest; her eggs are also round. The reason of this is that the eggs shall pack well in the nest, and all of them get a share of the warmth from the mother's body as well as ventilation.

Birds that lay their eggs in holes, as noted above, have round eggs. There are however, certain birds which incubate their eggs without any nest at all, upon the ledges of rocks. In this position it is very possible that danger would occur to the egg, by being accidentally moved by the parent bird, or maybe by the wind. If the egg was round, it would probably roll off the precipice, and, falling to the bottom, be smashed. In this case, of course, there would be no bird. Let us now see how the difficult problem of the preservation of this egg is managed by creative wisdom. The egg of the guillemot, to take a good example, is not round, but elongated at one end; the consequence is, that when it is touched the egg will not roll away like a billiard-ball, but it will simply turn around upon its own axis. This peculiar structure can be seen, and the action of the force upon the egg illustrated, by a simple experiment. Take a common screw, and place it near the edge of the table; touch it gently, so as to set it in motion. You will observe that the screw, instead of running off the edge of the table, will simply turn round on its small end—its own axis. I cannot conceive anything more beautiful, than this arrangement of the eggs of birds, which build on ledges of rocks, and which are very liable to destruction. This fact will, I think, afford excellent evidence (if more witnesses were required) to show creative skill even in such simple things as birds' eggs.

—Frank Buckland, in George C. Bompas's *Life of Frank Buckland*, 1885

July 30, 1852

What a gem is a bird's egg, especially a blue or a green one, when you see one, broken or whole, in the woods! I noticed a small blue egg this afternoon washed up by Flint's Pond and half buried by white sand, and as it lay there, alternately wet and dry, no color could be fairer, no gem could have a more advantageous or favorable setting. Probably it was shaken out of some nest which overhung the water. I frequently meet with broken egg-shells where a crow, perchance, or some other thief has been marauding. And is not that shell something very precious that houses that winged life?

—Henry David Thoreau, journal

Be it far from me to use caustic speech against any man or set of men; but it makes me both indignant and sick at heart to read the bloody chronicles of most of the so-called "collectors." How many embryo birds they slay merely to gratify their morbid craze for gathering "clutches," as they suggestively call a set of eggs! Not long ago a collector narrated in an ornithological journal, the harrowing story of his having rifled the nest of a hairy woodpecker five or six times in a single season, the poor bird laying a new deposit after each burglary, until at last she grew suspicious and sought a safer site for her nest. The writer described his part of the performance with apparent gusto, as if he has made a splendid contribution to science! If he must have a collection of hairy woodpecker's eggs, why not take a single "clutch," and then leave the bird to make her second deposit and rear her brood in peace?

—Leander S. Keyser, *In Bird Land*, 1897

Nuts for the Boys and Girls to Crack

1. Name five birds which walk.
2. Name five birds which sing on the wing.
3. Name five birds which sing in the night.
4. Name five birds which nest in holes.
5. Name five birds which nest in bird houses.
6. Name five birds that repair and use last year's nest.
7. Name five birds which creep up the trunks of trees.
8. Name five birds which have blue plumage.
9. Name two birds that carry their young as a cat does kittens.
10. What is a "Merry thought?"

Answers:

1. Cowbird, Ovenbird, Meadowlark, Titlark, Partridge
2. Bobolink, Bluebird, Goldfinch, Indigo Bunting, Purple Finch
3. Chat, Vesper, Sparrow, Carolina Wren, Rose-breasted Grosbeak, Mocking bird
4. Woodpeckers, Bluebirds, Swallows, Great-crested Flycatcher, Wren
5. Martins, Bluebirds, Wrens, Sparrows, White-bellied Swallows
6. Owls, Eagles, Fish Hawks, Bluebirds, Great-crested Flycatchers
7. Brown Creepers, Black and White Warblers, White and Red-breasted Nuthatches, Woodpeckers
8. Bluebird, Indigo Bunting, Kingfisher, Blue Jay, Black-throated Blue Warbler
9. Whip-poor-will, Wood Duck
10. A Merrythought is the forked bone of a fowl's breast, often called a wishbone.

—Anonymous, *American Ornithology for the Home and School*, Volume 2, 1905

From Gilbert White's Journals

June 9. A pair of swallows hawk for flies 'til within a quarter of nine o'clock; they probably have young hatched.

June 13. The house-martins which build in old nest begin to hatch, as may be seen by their throwing out the egg-shells.

July 11. Trenched out celriac, & some of the new-advertized large celeri. Planted out some endive. A pair of house-martins, that built under the eaves of my stable, lost their nest in part by a drip, just as most of the young were flown. They are now repairing their habitation in order to rear a second brood. Sparrowhawks carried-off also from a farm-yard a young duck larger than themselves.

Aug. 14. The bank-martins at the sand-pit on Short-heath are now busy about their second brood, & have thrown out their egg-shells from their holes. The dams & first broods make a large flight. When we approached their caverns, they seemed anxious, & uttered a little wailing note.

1782

June 5. My brother Thomas White nailed-up several large 'scallop shells under the eaves of his house at South lambeth, to see if the house-martins would build in them. These conveniences had not been fixed half an hour, before several pairs settled upon them; &, expressing great complacency, began to build immediately. The shells were nailed on horizontally with the hollow side upward; & should, I think, have a hole drilled in their bottoms to let-out moisture from driving rains.

1785

Aug. 23. Martins & swallows congregate by hundred on the church & tower. These birds never cluster in this manner, but on sunny days. They are chiefly the first broods, rejected by their dams, who are busyed with a second family.

1787

June 23. Brood of nightingales frequents the walks. The number of swifts are few, because they are stopped-out from the eaves of the church, which were repaired last autumn. The nest of a *Flusher,* or red-backed *Butcher*-bird was found near Alton. Pease, barley, & oats look well, especially the first, which show fine bloom: wheat looks but poorly. Wheat at market rises. Sheep are washed.

June 25. Nep. and niece Ben White brought little Ben.

June 27. A brood of little partridges was seen in Baker's hill.

1793

Apr. 6. On the 6th of last October I saw many swallows hawking for flies around the Pleastor, & a row of young ones, with square tails, sitting on a spar of the old ragged thatch of the empty house. This morning Dr. Chandler and I caused the roof to be examined, hoping to have found some of these birds in their winter retreat: but we did not meet with any success, tho' Benham searched every hole & every breach in the decayed roof.

Apr. 7. The chaffinches destroy the blossoms of the polyanths in a sad manner. Sowed a bed of carrots: the ground hard, & rough, & does not rake fine.

Connection

Beloved of children, bards and spring,
O birds, your perfect virtues bring,—
Your song, your forms, your rhythmic flight,
Your manners for the heart's delight;
Nestle in hedge, or barn, or roof;
Here weave your chamber weather-proof.
Forgive our harms and condescend
To man, as to a lubber friend,
And, generous, teach his awkward race
Courage and probity and grace!

—Ralph Waldo Emerson, *Birds*, 1867

When I entered college, I was devoted to out-of-doors natural history, and my ambition was to be a scientific man of the Audubon, or Wilson, or Baird, or Coues type—a man like Hart Merriam, or Frank Chapman, or Hornaday, to-day.

—Theodore Roosevelt, *Theodore Roosevelt: An Autobiography*, 1920

Some birds are even capable of attachment to the person that feeds them. How far they may be instructed by long assiduity, is obvious from a late instance of a canary-bird, which was shown in London, and which had been taught to pick up the letters of the alphabet at the word of command. Upon the whole, however, they are inferior to quadrupeds in their sagacity; they are possessed of fewer of those powers, which look like reason, and seem, in all their actions, rather impelled by instinct than guided by choice.

—Oliver Goldsmith, *Preface and Familiar Introduction
to the Study of Natural History*, 1763

Wednesday, September 27th

Many birds flying about in parties. Some of the goldfinches still wear their summer colors, yellow and black. Walking in the lane, we came upon a large mixed flock, feeding on the thistles and silk-weed of an adjoining field which is overrun with these weeds. There were goldfinches, glue-birds, sparrows, robins; and perched in a tree, at no great distance, were several meadow-larks apparently attracted by the crowd, for they sat quietly looking on. Altogether there must have been several hundreds in the flock, for there were frequently six or eight hanging upon one thistle-stalk. Some were feeding busily; others were flitting about, now on the fences, now in the road. It was a gay, pretty sight. We disturbed them, of course, passing in their midst; but they did not seem much alarmed. Taking flight, as we came close to them, they alighted again on the rails and weeds, a few yards beyond, repeating over and over the same move-ment as we walked slowly on, until more than half the flock had actually accompanied us in this way a good piece of road, a quarter of a mile. They seemed half convinced that we meant no harm to them. As we reached the end of the lane and turned into the highway, some went back to their feast; others, as it was near sunset, flew away in parties.

—Susan Fenimore Cooper, *Rural Hours*, 1850

Birds certainly gave me more pleasure than other animals, and this too is no doubt common with children, and I take the reason of it to be not only because birds exceed in beauty, but also on account of the intensity of life they exhibit—a life so vivid, so brilliant, as to make that of other beings, such as reptiles and mammals, seem a rather poor thing by comparison.

—W. H. Hudson, *Far Away and Long Ago*, 1918

Columbus, Ohio

There were some big doings in town today. A governor, or somebody, was to be inaugurated. Brass bands crashed, militia-men marched and counter-marched, officers of the day strutted and bawled orders, while Masonic grandees waved gorgeous plumes from top-heavy headgear (they tell me) and hoi polloi enjoyed themselves generally. I wasn't there. I'd rather see a squad of Tow-hees or an aerial procession of Blue Jays than a gubernatorial staff under full sail. The governor—dear man—the one sober, modest, capable person in all the chaos of regalia, and noise, and aspiration—he didn't miss me, much. Excited by reports of a winter bird paradise off north-east, I set out at 9 a.m., in spite of a brisk north wind and threatening snow, at a temperature of 21 Fahr. Arrayed in two sweaters and an incommunicable number of trousers, I was deter-mined to hold carnival with the birds. I took oath to report them faithfully, and their silent admiration was as flattering to my appre-ciative soul as the applause of the gaping crowds downtown could possibly have been to his excellency.

—W. Leon Dawson, *Wilson Bulletin*, 1902

On the Carrion Crow

Many an hour of delight do I experience, when, having mounted to the top of a favourite aged oak which grows on the border of a swamp, I see him chasing the heron and the windhover through the liquid void.

—Charles Waterton, journal, 1840s

The joy in life of these animals—indeed, of almost all animals and birds in freedom—is very great. You may see it in every motion: in the lissom bound of the hare, the playful leap of the rabbit, the song that the lark and the finch must sing; the soft, loving coo of the dove in the hawthorn; the blackbird ruffling out his feathers on a rail. The sense of living—the consciousness of seeing and feeling—is manifestly intense in them all, and is in itself an exquisite pleasure. Their appetites seem ever fresh: they rush to the banquet spread by Mother Earth with a gusto that Lucullus never knew in the midst of his artistic gluttony; they drink from the stream with dainty sips as though it were richest wine. Watch the birds in the spring; the pairs dance from bough to bough, and know not how to express their wild happiness.

—Richard Jeffries, *Wild Life in a Southern County*, 1881

When I saw the Oriole from his nest among the plum-trees in the garden, sail over the air and high about the Gothic arches of the elm, a stream of flashing light, or watched him swinging silently on pendent twigs, I did not dream how near akin we were. Or when a Humming-Bird, a winged drop of gorgeous sheen and gloss, a living gem, poising on his wings, thrust his dark, slender, honey-seeking bill into the white blossoms of a little bush beside my window, I should have thought it no such bad thing to be a bird, even if one next became a bat, like the colony in our eaves, that dart and drop and skim and skurry, all the length of moonless nights, in such ecstasies of dusky joy.

—Harriet Rohan, in T. W. Higginson's *The Life of Birds*, 1862

Particular species of birds, like different nations of men, have their congenial climes and favorite countries; but wanderers are common to both; some in search of better fare, some of adventures, others led by curiosity, and many driven by storms or accident.

—Alexander Wilson, *American Ornithology*, 1826

Like most Americans interested in birds and books, I know a good deal about English birds as they appear in books. I know the lark of Shakespeare and Shelley and the Ettrick Shepherd; I know the nightingale of Milton and Keats; I know Wordsworth's cuckoo; I know mavis and merle singing in the merry green wood of the old ballads; I know Jenny Wren and Cock Robin of the nursery books. Therefore I had always much desired to hear the birds in real life; and the opportunity offered in June, 1910, when I spent two or three weeks in England. As I could snatch but a few hours from a very exacting round of pleasures and duties, it was necessary for me to be with some companion who could identify both song and sight. In Sir Edward Grey, a keen lover of outdoor life in all its phases, and a delightful companion, who knows the songs and ways of English birds as very few do know them, I found the best possible guide.

We left London on the morning of June 9, twenty-four hours before I sailed from Southampton. Getting off the train at Basingstoke, we drove to the pretty, smiling valley of the Itchen. Here we tramped for three or four hours, then again drove, this time to the edge of the New Forest, where we first took tea at an inn, and then tramped through the forest to an inn on its other side, at Brockenhurst. At the conclusion of our walk my companion made a list of those birds we had seen, putting an asterisk (*) opposite those which we had heard sing. There were forty-one of the former and twenty-three of the latter, as follows: *Thrush, *blackbird, *lark, *yellowhammer, *robin, *wren, *gold-crested wren, *goldfinch, *chaffinch, *greenfinch, pied wagtail, sparrow, *dunnock (hedge, accentor), missel thrush, starling, rook, jackdaw, *blackcap, *garden warbler, *willow warbler, *chiffchaff, *wood warbler, tree-creeper, *reed bunting, *sedge warbler, coot, water hen, little grebe (dabchick), tufted duck, wood pigeon, stock dove, *turtle dove, peewit, tit (?coal tit), *cuckoo, *nightjar, *swallow, martin, swift, pheasant, partridge.

—Theodore Roosevelt, *Theodore Roosevelt: An Autobiography*, 1920

Swallow means porch-bird, and for centuries and centuries their nests have been placed in the closest proximity to man. They might be called man's birds, so attached are they to the human race. I think the greatest ornament a house can have is the nest of an eave-swallow under the eaves—far superior to the most elaborate carving, colouring, or arrangement the architect can devise. There is no ornament like the swallow's nest; the home of a messenger between man and the blue heavens, between us and the sunlight, and all the promise of the sky.

—Richard Jeffries, *The Open Air*, 1885

March 17, 1860

I see a large flock of sheldrakes, which have probably risen from the pond, go over my head in the woods. A dozen large and compact birds flying with great force and rapidity, spying out the land, eyeing every traveller, fast and far they "steam it" on clipping wings, over field and forest, meadow and flood; now here, and you hear the whistling of their wings, and in a moment they are lost in the horizon. Like swift propellers of the air. Whichever way they are headed, that way their wings propel them. What health and vigor they suggest! The life of man seems slow and puny in comparison,— reptilian.

—Henry David Thoreau, journal

The pleasure I receive from the warblings of the birds in the spring, so superior to my poor description, as the continual succession of their tuneful notes is for ever new to me. I generally rise from bed about that indistinct interval, which, properly speaking, is neither night or day; for this is the moment of the most universal vocal choir. Who can listen unmoved to the sweet love tales of our robins, told from tree to tree? or to the shrill cat birds? The sublime accents of the thrush from on high always retard my steps that I may listen to the delicious music . . . The astonishing care which all birds display in the construction of their nests, ill provided as we may suppose them with proper tools, their neatness, their convenience, always make me ashamed of the slovenliness of our houses; their love to their dame, their incessant careful attention, and the peculiar songs they address to her while she tediously incubates their eggs, remind me of my duty could I ever forget it. Their affection to their helpless little ones, is a lively precept; and in short, the whole economy of what we proudly call the brute creation, is admirable in every circumstance; and vain man, though adorned with the additional gift of reason, might learn from the perfection of instinct, how to regulate the follies, and how to temper the errors which this second gift often makes him commit. This is a subject, on which I have often bestowed the most serious thoughts; I have often blushed within myself, and been greatly astonished, when I have compared the unerring path they all follow, all just, all proper, all wise, up to the necessary degree of perfection, with the coarser, the imperfect systems of men, not merely as governors and kings, but as masters, as husbands, as fathers, as citizens.

—Crèvecouer, *Letters from an American Farmer*, 1782

We have no right to expect birds to tell one human being from another, so long as we, with all our boasted intelligence, cannot tell one crow or one magpie from another.

—Olive Thorne Miller, *A Bird-Lover in the West*, 1900

A neglected field that has run to seed, covered over with nodding thistles and "horse-knops"; in its corners are bunches of groundsel and dandelion and plantain. It is rarely visited, and never stocked. Now and then a lad comes with a sickle and lays low the glowing pride of foxglove and thistle; but somehow he never works systematically, and hence never changes the aspect of that particular field. The characteristic flora of the spot still holds its own, and the weed-harvest of each year is more abundant than that of the last. Bunches of nettles and docks and campions hide the nesting-places of the ground-birds and under that rotten stump resides a colony of hedgehogs. A pair of larks have their nest under an overhanging tuft, and a spotted flycatcher seems ever to sit on a spray over the stream which runs down the bottom of the field. In our "intack" a pair of corn-crakes have taken up their abode, and give out their "crake, crake, crake," far into the night. As we stand in the tall wet grass, the call seems to come from the middle of the field, then far out yonder, and anon the bird runs nearly to our feet. We always love to hear the call, however, as it betokens summer, evening fishing, and long night-walks.

—Anonymous, *Winter Birds*, 1889

Rooks, I am inclined to think, are not birds that give their conscience into keeping. Each one of them is his own sentinel.

—Edmund Selous, *Bird Watching*, 1901

for my part I love to look on nature with a poetic feeling which maginifys the pleasure I love to see the nightingale in its hazel retreat & the cuckoo hiding in its solitudes of oaken foliage & not to examine their cacasses in glass cases yet naturalists & botanists seem to have no taste for this practical feeling they merely make collections of dryd specimens classing them after Linnaeus into tribes & familys & there they delight to show them as a sort of ambitious fame with them "a bird in the hand is worth two in the bush" well everyone to his hobby.

I have none of this curiosity about me tho I feel as happy as they can about finding a new species of field flower or butterflye which I have not seen before yet I have no desire further to dry the plant or torture the butterflye by sticking it on a cork board wit a pin—I have no wish to do this if my feelings woud let me

—John Clare, journal, 1825

When wearied, with working my canoe against the impetuous current . . . I resigned my bark to the friendly current, reserving to myself the control of the helm. My progress was rendered delightful by the sylvan elegance of the groves, chearful meadows, and high distant forests, which in grand order presented themselves to view. The winding banks of the river, and the high projecting promontories, unfolded fresh scenes of grandeur and sublimity. The deep forests and distant hill re-echoed the chearing social lowings of domestic herds. The air was filled with the loud and shrill whooping of the wary sharp-sighted crane. Behold, on yon decayed, defoliated Cypress tree, the solitary wood-pelican, dejectedly perched upon its utmost elevated spire; he there, like an ancient venerable sage, sets himself up as a mark of derision.... The crying-bird, another faithful guardian, screaming in the gloomy thickets, warns the feathered tribes of approaching peril; and the plumage of the swift sailing squadrons of Spanish curlews (white as the immaculate robe of innocence) gleam in the cerulean skies.

—William Bartram, *Travels*, 1791

Those who are addicted to rambling in pursuit of natural curiosities may have observed that pine-woods are remarkable for certain collections of mosses which have cushioned a projecting rock or the decayed stump of a tree. When weary with heat and exercise, it is delightful to sit down upon one of these green velveted couches and take note of the objects immediately around us. We are then prepared to hear the least sound that invades our retreat. Some of the sweetest notes ever uttered in the wood are distinctly heard only at such times; for when we are passing over the rustling leaves, the noise made by our progress interferes with the perfect recognition of all delicate sounds. It was when thus reclining, after half a day's search for flowers, under the grateful shade of a pine-tree, now watching the white clouds that sent a brighter day-beam into these dark recesses, as they passed luminously overhead, and then noting the peculiar mapping of the grounds underneath the wood, diversified with mosses in swelling knowls, little islets of fern, and parterres of ginseng and Solomon's-seals,—in one of these cloisters of the forest, I was first greeted by the pensive note of the Green Warbler, as he seemed to utter in supplicatory tones, very slowly modulated, "Hear me, Saint Theresa!" This strain, as I have observed many times since, is, at certain hours, repeated constantly for ten minutes at a time, and it is one of those melodious sounds that seem to belong exclusively to solitude.

—T. W. Higginson, *Birds of the Garden and Orchard*, 1858

Our boat being now in readiness and our horses turned out to pasture, each one retired to repose, or to such exercise as most effectually contributed to divert the mind. I was at this time rather dejected, and sought comfort in retirement. Turning my course to the expansive fields, fragrant groves and sublime forests. Returned to camp by dusk, where I found my companions cheerfull and thoughtless rather to an extreme. It was a calm still evening and warm, the wood-cock (scolopx) chirruping high up in the air, gently descends by spiral circular tract, and alights on the humid plain: this bird appears in Pennsylvania early in the spring, when the Elm and Maple begin to flower, and here the scarlet Maple, Elm and Alder began to shew their blossoms, and the gay Azalea also preparing to expand its beauties.

—William Bartram, *Travels*, 1791

As I sat the other day in the deep woods beside a black brook which dropped from stone to stone beneath the shadow of our Rattle-snake Rocks, the air seemed at first as silent above me as the earth below. The buss of summer sounds had not begun. Sometimes a bee hummed by with a long swift thrill like a chord of music; sometimes a breeze came resounding up the forest like an approaching locomotive, and then died utterly away. Then, at length, a Veery's delirious note rose in a fountain of liquid melody from beneath me; and when it was ended, the clear, calm, interrupted cant of the Wood-Thrush fell like solemn water-drops from some source above.

—T. W. Higginson, *The Life of Birds*, 1862

There is precisely as much satisfaction in learning the ways and appearance of an unfamiliar bird, and in getting a clear sense of its individuality, as if the same species had not been watched by a thousand pairs of eyes. As someone has well said, every observer is for himself at least an original discoverer; and the same exhilaration of discovery is in store for each new beginner. It is entertaining to read others' accounts of bird-life, but this is a mild satisfaction compared with seeing for one's self what is transpiring in the woods and fields all about. However instructive the experience of others, one *realizes* only his own experience. It is the difference between shadow and substance.

—Howard E. Parkhurst, *The Birds' Calendar*, 1894

Biographies of Selected Contributors

CHARLES CONRAD ABBOTT
b. 1843 d. 1919

The grandson of botanist Solomon Conrad, Charles Abbott spent most of his life in northern New Jersey on the banks of the Delaware River. His writing about the area's natural history gained a national audience when it appeared in magazines including *American Naturalist*, *Popular Science Monthly*, and *Lippincott's Magazine*.

JOHN JAMES AUDUBON
b. 1785 d. 1851

Born on a Santo Domingo plantation as the result of one of his father's extramarital affairs, Audubon was adopted formally by his father and his father's wife on his arrival in France at age ten. He came to the United States in 1804, and settled near Philadelphia. He is thought to be one of the first to "band" birds, fastening silver threads to the legs of baby pewees to identify them on their return the following spring. Thirty years of travel and research went into his best-known project, the elephant folio of fine engravings, *Birds of America*.

FLORENCE MERRIAM BAILEY
b. 1863 d. 1948

Florence Merriam formalized her love of ornithology at Smith College, founding a chapter of the Audubon Society, inviting John Burroughs to campus, and publishing articles on bird behavior in the Audubon Society magazine while still a student. Her early book *Birds Through an Opera Glass* (1889) was followed by an account of western birdwatching, *A-Birding on a Bronco* (1896), and the popular bird guide *Birds of Village and Field* (1898). After marrying the naturalist Vernon

Bailey, she focused on western birds, writing the *Handbook of Birds of the Western United States* and *Birds of New Mexico*. She was the first woman associate member, and, later, fellow, of the American Ornithologists' Union, and also the first to receive its Brewster Medal (1931).

WILLIAM BARTRAM
b. 1739 d. 1823

Son of the botanist John Bartram, a Quaker and friend of Benjamin Franklin, William grew up on the Schuylkill River near Philadelphia. Between 1773 and 1777 Bartram traveled through the southeast United States under the patronage of Dr. John Fothergill of England. The 1791 publication of his *Travels Through North and South Carolina, Georgia, East and West Florida, the Cherokee Country, the Extensive Territories of the Muscogulges, or Creek Confederacy, and the Country of the Chactaws* made him famous on both sides of the Atlantic. Alexander Wilson later named Bartram's sandpiper (the upland plover) after this important early naturalist.

FRANCIS TREVELYAN BUCKLAND
b. 1826 d. 1880

Frank Buckland was best known for his work on fish and was, for fifteen years, the inspector of salmon fisheries for England and Wales. His nature writing appeared in the *Field* newspaper and in *Land and Water*, a journal devoted to the natural world, which he founded in 1866.

JOHN BURROUGHS
b. 1837 d. 1921

The name John Burroughs is almost synonymous with the study of natural history in nineteenth-century America. During a ten-year stint in the Treasury Department, Burroughs met and befriended Walt Whitman, who suggested the title of the naturalist's first book about birds, *Wake Robin* (1871). Described by the novelist Henry James as "a sort of reduced, but also more humorous, more available, more sociable Thoreau," Burroughs welcomed visitors to "Woodchuck Lodge," his summer retreat in the Catskills, and became the most widely read voice of nature of the century.

MARK CATESBY
b.1679? d. 1749

Englishman Mark Catesby arrived in America in 1712 as a specimen collector. He remained for seven years, returning to England only to gather sponsorship for another collecting journey, this time to South Carolina, Georgia, and Florida between 1722 and 1725. Catesby wrote and illustrated the resulting colorful three-volume text *The Natural History of Carolina, Florida, and the Bahama Islands* on his return to England.

JOHN CLARE
b. 1793 d. 1864

John Clare started writing poetry as an undergardener on the estate of the Marquis of Exeter in England. Fired from that position for writing too much, he worked as an itinerant farm laborer to support his family. Clare carried on vast correspondence with his readers and other writers after his "discovery" by the literary world, but financial success did not come, and he remained a farmer. Poverty was said to be a cause of a series of mental breakdowns, which led to extended stays in mental asylums, in one of which he finally died. His poetry is best known for the intimacy with which he portrayed the natural world of birds, animals, and the land around him.

SUSAN FENIMORE COOPER
b. 1813 d. 1894

Born and raised in Cooperstown, New York, Cooper accompanied her father, James Fenimore Cooper, on his international travels, serving for the later part of his life as his amanuensis. Based on a journal she kept in the last years of her father's life, *Rural Hours* (1850), an account of the natural life of the lake region near Cooperstown, was widely read, running through six editions in four years.

ELLIOTT COUES
b. 1842 d. 1899

After entering the army as a medical cadet in the Civil War, Elliott Coues served as an assistant surgeon in the U.S. Army from 1864 to

1881. He took advantage of his postings in the remote American West to observe and record bird species. While still in the army, he published his first, most famous work, *Key to North American Birds*, followed by *Birds of the Northwest* and *Birds of the Colorado Valley* in 1874 and 1878. In the 1880s, Coues explored spirituality, eventually founding the Washington chapter of the Theosophical Society. Later, he turned his energies to editing books on the exploration of the West, including a version of the Lewis and Clark expedition and *The Expeditions of Zebulon Pike*.

MICHEL-GUILLAUME-JEAN DE CRÈVECOEUR OR HECTOR ST. JOHN DE CRÈVECOEUR
b. 1735 d. 1813

After spending time in Canada during the French and Indian Wars, Crèvecoeur came to New York in 1759. He traveled widely before settling on a farm in Orange County, New York, in 1765. His essays on America were collected in *Letters from an American Farmer* in 1782. After losing his farm and wife to an Indian raid while he was visiting France, he became the French consul at New York.

WILLIAM DUNBAR
b. 1749 d. 1810

Although William Dunbar was born in Scotland, the state of Mississippi claims him as one of its own. After emigrating to America in 1771, Dunbar quickly made his way south, where he established himself in agriculture. He revolutionized the cotton industry by inventing the square bale and suggesting the production of cottonseed oil. An avid astronomer and observer of his natural world, he was asked by Thomas Jefferson to explore the Ouachita River country in 1804.

OLIVER GOLDSMITH
b. 1730 d. 1774

After an unsuccessful medical education, Oliver Goldsmith turned to writing. By turns journalist, dramatist, reviewer, novelist, and poet, he was among the best-known writers of the eighteenth century. His novel *The Vicar of Wakefield* (1766) and the play *She Stoops to Conquer* (1773) remain widely read today. Somehow, he made time to write and publish a study of natural history.

PHILIP HENRY GOSSE
b. 1810 d. 1888

The son of miniature painter Thomas Gosse, Philip Gosse traveled widely, collecting birds and insects for the British Museum. His wife, Emily, was one of the early religious charity workers among the poor in London's East End.

JAMES HALL
b. 1793 d. 1868

James Hall was born in Philadelphia and, after studying law, fought in the War of 1812. Afterward, he saw opportunity in the West and moved to the Ohio River in Illinois, where he built a successful law practice and edited and owned the *Illinois Gazette* in Shawneetown. He was active in society and, when appointed state treasurer, moved to the capital city of Vandalia. Hall is best known for his documentation of the history of the settlement of the Ohio Valley.

THOMAS WENTWORTH HIGGINSON
b. 1823 d. 1911

T. W. Higginson is best known as the early champion of Emily Dickinson's poetry. After graduating from Harvard at age seventeen, he became an ardent abolitionist and supporter of women's suffrage. In November 1862, he became the colonel of the first African American regiment in the Union army. His writing about birds and nature appeared in the *Atlantic Monthly* and his books include *The Birds of Pasture and Forest*, *Birds of the Garden and Orchard*, and *The Life of Birds*.

WILLIAM HENRY HUDSON
b. 1841 d. 1922

W. H. Hudson was born of American parents in Argentina and was brought up on the plains of the Rio de la Plata, where he, by his own admission, ran wild, exploring the world around him, especially the world of birds. He emigrated to the England of his grandparents in 1869, where he turned his attention to writing. His writing about birds included the scientific *Argentine Ornithology* (1888–89) and the more accessible, yet informative, *Birds in a Village* (1893). Perhaps his most famous work, though, is the adventure romance of Venezuela, *Green Mansions*, which appeared in 1904.

OLIVE THORNE MILLER (PSEUDONYM FOR HARRIET MILLER)
b. 1831 d. 1918

Early in her career, Miller wrote stories for children, turning her focus to birds in 1880, after moving to Brooklyn. In all, she wrote five books on birds, including the popular *Bird-Ways* (1885) and *A Bird-Lover in the West* (1894). Largely self-taught, she gained the respect of the predominantly male scientific establishment and at her death was regarded as one of America's best writers about birds and their behavior.

JOHN MUIR
b. 1838 d. 1914

Born in Scotland, John Muir was raised on a farm in Wisconsin. After leaving the University of Wisconsin without a degree, Muir traveled throughout the Midwest, walking much of the way. In 1868, he settled in the Yosemite Valley of California. His passionate writings about the natural world of Yosemite contributed to its eventual protection as a national park and furthered the popular cause of conservation.

ALFRED NEWTON
b. 1829 d. 1907

As a fellow of Magdalene College, Cambridge, Newton made many contributions to the emerging science of ornithology. In 1858, he traveled to Iceland to locate the last nesting place of the great auk. A founder of the British Ornithological Union, he is best known for his *Dictionary of Birds*, which appeared from 1893 to 1896.

THOMAS NUTTALL
b. 1786 d. 1859

Thomas Nuttall emigrated to Philadelphia from Liverpool in 1808. He first focused on botany, traveling with the Scottish naturalist John Bradbury up the Missouri River between 1809 and 1811. Somewhere, perhaps in his travels along the Arkansas and Red rivers between 1818 and 1820 or while curating the Botanical Garden at Harvard University in the twenties, Nuttall's attention turned to birds. In 1832, he published

A Manual of the Ornithology of the United States and Canada. In recognition of his contributions to the study of birds, the first ornithological club in America was named after him.

SIR RICHARD OWEN
b. 1804 d. 1892

A successful surgeon and lecturer in anatomy, Owen pursued interests in geology, natural history, and microscopy. His work as the curator of the exhibition of extinct animals at the Crystal Palace of the Royal Exhibition in 1855 placed him at the center of Victorian debates about evolution. The author of more than fifty scientific works, he is best known for his multivolume anatomy of vertebrates.

CHARLOTTE SMITH
b. 1749 d. 1806

Charlotte Smith is recognized as one of the earliest Romantic poets. She spent time in debtors' prison due to her husband's fiscal irresponsibility, and turned to writing as a way of clearing up his debts and supporting her twelve children. Her volumes of poetry include *Elegiac Sonnets* and *The Emigrants*, successful publications that influenced William Wordsworth, Mary Robinson, and Samuel Taylor Coleridge. Her *History of Birds* was published after her death, in 1807.

HENRY DAVID THOREAU
b. 1817 d. 1862

Thoreau is one of the few nineteenth century writers about birds whose prose has not faded into obscurity. In addition to writing his political meditation *Walden* (1854), the friend of Emerson and the Alcotts recorded his keen observations on the natural world in journals that supplied the heart of published texts like *The Maine Woods* and *A Week on the Concord and Merrimack Rivers*.

ALFRED RUSSEL WALLACE
b. 1823 d. 1913

A. R. Wallace became interested in botany and astronomy while working as a surveyor's assistant. He was one of the nineteenth century's most traveled naturalists, joining Henry Walter Bates for a voyage up the Amazon in 1848 that lasted, for Wallace, four years. His records and collections were destroyed in a shipwreck on his journey home, and Wallace set out to the Malay Archipelago to gather more knowledge and specimens. It was there that he thought through an idea of natural selection that he would share in correspondence with Charles Darwin, who was at that time working on his theory of evolution. The result was a landmark joint-authored paper delivered to the Linnaean Society in 1858. Wallace continued his friendship with Darwin and other scientific luminaries of the nineteenth century, including Charles Lyell and Herbert Spencer.

GILBERT WHITE
b. 1720 d. 1793

A longtime fellow of Oriel College, Oxford, and schooled in the Church of England, White did whatever he could to remain in or near his birthplace of Selbourne for most of his adult life. He passed much of that time at "The Wakes," a property he inherited from his uncle in 1763. White was a careful observer of the natural world and started to keep a "Garden Kalendar" in 1751, eventually expanding it to become his "Naturalist's Journal." At the urging of his family and friends, these musings found a more formal expression in his *Natural History of Selbourne*, published in 1789.

ALEXANDER WILSON
b. 1766 d. 1813

Upon his arrival in America in 1794, Wilson began a career as a schoolteacher near the Pennsylvania home of the naturalist William Bartram. Taking advantage of Bartram's library, Wilson learned much about the natural world and also of the shortcomings of ornithological literature. He raised support for what would later become *American Ornithology* by courting wealthy subscribers, including Thomas Jefferson. Later editions of the book, titled *Wilson's American Ornithology*, were expanded and edited by leading ornithological authorities, including Charles Lucien Bonaparte.

Illustrations

Page ii: Eighteenth-century birdwatchers. From Eleazar Albin, *A Natural History of English Song-Birds, and such of the foreign as are usually brought over and esteemed for their singing: To which are added, figures of the cock, hen and egg, of each species, exactly copied from nature.* London: A. Bettesworth, 1737.

Page 1: A sporting gent. From an advertisement for a binocular camera in the journal *The Nineteenth Century*, 1897.

Page 12: Ducks. From Thomas Pennant, *British Zoology.* Warrington: Printed by W. Eyres, for B. White, London, 1776.

Page 24: A nest and eggs. From Howard Jones, *Illustrations of the Nests and Eggs of Birds of Ohio; Illustrations by Mrs. N. E. Jones.* Circleville, Ohio, 1886.

Page 39: Nightingale. From Eleazar Albin, *A Natural History of English Song-Birds* (see above).

Page 47: Cañon finch. From John Cassin, *Illustrations of the Birds of California, Texas, Oregon, British and Russian America: intended to contain descriptions and figures of all North American birds not given by former American authors, and a general synopsis of North American Ornithology.* Philadelphia: J. B. Lippincott & Co., 1856.

Page 68: Hummingbird. From Thomas Nuttall, *A Manual of the Ornithology of the United States and of Canada, land birds.* Cambridge, Mass.: Hilliard and Brown, 1832.

Page 75: Swallows with rooftops in back. From M. and E. Kirby, *Stories About Birds of Land & Water.* Boston: Educational Publishing Company, 1910.

Page 82: Wrens, redbreast, and redstart. From *The Children's Picture Book of Birds.* Illustrated by W. Harvey. New York: Harper & Bros., 1861.

Page 107: Feathers. From Thomas Bewick, *The History of British Birds.* Newcastle: Beilby & Bewick, 1797–1804.

Page 112: Bird skeleton. From Thomas Campbell Eyton, *Osteologia avium; or, A sketch of the osteology of birds*. Wellington: R. Hobson, 1867.

Page 120: Peregrine. From Thomas Pennant, *British Zoology* (see above).

Page 134: Mockingbird. From Thomas Nuttall, *A Manual of the Ornithology of the United States and of Canada* (see above).

Page 148: Cormorant. From F. O. Morris, *A History of British Birds*. London: Groombridge, 1866–68.

Page 164: Golden-crested wrens. From M. and E. Kirby, *Stories About Birds of Land & Water* (see above).

Page 169: Dodo. From H. E. Strickland and A. G. Melville, *The Dodo and Its Kindred*. London: Reeve, Benham, and Reeve, 1848.

Page 180: Prairie hen. From M. and E. Kirby, *Stories About Birds of Land & Water* (see above).

Page 184: Mountain partridge. From Daniel Giraud Elliot, *North American Game Birds*. New York: F. P. Harper, 1897.

Page 193: Baby heron. From Thomas Pennant, *British Zoology* (see above).

Page 211: Chimney swift. From Jenny H. Stickney, *Bird World, a bird book for children*. Boston: Ginn & Co., 1898.

Page 218: Kite's egg. From William Chapman Hewitson, *British Oology*. Newcastle upon Tyne: Published for the author, by Charles Empson, [1831–42].

Page 224: Chick with grasshopper. From Walter Swaysland, *Familiar Wild Birds*, illustration by Archibald Thorburn. New York: Cassell, 1883.